I0662744

HARVEST CRUISE

REBECCA BENISON

Copyright © 2024 by Chicken House Press and Rebecca Benison

This book is a work of fiction. Unless otherwise indicated, all the names, characters, places, events and incidents in this book are either the product of the author's imagination or used in a fictitious manner. Any resemblance to actual persons, living or dead, or actual events is purely coincidental.

All rights reserved. This book or any portion thereof may not be reproduced or used in any manner whatsoever without the express written permission of the publisher except for the use of brief quotations in a book review or scholarly journal.

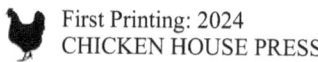 First Printing: 2024
CHICKEN HOUSE PRESS

Library and Archives Canada Cataloguing in Publication
CIP data on file with the National Library and Archives

ISBN trade paperback edition: 978-1-990336-65-2

Chicken House Press
282906 Normanby/Bentinck Townline
Durham, Ontario, Canada, N0G 1R0
www.chickenhousepress.ca

For the reluctant risk-takers.

It'll probably turn out fine, maybe even better.

HARVEST CRUISE

REBECCA BENISON

CHICKEN HOUSE PRESS

CHAPTER 1
WORK

"What the hell is wrong with you?" Lisa demanded, not even bothering to exchange pleasantries as Geri entered the office. Geri was startled by the outburst, before realizing that Lisa was probably referring to yesterday's date. *Word travelled fast*, she thought to herself.

"Nothing's wrong, we just didn't connect," she replied as she put down her bag, took off her jacket, and hung it over the back of her chair. As she got settled she assumed that Lisa would get frustrated and leave. Instead, Lisa got frustrated and stayed.

"It's hard to connect with someone when you're busy looking at your shoes all day," Lisa said sharply, staring her down. It was one thing to brush off a distant friend or acquaintance on a blind date, but Tom was family. And beyond that, he was a nice guy.

Geri closed her eyes. "You know how I feel about the whole dating thing," she began quietly, not making eye contact with Lisa as she spoke. "I'm awkward. It's hard for me to meet new people, and especially after Mark, it's hard for me to just start over."

"But Mark was years ago!" Lisa pleaded, running an impatient hand through her pin-straight blonde hair. "You need to move past it and get on with your life. Not everyone is going to string you along for years and then suddenly up and leave! It's just not something most people do!"

Staying silent, Geri finally met Lisa's eyes, then looked back at her screen and logged into her computer. Lisa stood over her for a few seconds more, watching her close friend and employee through a lens of frustration and pity before turning to go into her own office and slamming the door.

Geri put on her headphones, opened her email, and got to work.

The two had never met before Lisa first interviewed Geri as a marketing writer. She'd seen her portfolio online and liked her style. During the interview, Geri was noticeably nervous and very quiet. She wasn't much of a people person, that was obvious, but she had natural talent. She was also observant, eventually offering her own insights when prompted, albeit somewhat shakily. Though she lacked self-confidence, Lisa saw Geri as a person who could run with an idea and take it into new directions without too much hand-holding. Lisa liked that.

Over time, Lisa got Geri to warm up a bit, bringing her into her office for one-on-one meetings or working lunches and talking about life in between. They'd been working together for four years now, but they never saw each other outside of work. Nobody had ever seen Geri outside of work. While there were frequent office happy hours and milestone celebrations, Geri never took part, insisting that she had a lot of work to catch up on at home.

Today, the hours passed by quietly for Geri until just after noon, when Lisa stopped by her desk. Lisa waved a hand in front of the computer screen when she realized Geri couldn't hear her over her headphones.

"Hey," Lisa said, snapping her fingers now. "Let's go to lunch."

Geri tried to politely decline, saying she was busy, but Lisa wasn't taking "no" for an answer this time.

"You were busy enough yesterday," she said pointedly. "You're not going to be too busy today. Let's go." She took Geri's jacket from the chair and held it out for her like a mother would for a dawdling child.

Geri took the jacket, grabbed her purse, and walked with Lisa to the elevator. They silently went down the five floors to the lobby and out into the sunshine. They headed across the street to the diner on the corner. Geri passed by it every morning and evening but had never once stepped inside.

The wait staff got them settled at a small table, right by the window where they could watch the goings-on of the city while eating lunch. Geri was glad to be by the window because it gave her an excuse to look elsewhere while carrying on a conversation. Eye contact was an oddly intimate affair for her, so having a window to look out of was a welcome respite.

"Look, I'm sorry for going off on you before," Lisa began. Geri was about to say that it was okay, but Lisa held up her hand to signal that she wasn't finished. "It wasn't right of me to bring up Mark like that, and I *am* sorry." Geri looked at her now, taking in Lisa's sincerity and feeling quite surprised by it. "It's just so frustrating watching you go through the motions of life when I know that you have so much more to offer. You're young, you're gorgeous, you're talented—and I want you to have someone who appreciates that."

Lisa herself was just over 40 years old, physically fit, attractive, and ambitious. She'd been happily married for 12 years before her husband died without warning, killed by an aneurysm nobody knew was there.

Lisa knew how rare it was to find a true life partner, even if her own partner's life had been cut short. She wouldn't trade those years for anything, and she wanted Geri to have that experience.

"I know you want me to find someone, but I'm just not sure what I want for myself anymore," Geri said, looking away again. It was partially true. She saw herself starting a family with Mark, and travelling the world together. After a handful of years together she thought that getting married was a given, though she was too shy to actually ask. Deep down she knew that she was afraid of what his answer might be. What she didn't know was that Mark already had a family.

All those years of separate holidays because Mark said that Geri's family was stifling, and that he was too embarrassed by his own parents to even introduce her. All those weekends when he was too busy working to see her. It finally made sense when she found a wallet carelessly dropped on the floor of her old apartment. It wasn't Mark's wallet, and yet it was. A different wallet with a different driver's license and credit cards. Complete with a different, albeit similar, name. Mark Jefferson suddenly turned into Mark Jeffries. A quick search online found him posed with a lovely wife and two small children. He even had a dog and a picket fence.

Mark already had his fairytale ending. Geri was never even part of the story.

"Look," Lisa said, snapping Geri back to reality. "I think you're taking things too seriously. Why don't we try something different, just to shake things up? No more men or dating, let's just figure out how we can get you out into the world a little. I think we need a girl's night with some friends."

CHAPTER 2
GIRL'S NIGHT OUT

*G*eri begrudgingly agreed to meet Lisa at 8:30 p.m. that Friday, which was much later than Geri would normally leave her apartment. All week, she'd been dreading this night. She'd be staring at her computer screen and suddenly feel her stomach lurch as another anxious thought barged into her head. More than once, she'd been standing at the printer and was struck by the feeling that her legs were sinking under her. She gripped the table for stability as the floor undulated beneath her feet. She hoped nobody else noticed.

All week, the thoughts kept coming. What if Lisa actually hated Geri and wanted to humiliate her? What if Lisa liked Geri but her friends ended up hating her? What if Lisa and Tom were plotting revenge for her blowing off the date?

Even after she'd convinced herself that her paranoia was unwarranted, more realistic threats assailed her mind. What if she got sick during the night? What if there was no bathroom and she had to go? What if she spilled her drink all over herself?

By Thursday afternoon, she'd been thinking up excuses to get out of it.

She could pretend to feel sick during work on Friday and ask to go home early, giving her an easy out that night. Or, she could fake a family emergency that required her to travel back home to her parents' place for the weekend. She even briefly considered fostering a puppy from the local shelter just so that she'd have an excuse to be home; fortunately, she realized how absurd that plan was. Training a young puppy would be a lot more time consuming and stressful than simply going out for one night. Probably.

By 6:30 p.m. on Friday, Geri had tried on five different dresses in front of her full-length mirror, a few of them twice, before settling on the pair of black jeans and flouncy top she'd selected on Tuesday. If there was a breeze, she wouldn't have to worry about a dress getting caught up in it. If she had to take a cab, she felt much more comfortable disembarking while wearing pants—no wardrobe malfunctions here.

The outfit was tasteful, but wasn't exactly exciting for a night out. She had drawers full of jewelry she never wore, and decided that tonight was a good opportunity to bring them out. On went a chunky necklace she'd gotten from a cousin years ago, complete with an equally large bangle bracelet her mother had given her. She even played with some eye shadow she'd gotten as a Secret Santa gift last year, before rubbing most of it off in frustration.

She strapped on a pair of bronze gladiator heels that had been sitting in her closet for longer than she remembered, and as she looked in the mirror she hardly recognized herself. It had been so long since she'd let her hair down and dressed in anything other than grey business wear or sweats. She looked good. She'd had all of these things stowed away for years and never once thought to wear them together—or at all—until now.

At 8:00 p.m., Geri was standing outside the bar where they'd agreed to meet. There was an outdoor patio, so she picked a table and ordered herself a glass of white wine—which wouldn't stain if she spilled any on her blouse. She slowly sipped, aware of the groups of people arriving together as she sat alone, legs crossed on the patio. She pulled out her phone and absently scrolled through her Facebook feed, then checked her email, then went back to Facebook.

By 8:25 p.m., Geri was getting worried. Should she text Lisa? Did she go to the wrong place? Did she have the wrong day? Maybe they decided to go somewhere else and didn't tell her. Was her suspicion that Lisa hated her true? Was this all a setup? Maybe they got into an accident on the way there. Was Lisa alive?

Geri took a deep breath, weighing the possibilities. Lisa probably wasn't dead. If they didn't arrive in 10 minutes, she would text Lisa to see what was up. As the time ticked on, she hoped they'd arrive simply to alleviate the fear that they had all been killed.

At 8:35 p.m. Geri texted.

Geri: Hi, I'm here
Lisa: Great! We're just down the block looking for
        parking
Geri: Ok good, see you soon!

Geri breathed an audible sigh of relief. They were alive. And they were coming.

Two minutes later Geri saw Lisa and two other women heading toward her, excitedly waving and smiling. Lisa approached with a hug. This caught Geri off guard, though she reciprocated with arms that suddenly seemed too long for her body.

"This is Trish, and this is Mary," said Lisa. "Trish has been my best friend since college; we were roommates. And Mary is my sister, she's actually around your age."

Geri awkwardly shook each of their hands. "Nice to meet you," she said with a small smile.

Trish was like Lisa in that she was intense, lean, and appeared much younger than her years despite an obvious air of experience. In looks, however, they couldn't be more different. Whereas Lisa was a pale blonde with streaks of grey in her shoulder-length hair, Trish had ebony skin and raven-dark braids pulled back into a loose ponytail. Geri wondered if she had any grey hair to hide, or if she used dye to maintain her youthful appearance, but she wasn't about to ask.

Mary could easily be recognized as Lisa's sister. She had the similar piercing gaze, only her eyes were more blue while Lisa's were more grey. And while Lisa was naturally a dusty blonde, Mary veered more toward strawberry blonde. She was also a few inches shorter and a bit curvier than her fitness-obsessed big sister. Still, they had the same easy smile and laugh.

The women sat down at the table Geri had claimed and began their own introductions.

"Lisa says you're a writer," Mary said. She seemed excited to be there, unlike Geri who worked to maintain a friendly smile that hurt her cheeks.

"Yes, I am," Geri answered.

In between sips of her lemonade, Mary, the designated driver, asked about the type of writing Geri did, what she liked about her job, how she became interested in her career choice, and what her favourite assignment has been. She was certainly the bubbly one of the group, as Lisa and Trish listened while sipping their glasses of red wine.

"Alright Mary, enough of the interrogation," Lisa said with a sideways glance and a chuckle. "She's been so busy thinking of questions for you that she forgot to mention that she's a writer too," she explained.

"Are you?" Geri asked Mary, more interested now.

"Yeah, I'm a reporter for the *Gazette*," she said, smiling. "Sorry if I came across too strongly." She laughed. "I guess I'm still in work-mode."

Geri understood, and told her as much. While they had two different styles of writing and storytelling, she knew how easy it was to get lost in someone else's story. She'd done it herself more times than she cared to count.

The women conversed together now, with Lisa serving as ice-breaker. As more rounds of drinks were ordered, more stories were told, and more laughs were shared. Geri could actually see herself coming out to girls' night more often. This was much more entertaining than sitting at home watching another re-run of a 90s sitcom.

By the end of the night, as they got their bill, Lisa shooed away the other three sets of hands and put her card in the billfold. When the server returned to get Lisa's signature and tip amount, he passed her another receipt, too.

"We're entering all of our customers into a draw for a

free Caribbean cruise," he said. "It's a singles cruise for you and a friend. If you want to be entered, all you have to do is fill in your name and phone number and we'll call you if you win."

"And who said any of us are single?" asked Trish, raising an eyebrow. "Don't you know a double date when you see one?" She stared at him intently as he stammered an apology and left the table, leaving all four women laughing hysterically behind him.

"You're so bad," said Lisa, wiping a tear from her eye as she continued to laugh.

"I know," said Trish. "Sometimes I like to have a little fun. You think people are nervous around a Black woman? You should see how they act around a Black lesbian."

With this they all launched into hysterics again, taking even longer to compose themselves this time.

"Ah, my side hurts from laughing," said Lisa through gasps. "I want him back though so I can give him the form! I want that cruise!"

"And which one of us would you take with you if you won?" asked Mary slyly, clearly expecting the answer would be her.

"Geri," Lisa answered quickly. "She's the only one here who's never been a pain in my side!"

Geri laughed with the others, it was obviously a joke, after all. Of course Mary would be the one to go with her if Lisa actually did win. They were sisters, end of story. Geri could never see herself going on a cruise, anyway. Her anxiety was bad enough on land, she could only imagine how she'd feel stuck on a boat in the middle of the ocean.

Still, it was fun to joke. The four of them lingered just a little while longer, still laughing every time they caught sight of their server, who appeared to make every effort to avoid them. Eventually Lisa went inside the bar to hand in the bill and the entry form to the bartender directly.

They said their goodbyes, shared a few clumsy hugs, and went on their way shortly after. Mary offered to give Geri a ride home, but she was looking forward to a quiet taxi ride to decompress. It was a good night.

CHAPTER 3
SURPRISE

*B*y the following week, Geri was back to her usual grind. She felt a closer friendship with Lisa after Friday night, but she didn't know how to translate that into the workplace. She also didn't want anyone else to see her as a favourite with the boss.

They continued to go to lunch together and carry on their professional relationship. By Wednesday afternoon, though, something changed. Lisa was downright giddy. Finally, she stopped by Geri's desk and told her to come to her office because she had something to tell her.

It must be something good, Geri thought. She'd never seen her this happy at the office.

"Sit down," Lisa said, pursing her lips tightly in an attempt to contain her smile. "I have big news..." she added, emphasizing the word "big."

Geri complied and sat across from her, her mind racing. She imagined getting a raise or promotion. With more money, she'd be able to fix up her house. She couldn't help but mirror Lisa's excitement at the thought.

"Remember Friday night?" Lisa began in a conspiratorial whisper. Geri nodded, though she couldn't imagine what that had to do with anything.

"I got a call today... I won the cruise!" she shouted as her hands slapped her knees repeatedly. Geri's smile turned to slack-jawed shock.

After a few seconds of stunned silence, she felt obligated to speak. "You're serious?" she asked breathlessly.

"Yes! And you're coming with me!" Lisa exclaimed. She got up from her chair and grabbed Geri's hands to lift her to her feet, which had gone numb. As Lisa took her hands and shook them with delight, all Geri felt was terror. She feigned a smile for Lisa's sake, so that she could still be seen as a team player. Already, though, she was plotting ways to get out of this as tactfully as possible.

"What about Mary?" Geri finally blurted out.

"What about her?" Lisa asked dismissively. "She goes travelling all the time for work, and still finds time to plan week-long vacations with friends at least once a year. I doubt she could fit *another* trip in her itinerary. Besides, when's the last time *you* took a real vacation?"

Geri thought for a moment. "About 15 years ago, probably," she said. It had been a family trip to the Grand Canyon when she was in middle school. She still had the Polaroid pictures stored away in a shoebox under her bed.

Throughout the day, Geri remembered bits of that family vacation in between bursts of terror over the upcoming cruise. They'd stopped at a hot dog stand somewhere in the desert for a quick meal. They later pulled over at an ice cream stand. Geri made a mess of melted chocolate-vanilla swirl all over her pretty white dress. Then BAM—cruise panic.

When Geri got back to her home that night, she felt exhausted. Her workload had been light, but the news of the cruise had her nervously pacing between the water cooler and the ladies' room all day. She imagined her coworkers thinking she was either diabetic or pregnant based on her flurry of activity.

She kicked off her shoes in front of the green sofa, hung up her jacket and purse on the coat rack, and heavily trudged her way upstairs.

In her room, Geri crouched down and reached under the bed. She pulled out a beat-up black shoe box. She sat on the bed with the box in her lap, wiping dust from the bedspread and her black slacks.

For the next few minutes, she went through each photo, remembering other small details that she'd long since forgotten about that last family trip. They'd had a great summer together. It was the first and last time Geri had ever been on a plane. She was afraid, but ended up feeling proud of herself for facing her fear and not having a meltdown in front of everyone.

They could have taken a helicopter ride too, but that was too much too soon. Instead, they simply opted for a picture in front of the helicopter, which was the photo Geri was holding in her hand when her phone buzzed in her pocket.

It was a text from her dad. "Call me when you can," was all it said.

Geri didn't talk much to her parents. Her mother called once a week to check in and offer the latest updates on family gossip. Her father mainly just shouted "Hello!" while she was on the phone with her mother. Neither of them texted except for those rare occasions when they had a random question during working hours. Her mind raced to consider what might have caused him to text now. None of the scenarios she thought of were good.

CHAPTER 4
TROUBLE

*W*ith a hint of hesitation, Geri pushed the button to call her father. He picked up on the first ring.

"Dad? I got your text," Geri said, trying not to sound too nervous. Her free hand clutched the bedspread.

At the other end of the line her father sighed. "Margorie, hi, I wasn't sure if you were busy." He sounded tired and sad.

"No," she answered. "I just got home. Is everything okay?"

He paused, then replied, "Your mom's sick... She's stable," he added quickly, "but she's in the hospital."

He explained that she hadn't been feeling well for a few weeks, but wrote it off to stress. It was the end of the school year and as a teacher, that's the busy season.

"She was up late grading papers last night. She had a hard time breathing and felt nauseous," he said. "She didn't look good." He spared Geri the details, but told her that as soon as he saw her mother's grey complexion and felt her clammy skin, he'd made the call to 911, despite his wife's protests.

She'd had a massive heart attack, requiring a double bypass.

Geri listened to everything without saying a word. Her hand clutched the blankets tighter as her father spoke. Once he was done, there was a pause as Geri tried to think of what to say.

"Will she be okay?" she finally asked, her mind drawing a blank on anything else.

"They think so," he said. "They said it's lucky we caught it in time. They were able to do the surgery and get everything clear early this morning. She's in recovery now. It's just been a hell of a day," he said heavily. "She didn't want me to tell you until later, she didn't want you to worry."

Geri told him she'd book the next flight out of Boston and be there in the morning. She hadn't seen them in six months, since they headed south to Virginia. Her father had retired and wanted to lower their living expenses. Her mother kept working anyway; at 62, she considered herself too young to retire, and she loved being in the classroom.

The next few hours were a blur of Geri emptying her wardrobe in search of a carry-on bag that she was sure was in the back of her closet. Eventually, she just stuffed random shirts and pants into a tote bag she'd come across during the raid. She called a cab, gathered her things, and headed to the airport at 9:30 p.m. wearing the same outfit she'd worn to work earlier that day.

When she got to the airport, she realized that she'd never booked a flight before. She didn't know what to do or where to go. A staff member saw her looking around aimlessly and offered assistance. Step by step, they found a flight, secured a ticket, and Geri was guided through security. Her flight was scheduled for 5:45 a.m. By the time she got to the waiting area for her gate, it was near midnight.

She hadn't eaten anything since lunch, but she didn't feel hungry. Though she had hours to go until her flight, she worried that if she ate anything now, she'd regret it on the plane. This fear conflicted with the wisdom against travelling on an empty stomach. After about 30 minutes of deliberation, looking from her phone to the vending machine to the few bars that were still open in the airport, she headed to the vending machine and got herself a pack of sandwich crackers and a bottle of water. Back in her seat at the gate she quickly ate her dinner-snack, set an alarm so she wouldn't oversleep, and drifted off, hunched over her hastily packed tote bag.

At 4:45 a.m. Geri's alarm woke her. It took her a moment to remember where she was and why she was sleeping in public. The terminal had filled up substantially, and she was now surrounded by other people waiting for the same flight.

She checked her phone to see if she'd missed any calls or messages. Nothing. *No news is good news*, she thought to herself. She considered sending a quick text to check on things, but didn't want to bother her parents this early in the morning.

She remembered that she'd need to call in to work to let Lisa know where she was. Again, she didn't want to wake anyone, but she didn't know if she'd have time to call later in the morning. Instead, she sent Lisa a quick email letting her know that there was a family emergency and she'd probably be out the following day too.

Within seconds of putting her phone back in her pocket, Geri felt the familiar buzz.

Lisa had already responded to her email.

Hey, take as much time as you need! Hope everything is okay, let me know if you need anything. We'll hold down the fort! - Lisa

Geri remembered that Lisa got up early on Tuesdays and Thursdays for a six-mile run. She'd probably been getting ready to head outside when she sent the email. Good timing.

There had been so much on Geri's mind that she momentarily forgot how nervous she was about flying. Now, as she walked down the corridor toward the plane, all of that anxiety came flooding back. It crescendoed as she approached the plane door and nearly made her turn back around. She took a deep breath and walked through the threshold. As she was welcomed by the smiling flight attendants and guided toward her seat, Geri could feel her pulse settling. *It will all be okay*, she told herself. *Nothing to worry about.*

She was led to her row and seat number; she didn't realize she'd booked a middle seat. *It will all be okay*, she reminded herself. This was now her silent mantra.

A large, balding businessman sat in the window seat. He already had his laptop out, even though he'd have to stow the device in just a few minutes. Geri sat next to him and put her tote bag under the seat in front of her. There was nothing valuable inside, but she would have felt uncomfortable stowing the open bag in the overhead bin.

A few moments later, her other seatmate wandered

over and smiled. She was a middle-aged woman with a perfect bob of hair, wearing an expensive-looking cardigan be-dazzled with three brightly-coloured brooches. She seemed like a sociable woman; exactly the type that Geri tried to avoid in close quarters.

"Hi!" the woman beamed, holding out her hand to shake. "I'm Renee."

"I'm Geri," she answered, weakly taking the woman's hand by her fingers.

"Business or pleasure?" Renee asked.

This would be a long flight indeed.

CHAPTER 5
WHERE IS HOME?

*T*hough the flight lasted just under two hours, it felt as though Geri had been travelling all day by the time she arrived in Richmond. In fact, she wasn't too far off—she'd spent all night in an airport and all morning in the air.

She hastily stumbled through this new airport, looking for the exit and a taxi stand. Finally, she found her target and flagged down a cab to take her to the hospital. She had the address written on a scrap of paper somewhere at the bottom of her tote. Her cheeks flushed in the seconds it took her to find it, but the driver seemed used to waiting.

She shakily told him the destination, and he nodded as he pulled away from the airport. It was Geri's first time travelling alone. She was grateful that the cab driver wasn't much of a conversationalist.

As the cab pulled up to the visitor's entrance of the hospital, Geri got out her wallet and paid in cash, leaving a $10 tip since she didn't have small bills and wasn't comfortable asking for change. She thanked him and disembarked, her bags swinging at her sides as she approached the building. Once she told the receptionist who she was there to see, and verified her own relationship, she was brought through a maze of hallways to her mother's room.

Hesitantly, she stepped inside. When she saw her mother peacefully sleeping among the myriad of wires and beeping machines, and her father slumped over in a nearby chair, she backed out and quietly told her guide that she'd return a bit later so as not to disturb them. She was led to the main waiting room, where she rested her head against her tote and fell asleep.

About an hour later, she woke with a start and wanted to check in on her parents again. She couldn't quite remember the way to the room, but followed the hallways that seemed most familiar, occasionally turning around, trying to stay out of the way. Eventually, she found them.

"Margorie!" her father exclaimed, spotting her as she peered through the open door. He crossed the room and pulled her in for a strong embrace. She couldn't remember the last time she'd hugged either of her parents.

"Hi Dad, hi Mom," she said, putting her bags aside.

"Hi sweetie," her mother said. "I'm sorry you had to come all this way so early in the morning."

Of course her mother's first thought would be to apologize for the inconvenience of having a heart attack. Geri smiled.

Her father pulled up another chair and the three of them talked about everything that had happened. They discussed their fears, relief, and questions about what would happen next. At times there were tears, at others, laughter.

Nothing like this had ever happened in their family. Geri's grandparents were all deceased now, but had died gradually from the various troubles associated with old age—dementia, cancers being battled over decades, a stroke followed by a coma... the causes of death were all different, but ultimately they were all victims of time. Each had lived at least to their late 80s. Geri's mom was young by comparison, barely 62 years old. Nobody considered that she could face her own mortality so soon.

Geri was scared. She sat on her hands to keep them warm and to prevent them from shaking. In her head, she considered the logistics of moving to Virginia to be closer to her parents. Closer to home, wherever that was now.

Her mother could see the tension in Geri's body and turned the subject away from what had happened, to focus on Geri instead. She asked about work and what was new. Geri had much to tell.

"I was invited to go on a cruise, but I won't go," she began. This opened a flood of new questions.

Invited by who?

Cruise to where?

When will this be?

Why wouldn't you go?

Geri thought the last question's answer was obvious; clearly she couldn't go on vacation while her mother was ill. And she felt that the other questions were irrelevant since she wouldn't be going. Still, she found herself providing all the details she knew, along with numerous excuses for staying home.

"You cannot *not* go," said her mother firmly.

Geri rolled her eyes. How could she go anywhere at a time like this?

"This is a once-in-a-lifetime trip," her mother

continued. "Life is too short not to take that type of opportunity." She relaxed into her pillow and smiled warmly at Geri. "Honey, I'll be fine. I am fine. The doctors made me all better, and they said we're out of the woods here. We caught it before any real damage was done. I'm fine." She took Geri's hand softly in hers and held it, stroking her fingers with her thumb.

"I really didn't want to go anyway..." Geri said softly.

"I know," said her mother, matching her soft tone. "That's why you should. Get out in the world and leave your comfort zone. When will the cruise be?"

"I don't actually know," Geri answered with a shrug. "It's called 'the Harvest Cruise,' so I think it's in the fall."

"Well, that's perfect then!" said her mother, beaming from her pillow. "That's plenty of time for you to catch up with us, get bored, and then be on your way to a new adventure." She laughed.

Sometime in the afternoon, Geri got a text from Lisa asking how everything was going. Geri got her up to speed and asked if she could work remotely for a few weeks to spend more time with her parents. Lisa obliged, as she knew she would. Lisa was a firm woman, but a fair leader. She knew that she could trust Geri, and that she would put out good work no matter where she did it.

Over the next few weeks, Lisa and Geri maintained face-time with weekly video-chats in addition to texting, instant messaging, and emailing throughout the day. As expected, Geri kept up her usual pace, and perhaps was even more productive without the constant distractions of office life.

In the early mornings, Geri got into the rhythm of having a cup of decaf coffee with her parents. Her mother had been discharged days after her surgery, and had been told to avoid caffeine. They all sipped their coffee, read the news—her parents shared the newspaper while Geri scrolled through her phone—and eased into their days.

Geri worked from a spare room over the garage. It was hot and stuffy up there, but it was largely empty and unused. It was also quiet, and offered a view of the hillside that couldn't be found anywhere else. In between assignments and emails, Geri often found herself looking out the window just in time to see a deer pass below, or a tiny speck of movement that was probably a chipmunk in the leaf litter. Once, she even saw a hawk perched on a nearby branch, and wondered if it could see her through the window.

She hoped her own house was holding up well. There hadn't been any leaks when she left, but she kept having dreams that the place was flooded, water cascading through the ceilings in every room. She told Lisa where she kept the spare key, and asked her to check in every so often. Lisa would stop by on her way home, providing a live video feed as she walked through each room. Everything looked exactly the same as she'd left it, in a state of cherished disarray.

The only thing that looked different was the yard. The grass looked about a foot taller than when she'd left nearly a month ago. Weeds had overtaken the flower beds, which looked wilted from lack of regular watering. Lisa assured her that she'd hire someone to mow the lawn until Geri got back.

Lisa also kept her in the loop about the upcoming cruise, which would begin on August 6th, at the tail end of summer. Geri decided that after the cruise, she'd return to Boston to continue her life where she'd left off.

Although, looking out the window, she couldn't help but consider just staying here in her parents' home on the hill indefinitely.

As her next mortgage payment came due, however, she decided against that. Her house was her pride, and she couldn't just leave it to ruin—especially when it cost a significant portion of her paycheque each month.

CHAPTER 6
HARD GOODBYES

*A*ugust 5th came in a blink, and Geri found herself rushing to pack for the next day's endeavour. Her mother lent her an expensive luggage set, telling her that the tote bag she came with would *not* work for such a trip.

She also gave her some makeup since she hadn't brought any with her, and took her shopping for a tasteful vacation wardrobe. The whole time they were in the stores, Geri worried that the shopping trip might be too strenuous for a woman recovering from heart surgery, but this was her mother's speciality. She was a skilled bargain hunter with style, and she would not let her daughter go on a cruise in the tired clothes she'd been wearing.

As Geri cut off the price tags from dresses, shorts, shirts, and even a few new pairs of shoes, she had to admit, her mom had great taste.

Of course, she knew the real reason her mother wanted her looking good on the trip was in the event she happened upon an attractive stranger—it was a singles' cruise, after all. Her parents had long stopped asking about her romantic life, but Geri knew they still had hopes she'd find someone nice to settle down with. And as much as she avoided human interaction on a daily basis, she couldn't deny that she wanted that too.

After she finished packing, Geri and her parents went out to dinner to celebrate the time they'd shared. They went to a local diner where Geri ordered french toast, her mother ordered a vegetable omelet, and her father ordered a stack of chocolate chip pancakes. Having breakfast for dinner was a rare treat for everyone.

"You know, I think I'm grateful for having the heart attack!" Geri's mother laughed. "Who knows when I'd have gotten to see you otherwise," she smiled.

"Don't say that!" Geri said with a groan.

"It's true! I'm fine—better than fine—and I got to spend all this time with my daughter before she heads out on her first expedition!"

Geri's father agreed. "It has been good seeing you, Margorie. These past few weeks have felt like the old times."

Geri couldn't argue that. "Yeah, it's been nice being together these past couple of months. I really had missed you guys," she said seriously.

"Maybe we can visit you in Boston one day," said her mother hopefully. "How's the house coming along?"

"It's not much to look at," Geri said with a slight wince, "but it's livable at least. I'd love to have you guys there when you're up for travelling."

"I think we'll take you up on that offer!" said her father. "We have an air mattress in the garage we can bring with us so you don't have to worry about a spare bed or anything."

"And we can bring our own linens too!" her mother chimed in.

They smiled and laughed throughout the dinner, her father brushing away the waiter as he returned to ask if they were ready for the check. Once the planning had all been settled, he called him back over. Geri's parents would come to visit for Thanksgiving. They'd prepare a small turkey in her kitchen, and together they'd enjoy a warm holiday meal in Geri's own home.

With full bellies and genuine smiles, they returned to the house for coffee and to watch some TV before going to bed.

At about 11:30 p.m., they decided to call it a night. Geri needed to wake up in just a few hours to make her way back up to New York for the Harvest Cruise's evening departure.

As she turned out the light and got under the blanket, she realized she hadn't packed a toothbrush. Or deodorant. She tried to ignore the pang of worry, telling herself she'd pack them in the morning. Five minutes later, she got up, turned on the light, and rummaged through her things to get the last items packed. Finally content, she rolled back into bed and went to sleep.

CHAPTER 7
THE HARVEST CRUISE DEPARTS

*G*eri woke up at 5:32 a.m., waved good-bye to her parents from the back of a taxi by 6:03 a.m., and boarded her train to New York by 7:16 a.m. She planned on sleeping the whole way there, but found herself unable to close her eyes to the landscape passing by the window.

The train was packed, so it would have been hard to sleep anyway with all the activity going on around her. The next 10 hours were spent alternatively reading a new book—she'd packed five for the trip—walking back and forth to the dining car to stretch her legs and get snacks, and looking out the window.

By 5:38 p.m., she'd arrived in New York, where she met Lisa at the station for a quick embrace before they excitedly made their way to the dock to board the Harvest Cruise before its 7:35 p.m. departure.

Surprisingly, the energy of the day kept Geri from feeling too much anxiety about being trapped in the middle of the ocean for the next week. They approached the dock and looked up at the hulking ship ahead of them. It was a bright white vessel with fiery orange lettering that spelled out "Harvest Cruise." Around the letters were giant leaves painted the warm hues of fall. Underneath was a cornucopia filled with all the traditional items; apples, corn, squash, and more. It wasn't even September, yet the ship promised a full bounty. She snapped a quick photo to document the experience before being herded toward the ramp.

As she was pushed up the long path to the boat, squeezed in among the thousands of other passengers, she was suddenly hit with a flood of dread. The breeze had picked up by the water, and her hair whipped around her face, leading to further panic as she clawed the long locks out of her face and line of sight. She held it back with one hand while she continued rolling her luggage with the other. *Why didn't I put it up in a ponytail?* she admonished herself.

She looked around, feeling locked-in by the crush of strangers. There was nowhere to go but up to the boat. No escape.

Lisa had a hand on her arm to keep from getting separated, and gave it a squeeze as if she knew what was going through Geri's mind. Geri looked back at her, and Lisa smiled reassuringly, urging her on.

"We're almost there!" Lisa shouted over the crowd. Geri forced a smile and nodded in return. She was hot, clammy, and dizzy. But she had no choice other than to go forward. Finally, they reached the ship and were able to escape the throng of bodies that had been pressing against them the whole way up the ramp. On the ship, everyone branched out in different directions to explore and find their rooms.

Lisa found an attendant to guide them. They were brought through a dark, spacious lobby and down a narrow corridor. The floors were all carpeted, scarlet with gold accents, and the walls were covered with dark wood panelling and mouldings. It made a stately impression, though perhaps outdated. As they walked, Geri picked up the faintest scent of stale cigarettes. *It's a free cruise,* thought Geri. *It could be much worse.*

The attendant led them to the elevator and pressed the button for the 9th deck. Geri noted that the highest deck was 13. She'd been used to buildings that skipped the 13th floor entirely, and found it mildly off-putting that the ship's designers either hadn't considered the negative connotation, or hadn't cared. The elevator crept along, occasionally stopping to let off other passengers at their own decks. They reached deck 9, and the attendant led them down another musty, red-carpeted hall to their room, 926. It was a small but comfortable space with two full-size beds and a private bathroom. There was even a balcony, which was a refreshing surprise. Geri thumped her luggage onto the bed and made her way to the sliding glass doors. As she opened them, she inhaled the salty air and felt the cool mist on her face, immediately feeling a sense of relief and calm. She took long, deep breaths. Everything would be okay.

Stepping back into the room, she found Lisa already beginning to unpack her things on her own bed nearest to the door.

"I didn't even know we were getting a balcony room, how awesome is that!" Lisa said, beaming as she unloaded the contents of her bags. "This is a way nicer room than I thought we'd get for free."

"Yeah, it is nicer than I expected too," Geri said truthfully. She'd been picturing a tiny, dark, cupboard of a room. A claustrophobia-inducing nightmare. The bright, airy cabin they'd been brought to worked wonders in setting her mind at ease about the trip.

Geri followed Lisa's lead, neatly unpacking her things and finding appropriate places to put everything. They split the closet space between them and hung up their dresses and nicer clothes. They each picked a dresser drawer for casual items and undergarments. Within five minutes, the oversized bathroom vanity was crowded with toiletries, in addition to those provided by the cruise staff.

After everything was unpacked, the two women stowed their empty bags under their respective beds and headed toward the nearest bar, just downstairs and across the hall. Lisa opted for barstools rather than a private booth; she loved the chance to meet new people. They each ordered a Bahama Bay Breeze in celebration of the tropical excursion about to begin.

"So, how long have you been with the Harvest Cruise?" Lisa asked the bartender, a large bald man with tattoos going up each arm, the exact stereotype of what Geri expected a bartender to look like.

"Well they just hired me yesterday, so I've officially been here an hour," he answered without a hint of sarcasm. It was clear Lisa didn't like his tone as she arched her eyebrow at Geri. Geri just took a sip of her drink, uninclined to continue the conversation.

Eventually, more guests filled up the bar after they'd had a chance to get settled into their own rooms. The ship was now departing and everyone was settling in for the journey. Geri saw a man sit next to her out of the corner of her eye, but was careful not to turn her head to look in his direction, not wanting to draw attention to herself.

"How's that drink?" he asked, gesturing to her glass. *So much for not drawing attention*, she thought.

"It's okay, kinda strong," she replied, hoping the bartender didn't hear her. She never liked drinks that tasted too much like alcohol.

"Hmm, sounds good to me! I'll have what she's having!" he informed the bartender, who nodded wordlessly and made the drink.

"Are you a regular cruise-goer?" he asked Geri.

"No, this is my first," she answered, still trying not to look directly at him.

"Mine too! I won this trip at a bar back home, if you can believe it," he said.

"Same here!" she replied excitedly. "Well, actually she won the trip," Geri said, pointing to Lisa in the chair next to her. "She invited me to come along as her guest."

"Oh, funny, I didn't get a guest," he said. "I thought this was a singles' cruise?"

"It is!" Lisa piped in. "We're both single," she added with a wink, nodding her head toward Geri, which instantly made Geri blush.

"I'm Billy, by the way," he said, holding out his hand.

"Geri," she answered, taking his hand lightly in her own with a shy smile.

Billy asked about her home life, family, friends, hobbies, and anything else she cared to discuss. He even asked about Lisa and her backstory. Geri found herself answering every question, not even attempting to evade him. Lisa filled in any gaps when appropriate, but mostly tried in vain to engage the bartender. Not that she enjoyed his presence, she just wanted to keep Billy's attention on

Geri for the time being.

Surprisingly, Geri didn't mind at all now. Once she'd met his eyes, she found it hard to look away, trying to find the points where the colour turned from green to brown. There were even specks of blue toward the middle.

Lisa excused herself to go back to their room to freshen up, but not before inviting Billy to join them for dinner. She told them which restaurant to go to, and said that she'd made a reservation with the staff already. They should all head down in about 30 minutes.

Half an hour later, Billy and Geri found the restaurant and approached the maitre d'. He guided them to a private table and informed them that Lisa called to say that she was running late and that they should start without her.

Of course, Geri knew that Lisa had no intention of coming to dinner. Somehow, she'd staged another blind date on the fly. This time, with a stranger they'd both only just met minutes before. Geri had to hand it to her, Lisa had a rare knack for matchmaking. And this time, Geri was grateful.

Billy was captivating. He was only slightly taller than her, with dark hair and those eyes that were impossible to describe. By the end of the evening, they'd enjoyed a full three-course dinner that included a shared chocolate lava cake topped with vanilla ice cream and hot fudge that dripped down the sides and mingled with the molten chocolate inside.

When the check came, Billy quickly grabbed it from the table and pulled out his credit card.

"Oh, I hadn't even thought about whether food was included with the ticket or not," Geri said, feeling caught off guard by the bill.

"To be honest, neither had I," Billy said. "But, free cruise, so I guess they have to make up the money somewhere. I think the buffets might be included, though."

They continued talking for some time before they both realized it was near midnight. Billy walked Geri to her room, and told her he looked forward to seeing her at breakfast in the morning. She agreed, slowly opening the door and looking back, before saying goodnight and going inside.

On the other side of the closed door, she pictured him walking away, smiling. She was certainly grinning, herself. He didn't take the liberty of kissing her, which was a plus on his part—he wasn't too eager and seemed to want to get to know her before adding anything physical to the mix. She truly did look forward to breakfast.

Lisa seemed to have expected things to progress and had clearly planned accordingly; she'd made herself scarce for the night, leaving Geri the room to herself. She chuckled silently. Her boss was the best wing-woman she could ask for.

Geri was a pool of happiness. This was a high she hadn't felt in years, and she went to bed feeling renewed and excited about what tomorrow would bring.

CHAPTER 8
QUARANTINE

*G*eri awoke to sunlight streaming through the balcony doors. She smiled softly against her pillow.

After lying comfortably in bed, still snuggled into the cozy blanket for about 20 minutes after waking, she checked the time and saw that it was 7:43 a.m. Breakfast didn't start until 8:30, so she had plenty of time to shower, pick out an outfit, and pay her hair and makeup some attention.

She sat up and looked to her right toward Lisa's bed. It was still empty. She wondered where Lisa had stayed for the night. She was great at making friends, but the fact that she could find someone to bunk with on such short notice was amazing to Geri.

She carefully went through her dresser drawer, picking out the day's undergarments before heading to the closet to choose a dress. She went with simple but colourful options on both counts—she didn't want to seem too eager. Still, she made sure everything matched.

Today's colour would be pale pink.

After laying everything out on the bed, she hopped in the shower and began her morning routine.

Once she was scrubbed, rinsed, and moisturized, she towelled herself dry and got dressed, smelling of the lavender-vanilla scented toiletries that were pre-stocked in the shower stall. She made use of the cabin's hair dryer, thankful there was one available since she forgot to pack hers. She got dressed, secured the hair around her face with a couple of bobby pins, and got to work on her makeup; bronzy eyeshadow, a touch of mascara, the slightest hint of blush, and the perfect shade of pink lipstick to match her dress. She took in her reflection: a bubbly, carefree woman on her way to breakfast with a not-quite-stranger. She realized what a difference a little primping made in the morning. She liked the way she felt, being in control of her own image.

She headed downstairs at exactly 8:30 a.m., careful not to get there any earlier. She was relieved to find Billy already waiting for her outside the buffet. She didn't bother to hide her smile as they exchanged hellos. For the first time in a long time, she felt confident and excited for the day.

"You look great," Billy told her, scanning her up and down.

"Thank you," Geri said shyly, out of habit.

"Where's your friend? I figured she might be joining us today," he said. "Not that I mind either way, I kind of prefer your company," he assured her quickly.

Geri was caught off guard by the mention of Lisa. "I'm not sure where she is, she stayed out last night," Geri stammered. "I'll text her now." She took her phone from her wristlet. "I was hoping to find her here... not that I don't prefer your company too!" she added quickly. "I mean, I was just worried about her," she said, blushing and suddenly feeling hot.

Billy laughed. "I'm sure," he said playfully. "Well, you're stuck with me for this morning, at least. Let's head over to the buffet before all the good stuff is taken!"

They each filled their plates with scrambled eggs, bacon, and a few slices of melon before sitting at a table for two. If Lisa arrived later, they'd just add another chair to the table.

Geri texted her again to let her know where she was and ask what Lisa was up to. She got a reply seconds later.

Too much to drink last night, went back to our room to sleep it off. Go have fun today. Billy's cute :)

"Hmmm, Lisa said she's sick, so I guess it's just us today," Geri told Billy, feigning disappointment.

"Hope she feels better," he said. "There's a shore excursion later if you want to get off the boat."

"That sounds great! I'd love to get some fresh air," she answered.

They enjoyed a leisurely breakfast, continuing to talk about anything that came to mind. Billy was a great listener. He constantly asked Geri questions about herself rather than just talking about his own accomplishments. She found herself opening up quickly to him.

After they finished their meal, Billy suggested they tour the boat. There were 13 decks total, and they started at the top. They passed two cafés, five sit-down restaurants, three bars, and a spacious theatre. Each time they passed a place that looked good, they made a note to stop in at some point later in the trip.

At 11:30 a.m., the crew informed everyone that the shore excursion would begin in about half an hour, and included a guided tour of a small island off the Florida coast that Geri had never heard of.

Eventually the boat docked, and Geri went down the ramp with Billy. Though pressed by a throng of people again, this time, she felt excited.

As they stepped foot on the island, Geri realized she wasn't wearing the right shoes for a walking tour. She suggested heading back to the boat so she could change into another pair, but Billy proposed a different idea instead.

"How about we just walk along the beach?" he asked. "You can take your shoes off and we can walk on the sand, dip our toes into the water?"

"That sounds nice, but I'd hate for you to miss the tour just because I didn't think to wear the right shoes," she said.

"I'm not much of a guided tour person anyway," he said. "And according to the itinerary, it's mostly hiking the forest, and I'm not a fan of jungle spiders and mosquitos," he added with a laugh.

"Well, when you put it like that, the beach does sound better!" she agreed, laughing with him. She took off her sandals and held them in one hand while she looped her other hand through the arm Billy offered her.

They walked for what felt like minutes, but must have been the two hours they were allotted when they heard the foghorn informing passengers it was time to re-board. They quickly made their way back to the boat, splashing in the surf and laughing together along the way.

By the time they made it back, it seemed everyone else must have already boarded; nobody else went up the ramp with them.

It was now mid-afternoon, and Geri realized she was starving. They'd intended to stop by a beach-side bar for a quick snack, but time had escaped them. They decided to stop by one of the half-dozen restaurants they'd checked out that morning.

Geri texted Lisa to see if she was interested in joining them for a late lunch. Again, she got an immediate decline.

Already ate. Had toast delivered to the room. Enjoy.

It wasn't like Lisa to be so brusque in her texts, but Geri understood that she wasn't feeling well. She imagined it must be terrible being hungover and possibly seasick on a week-long cruise.

Geri updated Billy on Lisa's status and they headed to one of the more casual bistros for sandwiches and cold drinks to rehydrate after the long walk in the sun.

Geri decided it was time she showed some interest in Billy's life. She asked where he was from and where he lived now. He told her that he was from New York, Long Island specifically. He worked in New York City, but he'd recently been offered the chance to transfer to Boston.

Geri gasped with glee at the serendipity.

"Why didn't you tell me before?" she asked. "I can tell you everything about the city and where to go."

"That's *if* I transfer," he answered. "I haven't decided yet. I didn't know anyone there, before..." he added slowly.

Geri blushed. She realized that of course it was too

soon to think that he should move to Boston to be with her, even if it really was for his job. Still, she hoped that he would.

"Right," she said. "Well, if you do decide to go, I can help you figure out good places to stay while you get settled."

"Thanks," he said. "It's definitely something to think about." He smiled across the table.

Geri smiled back warmly. Maybe this could work. Even New York wasn't terribly far; just a train ride away. This could work.

They returned to lighter conversation, thinking about how to spend the rest of the day. Billy suggested they see an afternoon matinee at the onboard movie theatre, then have dinner at a fancier sit-down restaurant, before finishing the night by seeing a live musical performance. Geri had no complaints.

When it was time for dinner, however, she wanted to go back to her room to change into a more formal dress, and to check on Lisa. Billy assured her that the dress she was wearing was fine, but she felt it was too casual for the night. After some back-and-forth, Billy acquiesced, telling her he'd meet her in front of the restaurant when she was ready. He returned to his own room to freshen up in the meantime.

As Geri approached her cabin, she was nervous to see what state Lisa might be in. She was always squeamish about being around sick people—especially when nausea was a primary symptom.

She quietly opened the door and peeked around the dark room. She didn't see the expected lump of a sleeping body in Lisa's bed. In fact, the bed remained neatly made, still empty. She knocked on the bathroom door and heard no reply. Hesitantly, she opened that door, too, finding no sign of her roommate. At that, she sighed in relief. The possibility of finding Lisa unconscious on the bathroom floor had crossed her mind.

Geri turned on the lights around the room looking for any evidence of where Lisa might have gone, but didn't find anything. She texted to see where she was.

Lisa replied instantly.

Went to medic, feel really sick

Geri gasped.

OMG! Are you ok? What's wrong?

Virus. In quarantine til they find out. They disinfected room so you should be fine.

Geri now felt hot and nauseous herself. She was worried about her friend, but she also didn't want to stay in the room anymore, no matter how clean anyone said it was. One of her biggest fears leading up to this cruise was getting sick onboard. Not knowing exactly how sick Lisa was, or with what ailment, made her more nervous.

She sprayed her belongings with disinfectant and whipped hand sanitizer from her purse for a quick hand-wash. She then called reception and asked for a room change. Incredibly, they had one available. A porter immediately came to carry her luggage—once she'd finished packing it all back up—and escorted her to the new space. She couldn't believe how fast they were able to accommodate what she thought would be a difficult request. When she got there, her jaw dropped.

In front of her was a bright, spacious suite with a balcony even larger than the one she'd had in the previous room. She now had a king-size bed, a massive TV, and plush white carpet cushioning each step. This was the most luxurious space she'd ever been in, and it was hers for the next five nights.

She quickly picked a new dress and threw it on before texting Billy to let him know she was on her way.

She ran down three flights of stairs and had to get her bearings to remember where the agreed-upon restaurant was. When she found it, Billy was waiting patiently, reading the menu posted to the window.

She was catching her breath as she approached.

"Everything okay?" Billy asked, sounding concerned rather than irritated at her late and slightly disheveled arrival.

"It's a long story," she puffed. "I'll tell you everything once I have a chance to sit down."

They made their way inside the restaurant and were shown to a table before they could even reach the front desk to check in. Geri was relieved to find that their glasses had already been filled with water, which she gulped down a little too quickly. She began to cough as the cold liquid caught in her throat.

"Are you okay?" Billy asked again.

"I'm...fine..." Geri sputtered out between coughs. "Swallowed too fast...down the wrong pipe..."

She coughed a few more times, her face growing red from embarrassment more than anything. She finally caught her breath and explained the situation. She began with the texts between herself and Lisa, the room change to avoid getting sick, and the dash down three flights of stairs to the restaurant so she wouldn't keep him waiting too long.

"You should have told me," he said empathetically. "We could have met later, or rescheduled, or anything. I'm sorry you had to go through all that and then have to rush over here." He gently put his hand over hers, stroking her fingers.

"I wanted to see you," she said honestly. She found herself avoiding his smiling gaze, finding it too intense at the moment. "I just needed a minute to calm down, that's all. I'm good now."

They each ordered tomato soup with a grilled cheese sandwich on the side. Billy suggested that for the rest of the trip they not order anything that didn't require cooking, such as salads or fruits, to avoid any chance of food poisoning in case that's what made Lisa sick. Geri was more than happy to stick to that plan.

They shared a bottle of wine throughout dinner, and afterward, a slice of raspberry swirl cheesecake. About halfway through the cheesecake, Geri realized it was probably pre-prepared and frozen, and therefore a potential source of food-borne illness. Still, she'd already eaten half of her portion, she might as well finish it, come what may.

Whether it was the wine or the company, Geri wasn't sure, but she had calmed down considerably over dinner. After they'd finished, she looked around the restaurant on the way out and realized the place was barely half full. She found that odd for a cruise ship at dinnertime, but was grateful for the peaceful meal.

Though they had planned to see an after-dinner show, Geri found herself thoroughly exhausted. It had been a long, stressful day, and she didn't normally drink that much wine. Billy offered to walk her back to her room, and she appreciated the support as she found herself leaning on him and struggling to stay upright. They took the elevator up to her floor, and slowly made their way down the hall to her new room.

Clumsily, she fumbled through her purse to find the room key. Billy had to help her slide it into the door.

"I can stay with you tonight, to make sure you're okay," Billy said.

"No," Geri said. "I'm fine, just need to sleep this off."

"Okay, call me if you need anything," he said. He put her purse on a nearby chair and helped her take off her shoes as she melted into the bed. She was out before he could even cover her with a blanket. He smiled as he looked down at her. Then he quietly made his way toward the door, slipped her key card into his back pocket, and turned off the light before exiting the suite.

Lisa sat in darkness, bound at the wrists and ankles. She couldn't tell if the room was dark or if there was something over her eyes. The floor was hard and cold, possibly damp. She had no idea where she was, but was blissfully calm.

She heard scurrying every so often. She imagined large rats or insects moving freely around whatever room she was in. She was normally afraid of such creatures, but she wasn't panicking now. She didn't even flinch when something grazed her leg.

Eventually she heard a door open, and the shuffling of shoes and the grunting of people carrying something heavy. Then a thud and a muffled moan to her right. She didn't bother to turn her head; she couldn't see anything anyway. Was she blindfolded?

As the heavy-sounding door creaked closed, she heard the first words she'd heard in hours, or maybe days, or even weeks. She didn't know how long she'd been here. She didn't even know where "here" was.

"So, who's next then?" a bright female voice asked.

The door shut before she could hear an answer. As the moaning next to her continued, she became aware of her open mouth and the trail of saliva leaving a thin, cold line down her shirt. She closed her mouth slowly, but couldn't do much else.

After a moment of muddled thoughts, she opened her mouth again, this time to speak.

"Hhh-llo?" she whispered into the darkness.

She was answered by a moan on her right, and another on her left. She hadn't realized there was another person on that side of her before.

Unable to do much else, she dozed back to her unnatural sleep.

CHAPTER 9
HANGOVER

*G*eri awoke heavily, unsure of where she was. The light was blinding and she didn't know where it was coming from.

As her eyes adjusted, she recalled being on a ship. A cruise. She was in her new cabin. She hazily thought back to last night's dinner with Billy. Did she drink that much? The pounding headache said so.

Geri looked over at the clock on the nightstand. 11:13 a.m. She'd slept through breakfast. She held her pounding head in one hand as she pictured Billy waiting for her at the buffet. She clumsily grabbed her phone to text him but had to wait a moment for her vision to focus. Even her fingers felt like they weren't her own. Eventually she could see the screen, and the three texts waiting for her from Billy.

Good morning, I'm downstairs.
Hey, everything okay?
Do you want breakfast today?

She groaned with disappointment and embarrassment. She hoped he'd understand. She must have drunk far too much the night before. As she laid back in the bed and pondered what to do or say, she smelled something sweet. She sniffed at the air, unmoving for a few seconds before again sitting up slowly, careful not to jar her aching head too much.

As her eyes settled on the kitchenette counter, she could see a dish piled high with pancakes dripping with syrup, fruits, scrambled eggs, and bacon. On shaky legs, she cautiously rose and made her way to the counter. Next to the dish was a note, along with her keycard.

I forgot that I still had your key card from last night in my pocket. You seemed pretty rough, so I thought you might like some food brought to you this morning. You're fast asleep so I'm leaving it here when you're ready. Let me know if you want some company. —Billy

Geri smiled at the thoughtful gesture. She wasn't hungry, but surprisingly she wasn't nauseous either. Maybe she'd had the sense to take Dramamine before she passed out last night. She decided that she should eat *something*, and picked at the now-soggy pancakes. That was how she preferred them, anyway.

She went to the coffee maker and found a cup already made next to it. She silently thanked Billy for that too. She didn't even need to add sugar or cream, he'd made it perfectly light and sweet, the way she liked it. She sipped slowly even though the brew was now cold, savouring the moment before she had to face her hangover head-on.

She took a warm shower, got dressed in an easy pair

of shorts and a t-shirt, slipped on a pair of flip-flops, and texted Billy to thank him and ask if he'd like to meet.

"Of course," he assured her.

Though she didn't feel like going out, she knew there was another tropical shore excursion that afternoon. It felt silly to go on a cruise and stay in the cabin, so she forced herself up and out.

Billy met her on deck by the pool, where they could sit outside while waiting for the boat to dock.

"Hey, glad to see you up and about!" Billy greeted her with a wave, getting up from his lounge chair.

"Hi," Geri replied, her eyes shielded by sunglasses. "Sorry, I'm out of it today. I'm not much of a drinker. Must have had too much last night."

"Well we finished the bottle," Billy replied with a chuckle. "Here, let me get you some Gatorade, that should help."

He got up and made his way over to the poolside shop, where he purchased a bottle. He brought it back to Geri, who applied the cold bottle directly to her forehead for a few seconds before opening it.

"Thank you," she said, her eyes closed beneath the sunglasses. She sipped slowly, periodically opening her eyes to observe those around her. The deck had a number of people lounging in chairs, as she and Billy were. Very few people were speaking. Next to her, she saw a young woman who looked as miserable as she felt. The woman's brows were knitted in pain above her sunglasses, and she had the back of her hand pressed to her forehead. A sloppily-tied bandana held her hair back from her face and off her neck.

Geri usually wasn't much for pleasantries, but she was feeling oddly sociable in her discomfort.

"Rough night?" she asked.

"Must have been, I don't remember it," the other woman replied with her eyes still closed.

"Same here," said Geri. "I'm normally not much of a drinker, I guess last night I must have gone overboard—no pun intended."

The woman laughed. "Oh, normally I can drink guys under the table, I don't know what they must've put in that wine," she said playfully. "I'm Macie, by the way."

"Geri," she said with a small wave, though Macie still hadn't opened her eyes. She then gestured to her male companion. "And this is Billy."

"How'ya doing, Macie," he said by way of greeting. "You up for the shore excursion later?"

"I had been looking forward to it," she answered. "I'm not feeling great now, but I really don't want to sit it out. I'll probably be there."

"We can nurse our hangovers in between photo ops!" Geri giggled.

Geri and Macie continued to talk through closed eyelids, lounging in their chairs while sipping bottles of Gatorade as if they were cocktails. Billy stayed mostly quiet, soaking in the sunshine in his t-shirt and shorts. Eventually it was time to line up for the excursion and the three slowly made their way down to the ramp.

As they stood waiting to disembark, Macie introduced Geri and Billy to a few other people she'd met earlier. They decided to tour together as a group. Billy was uncharacteristically silent as they prepared for the tour. Geri wondered why he seemed uncomfortable with everyone. He'd been so upbeat earlier in the day… Still, she liked the idea of making more friends while she was here, especially given Lisa's absence.

Thinking of Lisa now, Geri pulled out her phone to send a quick message.

Hey, hope you're doing okay. I'm going on a shore excursion, but I was thinking maybe I can visit you later? Let me know how you're feeling.

A moment later Geri's phone buzzed in response.

I can't have any visitors yet. Feeling better, but still in quarantine. Have a great day!

Geri felt terrible for Lisa, winning this trip and not even being able to enjoy it. She also felt more alone knowing she wouldn't be able to see her friend for much of the trip.

Geri didn't want to become too reliant on Billy for companionship, there was no telling if or when he'd become bored of her. As much as she was excited by the prospect of this new relationship, she didn't want to get her hopes up too soon. It had only been two days, after all; though it was hard to believe how close they'd become in that short amount of time. It scared her a little when she realized how vulnerable she was. She'd been through this before, hadn't she?

Deep in thought, she hardly noticed as she was guided down the ramp by the crowd surrounding her. It wasn't until her feet shifted in the sand below her that she was brought out of her reverie.

CHAPTER 10
THE ISLAND

*H*undreds of people spilled out onto the beach to take in the fresh air and splash in the warm water. Geri, Billy, and Macie formed their own little group, and were joined by a middle-aged brother and sister wearing matching Hawaiian shirts and khakis. Their names were Leslie and Joe. They came from Minnesota—and had the accent to prove it. Their small group also included a single man who looked to be in his mid-thirties. He had a well-trimmed beard and an ear piercing. His name was Brett, and Geri suspected that Macie was especially interested in him by the way she touched his arm and looked up at him. He seemed standoffish to Geri. He didn't smile or say much to the group, and he hardly even acknowledged Macie on his arm.

The six of them set off together, and at Billy's suggestion, opted for a guided tour of the island. They joined about 50 others who'd opted for the tour. Though it was described as a "hike," the terrain was mostly flat and easy to navigate. It was shady under the canopy of so many palm trees, which was a pleasant respite from the hot sun. In the distance was a sleepy volcano that hadn't been active in centuries.

After walking for about an hour, the group stopped in a clearing for a quick break. There were fallen trees arranged in a large circle to provide seating, and each person was handed a soggy turkey sandwich and a small bottle of water. As everyone ate, the guide engaged them in conversation about the island and its wildlife.

"Are there any people on the island?" Macie asked.

"Just us," answered the guide brightly. "Nobody's ever lived here, but we do get frequent visitors who enjoy the local fare." He smiled.

Geri wondered what local fare he was talking about. The only food she'd seen during their outing were coconuts and bananas. Maybe there were shellfish along the coast?

After a few minutes, Billy got up and gently took Geri's arm to lead her away from the group. She didn't want to disappoint him by not following, but still had a headache and didn't want to get left behind if they got lost. She quietly called to Macie and the rest of their small group to follow, and after exchanging looks between them, they hesitantly got up to leave.

"Don't go too far," the guide cautioned. "The island is bigger than it looks. And watch out for snakes!" Geri looked at him, and again he was smiling. Was he serious? Or was he being dramatic?

"Maybe we should stay with the group," Geri suggested quietly to Billy.

"Don't worry about it, he's just joking about the snakes," he assured her. "Don't you want to see more of the island before we leave? We'll cover more ground if we start walking now instead of waiting for everyone else."

"As long as we're here," Macie piped in, "we might as well get the most out of this trip. Let's buddy up so we don't lose each other," she said with a wink, then hooked her arm around Brett's. He looked down at her, but didn't pull his arm away. Geri smiled nervously and looked to Joe and Leslie.

"Well, I don't think we need to hold hands," said Leslie brusquely, "but I like the idea of sticking together."

"We'll all be on the look-out for snakes!" said Joe, dramatically looking around at the ground below them and the trees above them.

"Great, let's go," Billy huffed, obviously unhappy with the additional company. Geri suspected he didn't like the group, but in an unfamiliar place with unknown risks, she was grateful to have extra sets of eyes and ears.

"What time do we have to be back at the boat?" Macie asked.

"Three-thirty," the rest responded in unison. They had just over an hour left to themselves.

Billy wanted to get closer to the volcano, and they were all curious to see what it was like. The first 10 minutes were easy going as they stayed on a trail. After that, the foliage began closing in and the air was thick with moisture and mosquitos. Twenty minutes in, and everyone wanted to turn around and rejoin the larger group.

"You guys can go," Billy said calmly, "but we're so close to the volcano. I'll keep going with Geri, you guys let the group know we'll be back soon."

"I don't think we should split up," Geri said quickly,

afraid of getting lost and being abandoned by the ship.

After a pause, Billy exhaled through his nose, and then agreed through closed eyes. "You're right," he said. "It's probably best we stick together. Alright, let's head back."

Brett and Macie led the group this time, arm in arm as she regaled him with stories of hiking trips she'd taken in the gorges of Watkins Glen, New York, where she grew up. Brett listened silently.

Joe and Leslie followed at a slight distance. As they walked, they pointed out birds, large spiders, and interesting flowers to each other. They each had a camera around their neck to document the sights along the trail and take pictures of each other in front of the tropical backdrops all around them.

Billy and Geri pulled up the rear. They didn't talk much, a first for them on the trip. She knew he was brooding about something, but didn't want to ask in front of the others. She'd bring it up later when they returned to the boat and had time to settle down.

Suddenly, an ear-splitting scream shattered the quiet of the island. Geri and Billy froze mid-step.

Geri looked ahead. Joe and Leslie were crouched to the ground, ready to run or lay flat at any moment, seemingly unsure of which was a better option. Then she saw Macie, one hand clutched over her mouth with the other pointing to something on the ground. Geri looked to Billy, who looked back to her before giving her arm a squeeze and slowly walking over to where Macie stood.

As Billy approached Macie, Geri realized that she didn't see Brett with her anymore. She looked around but didn't see him anywhere among their small group.

Billy followed Macie's gaze and where her finger

was pointing. On the ground was a human hand, cut off cleanly at the wrist. Beneath it, the ground was stained black with dried blood.

"Shit," said Billy.

"What is it?" asked Geri shakily.

Billy put up his own hand to signal her to stay back so she wouldn't have to see it herself. "A hand," he said. "A fucking hand, on the ground." He shook his head in disbelief and looked up at the canopy of trees above them, unsure of what to do next.

Leslie and Joe got up from their hunched positions and went over to confirm what they'd just been told. Upon seeing the disembodied extremity, Leslie's body appeared to melt beneath her as she fainted, while Joe turned to vomit into a nearby tangle of vines.

Geri rushed to Leslie's side. She checked her neck for a pulse and tried to feel if she was still breathing. She'd never seen anyone lose consciousness before. She rubbed Leslie's hand, rocking back and forth anxiously until Leslie's eyes began to flutter back to life. Once Leslie was able to slowly sit up without assistance, Geri turned her attention back to Macie, who was still standing, stuck in time, pointing her own finger toward the ones on the ground, curled slightly upward from the open palm.

Geri waved a hand in front of Macie's face, then rubbed her upper arms and gently pulled her away from the scene. At this, Macie screamed again, making Geri leap backwards in reflexive terror before pulling Macie into an awkward embrace for comfort. Macie cried loudly as she hugged Geri tight.

"What the fuck happened here?" she asked between sobs.

"I don't know," said Geri truthfully, still trying to

process what they stumbled upon.

"Maybe someone was clearing the plants away and had an accident," suggested Billy. "It could be nothing."

"Nothing?" cried Macie. "Losing a limb is not fucking nothing!"

As Joe wiped his mouth on his sleeve, he recovered enough to talk. "Alright. Let's take some pictures of where we are," he said. "We'll take pictures of the hand, and these trees, and we'll give them to the ship's crew so they can have someone look into this."

"Good idea," said Geri. "Let's take some of these banana leaves and make a big 'X' in this clearing so they'll know it when they see it."

"We should have stuck to the trail," said Leslie dazedly, still sitting on the ground where she fell. "We should never have left the group."

At this, Billy's jaw and fists tensed, but he said nothing. It was his idea to leave, and Geri reasoned it would be understandable if he felt any guilt or blame.

"Let's just focus on getting back to the group now," said Joe. "I've taken a lot of pictures. It's up to them to figure out what to do with 'em."

"What if they think we did it?" asked Macie, her eyes still wide with shock.

"If we did it, we wouldn't be telling them about it," said Geri matter-of-factly. "That being said, has anyone seen Brett?"

"Brett's gone?" Macie gasped, her fingers reflexively going to her mouth in panic. "He was just here! Where did he go?" She was panting with adrenaline now, unsure of what to do or where to turn.

Billy exhaled loudly, running a hand through his hair. "Aw, fuck," he said.

"He probably got scared and ran off when you screamed," said Joe. "I almost did the same thing myself."

"Me too," said Leslie. "I almost wish I *had* run off instead of seeing...that," she gestured toward the hand on the ground, but avoided looking in that direction. "He probably ran back to the group. Let's just start going back that way and hopefully we'll run into him."

"Okay," said Geri. "If he's not there when we get back, we'll tell the crew about it and they'll send out a search party. I'm sure they wouldn't leave without him."

"Right," said Billy. "They wouldn't leave anyone behind.

"God, I just want to go home," said Macie.

The five of them retraced their steps. Joe and Leslie were in the lead this time, having paid attention to the plants around them which now acted as landmarks to guide their way. Geri stayed close to Macie, holding her arm to keep her grounded. Billy pulled up the rear, constantly looking around as if waiting for someone to burst through the foliage at any moment.

After about five minutes of walking, he heard a snap behind them. He stopped. Nobody else seemed to notice. Not even a second later, another scream broke the island's silence, this one from somewhere in the distance. This prompted an answering scream from Macie, and jolted everyone into a sprint as they sought the safety of the larger group.

As she ran, Geri pushed back vines that threatened to ensnare her. She could feel her skin being scraped by thorns and she struggled to see through squinted eyes. Her sunglasses had been lost in the commotion, and she'd forgotten whatever headache she'd had that morning. Her focus was on avoiding the many leaves and branches swatting her face, and staying ahead of whatever might be in the brush with them. The group was a mass of flinging arms and legs, all running from a danger they couldn't see.

Suddenly, Leslie tripped and fell forward. Joe followed her down. Geri and Macie were running too fast to avoid them and tumbled over the two bodies, which set everyone into another confused frenzy of activity as they all struggled to get to their feet. During the chaos, Geri felt a shock of weight fall on her from above, pinning her where she lay.

"What's happening?" Macie cried.

Geri couldn't turn her head against the pressing mass, but looked about them from her current position, splayed atop Joe's back.

"It's a net!" Geri shouted huskily. "Billy, are you there?"

Billy had watched the net fall from the trees above them. He'd been steps behind and was now standing behind the trapped group.

"I'll go get help," he said, before running onward through the tangle of vines.

"Wait!" Geri shouted. But he was gone. She was sure he heard her, but he didn't turn around.

"Ugh!" Leslie grunted. "Let me see if I can get out from under somehow."

Before she could find an opening, Geri shushed everyone. She heard footsteps approaching from behind.

"Brett, is that you?" Macie asked desperately.

"No," answered an unfamiliar voice.

CHAPTER 11
CAPTIVE

*E*verything went silent. Was this a rescuer or a captor?

"Who are you?" asked Macie shakily.

"I'm your guide for the evening," he replied sarcastically. "Don't worry about my name, it don't matter." He whistled, long and high, to which distant barking answered.

"Oh God," said Joe quietly.

The stranger chuckled. "Don't worry about *Him*, either," he said. "He won't help you now."

Geri could feel herself shaking. She wasn't sure if the tremors were her own, or Joe's, or a collective shiver from the group trapped beneath the heavy net. She was pretty sure it was the latter.

The barking grew closer, yet it sounded choked and restrained, as if the dogs were being held back from an all-out assault. After what felt like 20 minutes, but was probably closer to two, the first leashed German shepherd appeared before them. It strained against its tether, and its bark was replaced by a snarl as it closed in on its target. From the sound of the low growls and occasional whines to the sides and rear, the group was surrounded.

Each dog was held back by a handler. Geri wondered why, but asked nothing of the man, or the dog handlers who now joined him. From her position, spread flat against Joe on the ground, all she could see were the lower halves of peoples' legs, and those of the dogs trying so hard to reach them through the heavy knit of the net. The men wore matching combat boots and camouflage pants.

"Alright!" yelled the lead man who'd first approached them. "Let's get 'em up and loaded," he ordered his troop. "Don't try to run," he warned the captive group on the ground. "These dogs are a lot faster than you. You're worth more whole, but we don't mind giving the dogs a treat every once in a while." He smiled a yellow-stained grin, though nobody on the ground could see it.

Geri shuddered. She didn't know if he was being literal, but she thought back to the hand they'd found in the clearing and wondered if the dogs had anything to do with it. Macie must have had the same thought, because she began hyperventilating then retching atop Leslie, who groaned and squirmed in disgust and fear.

The dogs were commanded to sit and stay, which they did obediently. Their handlers worked to free each person from the tangle of rope around them. Geri felt a rough hand pull her up by her arm. Her hair had caught in the rope, but she was pulled with such force that the trapped hairs ripped from her head. She yelped in shock, then crossed her arms around her torso, standing hunched in the clearing and feeling exposed.

Geri looked at the dogs, not wanting to make eye-contact with any of them. There were five in total. They sat watchfully, each of them focused on their handlers and their charges. There were six men surrounding them, including the first man who appeared to be their leader. Each had a gun holstered to a hip, and what looked to be an electric cattle prod on the other.

Within seconds, Macie, Joe, and Leslie joined Geri, standing on wobbly legs in the clearing. Macie was still crying, tears streaming down her face, her mouth agape. Leslie was worryingly pale, and Geri prayed she wouldn't pass out again. She doubted these men had the patience for such matters. Joe was silent, instinctively holding on to his camera for security—until it was brusquely taken by one of their captors.

"Take out your phones and whatever else you have on you," ordered the lead man.

Without hesitation, the group searched their pockets and handed over their devices. Leslie had brought a backpack, which was taken in its entirety. Geri handed over the cell phone from her pocket, remembering the work-issued phone in her back pocket. She decided to keep that one there, and claim that she'd forgotten about it if it was discovered later.

All of the confiscated property was dumped into a large canvas sack and hauled over one of the men's shoulders.

"Let's move!" shouted the leader.

Geri was paralyzed by a searing heat that travelled from the middle of her back, through her whole body. She couldn't even scream as she was pushed forward, falling to her knees before quickly stumbling onward.

So it *was* a cattle prod.

Though the four of them trembled with each step,

they made sure to keep pace with those surrounding them. The dogs were surprisingly silent, which was a relief.

Geri kept her head down, but occasionally stole glances at the men on either side. None of them wore masks, which surprised her. They all had deeply tanned skin and weather-worn faces. It was hard to judge their ages, but she guessed they were at least a few years older than her, though years of sun damage made them appear older than that. None of them had spoken since they'd arrived.

As Geri looked ahead of her, she could see they were moving back toward the volcano and away from any chance of running into the ship's crew or other passengers. She steeled herself for whatever was to come. She looked to Macie next to her, and saw that while she had a glazed over expression, she had at least stopped crying.

As they approached the base of the volcano, they began veering left. The terrain became more difficult to pass as they started a slow ascent over exposed, uneven rock. Geri carefully watched her feet with each step, trying not to focus on Joe stumbling ahead of her.

As the trail narrowed, the lead captor and one of the dog handlers took up the front while the other four kept to the rear. There was only enough room for two people to walk side-by-side. To the right of them was the mountain face. On the left, a steep cliff that dropped to the island's floor as they continued to climb higher.

Though she didn't like being so close to the edge, Geri kept herself between Macie and the cliff. She knew that Macie was close to breaking, and wanted her to feel as secure as possible under the current circumstances.

One wrong move could endanger everyone. She had to stay grounded.

Suddenly, a distant pop sounded above them, from further up the mountain. Then another. Then a third. Geri had never heard a gun being fired, but guessed that's what she was hearing now. Leslie and Joe hesitated for the briefest moment before continuing onward. They were already surrounded by guns where they were, what difference did it make if they were headed towards one more?

Geri didn't break stride, and looked to her right to make sure Macie was still with her. Thankfully, she still had that glazed over look from earlier. Maybe she didn't hear anything.

They continued walking, making a slow, curving ascent. Geri's legs burned, trembling from exertion and fear. The sandals she'd chosen this morning weren't meant for hiking, and they blistered her feet, leaving them a bloodied mess. She'd take off the shoes if the terrain wasn't so jagged underfoot. Or if she wasn't afraid of another cattle prod to the back.

As she again looked at her raw feet, a scream set her on high alert, even more so than the gunshots. They were closer to the source this time. And the scream itself rang out clear and loud on the otherwise quiet mountain. It almost seemed to echo, reverberating against the rock face before being silenced by some unseen force.

"We're almost there now," their guide chuckled.

Next to her, Geri saw Macie clutch her chest and begin to hyperventilate again.

"It's okay," Geri tried to reassure her, as quietly as she could. She reached out to touch her arm.

"No!" Macie shouted, swatting Geri's hand away.

"No! I'm not going!" She then turned, her back against the mountain. Wide-eyed, she looked past Geri, toward the expanse of trees below them.

Geri shifted forward, afraid of being tossed from the volcano's side as an afterthought if Macie tried to jump. Geri wasn't the only one who saw the direction of Macie's gaze, however. Before she could do anything, a shock in her hip cemented her where she was. Once the rod was pulled away, her arms were deftly pulled behind her so her wrists could be zip-tied together.

The dogs snarled and pulled in response to the sudden flurry of activity, creating even more tension among the group. Geri felt her heart hammering against her chest. She was sure she'd feel it stop at any moment, it was beating so hard and fast. She became lightheaded and wanted to sit down, but couldn't move. Instead she watched as a thin cord was tied from Macie's wrists to one of their captors' belts. They had her on a leash now, just like the dogs.

A quick "Hey!" from the leader silenced the dogs immediately. "There will be no running or jumping from this cliff. This mountain will be your home for the next few days. Breathe in the fresh air now. You won't be seeing daylight again for a while. And if you try that again," he turned, speaking directly to Macie, "I won't hesitate to put a bullet in your head myself. You're worth more alive, but people will still pay for your body as long as we keep it looking pretty."

At this revelation, Geri wanted to vomit. They were going to be sold. Alive or dead, it didn't matter. She wasn't sure either option was better than the other.

Ahead of Geri and Macie, Leslie gasped, and put her hands on her legs as she hunched over, panting for breath.

Joe sighed and rubbed her back. What more was there to do now?

"You two won't be worth much either way," the lead man said dismissively to the siblings. "But who am I to turn away business?" After a pause, he boomed, "Now, break's over! Pick up your feet and let's go!"

Again, they walked. Tears streaked Macie's face as she hung her head in defeat, leashed like an animal. Geri took note of everything around her, making sure she was aware of every boulder and divot in the ground. She doubted she'd make it out of whatever prison they were being led to, but she had to stay alert, just in case.

In just a few minutes, they rounded a bend and were standing in front of a small cave. It was guarded on either side by men with automatic rifles strapped across their chests.

One by one, they ducked into the dark opening, continuing through a damp, musty tunnel before finally reaching the hollow cavern within.

"Welcome home," said their guide with a mischievous grin.

CHAPTER 12
WAKING UP

*L*isa felt like she'd been sleeping for days. Her head ached as she struggled to focus. Where was she?

She looked around hazily, slow to move her head, which felt too heavy for her neck. She was in a grey room with pipes along the walls. It was a small space and felt either damp or cool, it was hard to tell. There were a number of bodies surrounding her on the floor. A person wearing a ship's staff uniform was bent over one of the bodies, injecting something into the lifeless figure. Within seconds, the person began stirring.

Lisa followed the crew member with her eyes as he repeated the process. Even in her confused state, she noted that he used the same needle for each person. The floor was now alive with squirming bodies who groaned in discomfort.

"Whh…...wheaah…" Lisa dyrly vocalized. She'd wanted to ask where they were. Her mind was waking up, but her body wasn't quite her own yet. If she focused, she could move her fingers, and then her toes, but her arms and legs were still too heavy to lift.

The crew member left the room before Lisa could pronounce the question on her tongue. Though she wanted to close her eyes and fall back to sleep, she knew something was wrong that shouldn't be ignored. Still, she was too groggy to begin to guess what was happening around her.

Lisa tried to remember what she had been doing before she found herself here—wherever here was—but couldn't process a single thought. She looked at the people around her, in various states of waking. She tried to find some spark of familiarity but was coming up short.

She looked at her right hand, and slowly curled and uncurled her fingers, trying to regain some control over herself. Her legs ached, and the area between them burned. She didn't bother to wonder why, she simply wondered when, and how often, she'd been visited during her unnatural sleep. And by whom.

With great effort, she pulled a leg toward her and used it as leverage to hoist herself into a higher sitting position. Her whole leg tingled with the electric feeling of having slept on it for too long. She winced and gasped at the sensation.

Similar grunts of effort sounded around her as the other people struggled to get themselves upright. There were heavy-lidded blinks, and slow headed turns as each person tried to figure out where they were. None were successful. Gradually, however, they were all able to regain some level of balance and feeling in their extremities. After what could have been minutes or hours, the guard from earlier returned with reinforcements. Lisa noted the guns on each of their hips.

CHAPTER 13
ACCOMMODATIONS

*T*he first thing that struck Geri about the cave was its oppressive heat. The further they went through the tunnel, the hotter it seemed to get. She'd expected the opposite; usually caves were dark, damp, and cool. This one was dark, hot, and humid. Was the volcano still active, after all?

As the tunnel widened and opened to the cavernous interior, Geri looked around to find large dog kennels scattered throughout. Instead of dogs, however, they were filled with people. At least three people per kennel.

The cave itself was dimly lit with hanging lanterns. There was no electricity on the island that she was aware of. As she continued to take in her surroundings, Geri was caught off guard by the rough hand suddenly gripping her arm. She didn't fight, and clumsily followed the person leading her to a cage along the cave's wall. Her arm was freed just long enough for the other person to slip a key into the padlock and open the gate to shove her inside.

"Welcome to hell," said one of her two kennel-mates.

Geri smiled nervously and introduced herself. The woman who had addressed her said that her name was Kate. She looked about 35 and was blonde and blue-eyed with a lean build.

The other woman looked younger, no older than 20. She was a petite, curvy woman who looked like she could have been a Sports Illustrated model with long, dark wavy hair that fell around her. Her name was Ximena, but she told Geri that everyone just called her Mina.

"How long have you both been here?" Geri asked.

"I've been here about two weeks," said Kate. "Mina just got here a few days ago, but she was on another island for about a week before that."

At this revelation, Geri's mouth dropped. "There are other islands like this?"

"It's not so much the islands that are the issue here," Kate explained, rolling her eyes. "It's the cruise line. They pick out people who don't have family or friends and they pick them off and bring them here."

"But I have family!" Geri countered, a bit too loud. She quickly covered her mouth and looked around, but nobody was looking at her.

"Just your parents though, right?" Kate asked. "And you don't live near them, do you?"

"No," Geri admitted. "I live in another state. We don't see each other much."

"Exactly," said Kate. "They've done their research on all of us. They know who we are, what we do for a living, who we talk to, and how often we see other people. They pick the people who nobody will notice never got back from the cruise—for at least a few weeks. By then, anything could have happened to them. Happened to us."

Geri couldn't understand how this was possible. "But wouldn't the cops notice that all of these people went on a cruise, and were never heard from again?"

"If somebody actually calls the cops, maybe," Kate said. "But none of us are close enough to anyone for anybody to notice we went missing in the first place."

"What about you?" Geri addressed Mina directly. "You don't have family?"

"I ran away two years ago," she said, pulling her arms around her legs as she sat on the ground in the corner of the cage. She tilted her head away, looking at nothing in particular. "The only people who'd look for me are people who don't really care what happens to me anyway."

Geri felt for the girl, who was all alone and too young to be isolated this way.

"Why did they move you from another island, do you know?" Geri asked.

"The auctions only happen here," Mina said. "They take people from everywhere, but eventually everybody comes here."

"How often are the auctions?" Geri asked.

"Every two weeks," Kate replied. "And the next one is in two days. You're lucky, you don't have to stay here long. I can't *wait* to get out of here."

"But what happens when you get sold? Where do you go?" Geri asked.

"Honestly, I don't care," laughed Kate. "I've been sweating in this hell hole for almost two weeks, eating nothing but whatever crap they're giving us and breathing in the same goddamned stink every minute of the day. All I want is to get outside. I don't care where I go after this."

To that, Geri had no reply. She didn't want to be locked in a cage. She didn't want to suffer in this heat, with the stench of a hundred sweaty bodies permeating every shallow breath. But she also didn't want to be sold as cargo. She didn't know who the buyers were, or what their plans could be, but she doubted the auction would end well for anyone.

Geri's skin was already damp and she felt lightheaded from the high temperatures of the cave. Her mind raced with possibilities she didn't even want to fathom. She considered herself and her cellmates. Attractive young women. She guessed it was obvious what they'd be used for. But what about the others? Leslie and Joe? Physical labour, perhaps? What did modern slaves actually do? She felt naïve at how little she knew of the world and its darker parts. She never saw it as something she'd become entangled in herself—human trafficking always seemed to be a foreign problem. How wrong she was.

As she sat at the front of her cage, Geri looked into the other cages to see where the members of her group ended up. Joe was closest, two kennels away. He had one other man in his cage, of a similar age and build. Next she spotted Macie. She was sitting on the ground with her legs pulled up and her arms crossed over her knees. Her head was buried in her arms, likely to hide her crying. Her two cage mates appeared lifeless at the bottom of the cage, laying on their sides. Only by the movement of their rib cages was Geri able to see that they were, in fact, alive. They were both so thin, Geri could count every rib. She wondered how long they'd been here.

After searching another moment, she spotted Leslie in a cramped kennel with three other women. Like Joe's cage, Leslie's cage was stocked with heavier individuals. Looking around the cavern, she realized that all of the cages were sorted in this way. Everyone appeared to be grouped by sex, age, and size. She supposed it made it easier for the buyers to zero in on the type of person they were interested in.

"Arms!" A shout startled Geri from her thoughts. She looked up at the woman standing outside the cage, a cigarette hanging from her lips. Geri didn't know what she wanted. Kate and Mina came to the front of the cage and each slipped an arm through the bars. Geri followed their lead. When she saw the woman pull out a needle, she recoiled.

"Don't make me pull out the taser," the woman warned.

"It's okay," said Kate. "They do blood tests every time there's a new shipment to check our health."

Geri looked back at Kate, unable to form a response. She hated needles. She avoided doctors for that reason. Now this brusque woman was going to stab her in the arm in this dark, unsanitary place?

Hesitantly, she produced her arm again. The woman took another syringe from the pack on her waist and started searching Geri's arm for a good vein. She found one quickly, and not-very-gently inserted the needle. Geri turned her head away and closed her eyes from the scene. Once the vial was filled, the woman pulled out the needle and moved on to Mina, then to Kate. No bandages or anything to stop the trickle of blood from running down her arm.

She looked at the vials, now filled with scarlet, and saw they were labeled with numbers rather than names.

"What's my number?" Geri asked Kate.

"You'll find out when she comes back for a urine sample," she replied flatly.

Geri thought she was joking and wondered whether Kate knew her own number. A few minutes later, the woman did indeed come back, along with a bag full of sterile urine cups.

"Pee in this," the woman said simply.

"Now?" Geri asked incredulously.

"Now," the woman said.

"Here?" Geri asked, looking around her, truly shocked by the reality hitting her.

"Here," the woman impatiently replied. "Just make sure you get it in the cup."

Geri again felt her heart hammering and her head buzzing. How could they expect anyone to produce a sample in this situation? She hadn't even considered the possibility of relieving herself in this cage.

She looked around to the other cages where other prisoners were alternately squatting over a single bucket in each cage, peeing first into the cups they were given before finishing up in the bucket. She looked back in her own cage, where she saw that there was indeed a bucket in the back corner that she hadn't noticed before. Mina was using it now. Geri averted her gaze, on the verge of crying out in disgust and frustration.

After her two kennel-mates had finished, it was her turn. She looked at the cup in her hand. #292. She sheepishly walked over to the bucket and squatted above it before attempting to pull down her shorts just enough to urinate without leaving herself fully exposed. She regretted not putting on a dress this morning, which could have at least saved her some humiliation—although the shorts made it possible for her to keep her spare phone hidden in her back pocket.

It had been a long time since Geri had been asked for

a urine sample. She'd forgotten what a shy bladder she had. As she perched uncomfortably over the bucket, she found it next-to-impossible to produce a sample. Nothing was coming.

The woman outside the cage tapped her foot impatiently. Geri felt her face getting increasingly hotter. She hadn't used a restroom all day, surely her bladder was full.

"Let's go, bitch!" the woman seethed through her cigarette, finally removing it from her mouth to add, "I'm not standing here all day waiting for you to piss!"

Geri saw all eyes actively avoiding her. She strained, willing her bladder to squeeze itself empty. She took her free hand and pressed it to her stomach, finally loosening whatever had been holding back the stream. She filled the cup and mortifyingly finished into the bucket for what felt like a full minute or longer, before closing the lid on her sample and handing it back to the woman, who took it with a grunt before putting it in her bag and leaving.

"Guess we should've warned you," said Kate empathetically. "We're used to it now. There's no sense of modesty here." As she said it, she took the bucket, now filled with the urine of three women, and dumped it out through the bars. Geri felt warm droplets splash off the bars and against her arm.

For the first time throughout the whole ordeal, Geri cried. It was bad enough living with crippling anxiety in everyday life. Here, she had no choice but to be on constant display. There were no doors or excuses to hide behind anymore. Suddenly, she understood why people would rather get sold to an anonymous stranger than stay here for another day or hour. How could she live this way? How did anyone live this way?

CHAPTER 14
FINDING HER FOOTING

"Wakey, wakey!" shouted an over-enthusiastic woman as she entered the room, led by the guard who'd administered the mystery injections to Lisa and all the others sprawled around. Lisa's head pounded with the reverberations of the woman's voice. It felt like they were in a room made of metal the way the sound echoed off each wall. Looking at all the pipes along the walls and ceilings, it wasn't too far off to think so.

Armed guards walked in, all wearing matching uniforms.

"Time to get up," the woman boomed as she clapped her hands. The guards hastily began yanking people by their arms. Lisa whimpered as she was pulled up by her collar, trying to feel her feet under her to balance into at least a semi-erect stance. She was unsuccessful, falling back to the ground twice before finally settling into a crouching position.

In her confused state, she couldn't count the people on the ground, or the number of guards harassing them. She focused instead on herself and gaining control of her unwieldy limbs. She could feel her toes, which she now noticed were covered in only socks—where were her shoes? And what shoes had she been wearing before... this? Looking around her, she saw that only the guards were wearing shoes; steel toed boots, it appeared.

One guard used his boot to kick a man who'd stayed on the ground too long. He didn't seem to be moving at all. Another kick to the ribs elicited no response. The guard bent down and checked the man's neck for a pulse. Whatever he found must have displeased him, because he kicked the man directly in the face with a resounding crack, causing the whole body to move in one stiff motion. Lisa was thankful he was turned away from her so she didn't have to see his face before or after the breaking blow.

She let out a deep breath, unaware that she'd even been holding it. She again focused on her toes, then the balls of her feet and her heels. Her legs still burned, more so now from the crouching position. She slowly straightened her knees, her back still bent forward and her arms resting on her thighs for support. She was hunched over, but standing. The rest of the people who had been on the ground with her were now similarly positioned, occasionally prodded by boots or the butt of a gun if they took too long.

"Alright, time to go!" shouted the woman, who appeared to lead the other guards. Lisa felt a large hand close on her arm just long enough to shove her toward the door. She stumbled, but remained on her feet. A small victory.

The group made their way through the open door, which led them through a dark hallway with more pipes and metallic sounds. Lisa had no idea where she was, though she imagined this was what it must be like to be on a submarine.

The group continued on for some time, going up two flights of stairs and more hallways that branched right or left as you got to the end. Finally, they approached a dead end that had a single steel door.

It took two guards turning a rusted wheel in order to unlock it. As the heavy door creaked open, Lisa was blinded by a sudden burst of light.

CHAPTER 15
SURVIVING

There was no way to tell how much time had passed in the cave, unless you were wearing an analog watch, as Geri was. All digital and electronic devices were confiscated before anyone entered the cave. Fortunately, Geri preferred to do things the old fashioned way, and that included keeping track of time. Even so, nothing in the cave was simple. The unearthly glow of dim lights along the rocky walls made it hard to see anything clearly, and impossible to tell whether it was day or night.

Geri had curled up on the dirt floor like everyone else in captivity. There wasn't much to do here but sleep, it seemed. She was awakened by voices at 8:15. She had no idea if it was still evening, or if she had slept through to the next morning.

"Dinner time," said a guard walking by. *That answered that*, Geri thought. In his hand were a number of canvas sacks. He slipped one through the bars of Geri's cage.

Geri hesitantly lifted a corner of the sack, not sure what she'd find inside. Kate and Mina quickly joined her and dumped the contents onto the bare dirt floor. Three bananas, one coconut, and some dried strips of jerky. There were also three metal drinking cups, though there was no water in the bag. Geri picked up a cup and held it in her hand.

"It's for the coconut," Kate explained. "We crack them open, pour out the liquid to drink, and then we eat the meat from it."

Geri looked at the small coconut, which had thankfully already been removed from its husk.

"This won't provide much, will it?" she asked, already knowing the answer.

"They don't care about our hydration," Kate rolled her eyes as she said it. "We just have to stay alive long enough for people to buy us. It's not like we're here for long."

Mina silently took the coconut in both hands and deftly hit it against a rock jutting out from the wall. After two strikes, she had a crack big enough to work with. She brought the coconut back to the centre of the cave and arranged the three small, metal mugs on the ground before using both hands to peel back the top of the fruit where she'd broken it. Then she carefully poured the liquid into each cup as evenly as possible.

Geri thanked Mina, who nodded in return. They each took an overripe banana from the pile. Geri never ate bananas that had any hint of a brown spot. She hated the overpowering flavour of a banana once it was sufficiently ripe. With a slight grimace, she peeled the top, getting an immediate whiff of the fruit. She tentatively took a bite, then made a disgusted face as she put it back into the pile.

"You guys can have mine," she said, turning her attention to the jerky. She took a piece and gnawed at it until her jaw hurt. It didn't taste like any jerky she'd ever had before, but it was easier on her palate than the banana. Once she'd finished that strip, she shared the coconut meat with her cellmates before washing everything down with her meagre cup of coconut water. She hadn't eaten since breakfast, but she really wasn't hungry after the day's events. The only thing she found herself wanting more of was the juice—or water—anything to quench her thirst. Her mouth was dry and her headache from earlier was coming back again. Unfortunately, she didn't expect a respite any time soon.

Instead, she sat backed up against the corner of the cell, her head pressed to one of the bars. She'd expected the metal to be cool on her skin. Instead, it was uncomfortably warm, just like everything else in the cave. There would be no escaping the heavy heat, nor the pain throbbing in her skull. She couldn't think of a single time in her life that could compare to this experience. She closed her eyes, crossed her arms over her chest, and tried to clear her mind of everything for the remainder of the night. All she could think of was her own discomfort.

Sometime later, she was roused by whispers and shuffling. She opened her eyes and checked her watch. 5:40. She assumed it was early morning. She then checked her back pocket, making sure the phone was still safely tucked away. It was. At least that was a plus.

She looked around to find the source of the whispers, and found two guards standing over Macie's cage, which was shared with the two very thin female prisoners. Again, they appeared dead, save for the shallow breaths seen with the rise and fall of their ribcages.

"Neither of them have eaten or drunk anything in a week," said one of the guards. Without water, the women would probably be dead in hours. Geri was surprised they'd made it this long in their condition.

The other guard kicked the cage bars nearest the women. Geri saw Macie shudder at the sound, while continuing to look away from the scene, her head hidden beneath her arms.

"Is this a hunger strike?" the guard asked the women on the ground. "Because you can't just starve yourself to death here, we have other ways to deal with that," she said ominously. Forcefully, she added, "If you don't eat anything by this evening, we'll shove it down your throats just to keep you alive until the auction. Don't test me."

The guard delivered one last kick before walking away, inspecting some other cages. Macie curled into herself, making herself as small as she could in the corner. Geri continued to follow the guards while trying not to attract their attention by staring. She listened while occasionally glancing to see where they were. When they changed direction toward her, she pretended to sleep.

"Bring a funnel tomorrow," one guard said to the other. "If they haven't eaten anything, mash up the coconut and bananas and force-feed them."

The other guard hesitated before asking, "Do you think they'll even sell? Is it worth it?"

The first guard glared back. "People will pay for anything." She then added, thoughtfully, "and if they don't, we'll just use them for dog food." There wasn't a hint of humour in her voice.

Geri closed her eyes tightly and felt bile rising in her throat, but swallowed it down to avoid unwanted attention.

She'd never considered suicide before, but knowing that even that wasn't an option filled her with unexpected dread. There was truly no way out of here, save for the approaching auction. Even the freedom to die had been taken from them.

When Geri was sure the guards were gone, and it seemed that everyone around was asleep again, she pulled the hidden phone from her pocket and brought it under her shirt. She pulled her arms in through the sleeves and held the phone in her hands. She'd always kept it on silent, and was grateful for that habit now. She only had 21-percent battery left, and no service in the cave. She composed a short text to her mother, knowing that it wouldn't send until she moved to a location with cell service. At least the more time-consuming task of writing the text would be done already. Once she was in range of a signal, she would turn the phone back on and hope the message reached its destination.

Her text was simple.

Kidnapped. Have police track harvest cruise for missing people. Love you both so much.

There was still so much she didn't know, which made it easier and harder to think of what to say. She decided that the less detail, the better for now. Once the authorities began their search, they'd likely find out more than she'd ever be able to guess.

She turned off the phone to conserve its battery. She needed it to have some life left in order to send that message later. She just hoped she'd be able to find a signal once she made it out after the auction. *If* she made it out after the auction.

As she put the phone back in her pocket, she looked up to find Mina looking back at her. They stared at each other for just a moment before Mina closed her eyes to go back to sleep. Geri did the same, keeping a hand securely over the phone as she did so and drifting off in under a minute. The exhaustion that came from doing nothing all day was more than anyone could fight.

Geri dreamed she was on a date with Billy. They were enjoying themselves, seated at an outdoor café, when they were suddenly attacked by wolves. The wolves tore apart the other guests at the café while Geri watched helplessly. When she looked across the table to Billy, she saw that he was gone. She frantically searched, finally finding him jumping over a table and out of harm's way. Geri then caught the yellow eye of one of the wolves, which began a slow, deliberate walk toward her. Just as it got close, someone came out from the kitchen, clanging pans and scaring away the wolves.

The clanging continued, and at 7:15, Geri was again startled awake by a heavy boot hitting the cage bars.

Time for breakfast.

There were two coconuts to be shared among three captives. Mina wordlessly went to work, scooping up the coconuts, cracking each against the rock wall behind them, and doling out the contents inside.

Neither Geri nor Mina looked at each other, which wasn't out of the ordinary for the short amount of time they'd been housed together. Geri wondered if Mina remembered the phone, or if she really saw anything at all. There was no way to tell, and she wasn't about to ask. Instead, she turned her attention to Kate.

"Is the auction tomorrow?" Geri asked.

"Should be," Kate answered while scooping up

coconut meat with her fingers.

"Is there anything we should know?" Geri continued, before adding hesitantly, "anything we'll need to do?" She was nervous to hear the answer, but wanted to be prepared. After her first day's introduction, she didn't want to be caught off guard again.

"Make yourself pretty," Kate said sarcastically, rolling her eyes. "I don't know, I wasn't here for the last one," she added. "I'm sure they'll give us directions if we're supposed to do anything—other than staying alive, at least."

At this, Geri turned to look back at Macie's cage mates. The emaciated pair were still breathing, but didn't appear to have moved since she last saw them early that morning. They didn't seem strong enough to move even if they wanted to. In the back of the cage, Macie struggled to break open a coconut by herself. She picked it up, and threw it onto the ground. Over and over she did this, almost robotic in her motions.

As Geri looked on, she saw a good rock with a sharp edge in Macie's cage. She waited for Macie to see it too. Finally, as if she willed her to do it, Macie looked from the coconut to the rock. As she cracked the fruit against it, Geri smiled.

Macie sipped the liquid straight from its vessel. It was the first drink she'd had in almost 36 hours. She ravenously gulped all she could. There was still one other coconut in the cage, and this one was broken easier now that she knew what to do. Once she had it open, Macie brought it to the other two girls in her cage. She poured a bit of the juice into her hand and tried to bring it to their lips, but it was running through her fingers. She then found the metal cups on the ground and poured the remainder into them.

Macie cradled one girl's head in her lap, delicately holding her up. She slowly brought the cup to the girl's mouth, dripping in the liquid drop by drop to avoid choking her. The girl sputtered, then licked her lips. Macie dripped in a bit more. Once the girl had at least gotten some liquid into her, Macie moved to the next. Again, she cradled her head in her lap and slowly poured the liquid from the cup into the girl's mouth. Unlike the other, this girl spit out what little bit was given and shook her head with a small groan. She used what little energy she had left to wave away Macie's efforts and roll to her side.

Macie hesitated, before giving the rest of the juice to the first girl. Geri had watched all this from behind her own cage bars, proud of Macie for her efforts, and sad for both of the girls in her charge. Their misery would be over soon, she told herself.

Hours later, she would realize that their misery had only just begun.

Once again, Geri was startled by the sound of boots striking metal bars.

"Time for lunch!" the guard from earlier shouted, obviously directed toward the starving women in Macie's cage. Looking closer at her uniform, Geri noted an insignia the other guards lacked. *She must be their captain*, Geri concluded.

"They had some coconut this morning," Macie told her sheepishly, gesturing toward the broken fruit on the ground.

"A little coconut now won't keep them alive until tomorrow," the leader growled. She then looked around the cave before yelling, "Let this be a lesson to all of you!"

Two more guards joined her. One had a funnel and

pitcher of whiteish slush. The other had IV bags connected to tubes. The guard with the IVs went to work first hanging the saline bags from the top of the cage and then inspecting each woman's arms for a good vein. As dehydrated as they were, this proved to be a challenge. After going over each arm multiple times, he sighed, then directed the guard with the funnel to begin working first.

The funnel was positioned on top of the cage, with a long, thin tube extending down. The second guard positioned himself on the ground, and pulled the first girl onto his lap, with the back of her head resting on his chest. He took the end of the funnel's tube, held open the girl's jaw with one hand, and quickly slid the tube down her throat. She gagged, but was too weak to struggle. The captain who had been overseeing the process picked up the pitcher of thick slush and poured it into the funnel.

Geri fought against a dry heave and turned away from the spectacle, as did everyone else in their cages. Nothing could block the gurgling sound of the woman being force-fed and choking on the viscous material. It went on for minutes. Nobody could help them. Geri didn't dare look back at Macie to see how she was holding up, but she was sure she could hear her retching too.

Just when it seemed to be over, they moved to the second girl. She groaned weakly, aware of what was coming but unable to stop it. The torture began anew, and again, nobody could watch. Geri closed her eyes tightly and wished there was something to drown out the sound.

Once it was done, the first guard with the IVs returned to the cage. He sat each woman up against the cage and loosely zip-tied them to the bars around their necks and waists to keep them sitting upright. After watching what happened next, Geri found out that this step served two purposes: it made them less likely to vomit, as gravity helped keep the contents of their now-distended stomachs in place; and it gave the guard better access to insert the IVs directly into each woman's jugular.

CHAPTER 16
SPLASH

*L*isa was blinded for a terrifying few seconds as her eyes adjusted to the brightness of daylight. She looked down toward the floor below her as she was pushed forward by the tight crowd of guards and other confused captives.

Stepping through the door, the first thing she noticed aside from the light was the strong scent of saltwater. Still looking down, she could see they were being led along a ramp. Below them, the ocean lapped at the side of the ship about 20 feet down from where they were currently standing.

The ship, Lisa remembered. She'd been on a cruise. Her mind flooded with memories as she recalled boarding with Geri, meeting a man—*what was his name?* And drinking alone at a bar while giving Geri and the new guy some space. That was all she remembered. How long ago was that, and what had happened since?

As she took in the scene, Lisa realized something was very wrong. These people prodding her with guns were not typical cruise ship security guards, and wherever they were heading—an island, from the look of things—was not on any agenda.

Suddenly, Lisa was overcome by a wave of heat and dread. She could feel her heart thrumming in her chest as her head buzzed with a surge of panicked energy. She looked over the railing of the ramp, and roughly judged the distance to shore. About 500 feet or so, she thought. She couldn't see how deep the water was, but decided to take her chances before they got any further.

Before anyone could react, Lisa was over the side of the ramp. It felt like she was suspended in the air for minutes rather than seconds. She saw the water below getting closer and closed her eyes before colliding with the hard surf. Her whole body screamed in pain as she smacked into and then sunk below the water's surface. She gasped a mouthful of water before kicking back to the surface to cough it up and take a breath.

She didn't hear the screams and commotion above. Nor did she hear the guns cocking as she sputtered, heaved, and gasped before again ducking under the cover of the sea.

On the ramp, the guards each grabbed the nearest captive to prevent them from following the escapee. Most of their charges were still too delirious to even realize what had just happened. They simply stayed put and followed the harried orders not to move. The female guard, the captain who led the bunch, had been walking ahead and didn't see Lisa jump. She did, however, hear the smack of something large hitting the water. She looked down in time to see Lisa breach for air.

"Guns!" she shouted. "Shoot!"

Lisa didn't hear the gunshots, but she was aware of

the bullets striking the water all around her. She didn't even feel the one that had gone through her hand. She had just enough time to cough out seawater and take one meagre breath before being forced to retreat back below the water's surface.

With nowhere else to turn, Lisa took what shelter she could find—which happened to be the underside of the ship. Her lungs protested the situation, and burned for lack of oxygen. The ship was wide, but she decided that her best option was to swim across and as far back as she could to avoid detection by the guards above.

She was still groggy from whatever they'd been giving her aboard the ship, and her arms and legs felt like lead in the water. Lisa saw threads of blood trailing around her like delicate ribbons, but didn't have time to consider where they were coming from. She simply kept going until she made it far enough that she felt it was safe to surface.

Her lungs felt like they were ready to explode when she finally came up for air with a gasping breath. Her hair was stuck to her face, blocking her eyesight. As she moved it aside with her hand, she finally saw the gnarly wound that went straight through to the other side. She hadn't felt any pain until that moment. Now, the raw flesh and salty seawater sent a throbbing pulse through her hand and down her arm. She hissed with pain, still very much aware of the danger above. She did her best to maintain even, quiet breaths, staying as close as she could to the ship's side. She heard shouting from the other side, and then hushed voices. In a moment, she could hear echoing footsteps above her as she took one more deep breath and again hid under the ship.

She saw the bullets travel through the water in front

of her. Seconds passed, then a minute. She slowly emerged about 20 seconds after the last bullet was fired. She heard footsteps again, this time louder. She looked to the side and saw the guards escorting the rest of the group down a dock. She watched as they were led to the beach, across the sand, and out of sight through the trees. She expected to hear more gunshots at any moment, but was equally disturbed by the silence that followed. She looked all around and saw no place to hide nearby. After some deliberation, she decided to take a chance and swim parallel to the shore for as far as she could before eventually making landfall and heading for the tree line.

Her hand burned with every stroke. Her body protested the sudden burst of activity after days of toxic sleep. Her legs were all but numb as they kicked through the water. Finally, she reached a point where she felt comfortable enough to head toward shore. She hadn't seen or heard any other people for some time. She chose a quiet, rocky ledge with reasonable cover, and a short climb to the nearest palm trees and vines.

She held her mangled hand close to her body and reached with the other to climb up the jagged rocks. The sudden heaviness of gravity combined with water-laden clothes and the grogginess of residual drugs in her system made the ascent torturously slow and arduous. She was barefoot, and found her footing carefully to avoid any further injury. Still, she could feel the poke of small, sharp stones with each step.

She climbed, aware of how simple this would be under normal circumstances, compared to how difficult it was now. Back home, she ran for miles each day and did weight training twice a week at the gym. Here, as she slowly made her way toward the tree line, it felt as though she'd been languishing in a bed for months and was now competing in a triathlon—one where losing could mean death.

Lisa stretched herself over the boulder ahead of her and was finally able to relish the feeling of sand beneath her arms and knees. She crawled the rest of the way, occasionally using the elbow of her injured arm as a brief support, and wincing from pain each time.

Reaching the protection of the trees, Lisa allowed herself to sit beneath a small palm to catch her breath and take in her surroundings. She looked back toward the ship, which was further away than she realized. She'd swum well, putting considerable distance between herself and whoever was left on the boat. She hoped nobody aboard saw her.

From her low vantage point, she couldn't see much of the island around her. She remembered briefly seeing some kind of mountain earlier, but she didn't know where she was in proximity to it now. All she saw were the rocks behind her, and bursts of green life ahead of her.

CHAPTER 17
AUCTION DAY

*T*he day began as it had the previous morning. A clang against the bars jarred Geri awake in time to see two bananas, three strips of jerky, and a coconut land on the ground in front of her.

"Eat up!" yelled an unfamiliar guard. "This is your last meal here. We don't want any leftovers," he said with a dark smile.

Geri avoided the bananas and went straight for the jerky while Mina worked on the coconut.

"What if we don't get sold?" Geri wondered aloud.

"You heard him," said Kate, "No leftovers—we won't be staying here either way. I don't know what happens next, but I think getting sold is the best option."

Geri contemplated alternatives, but didn't come up with much. They'd probably end up enslaved either way, so did it matter who cracked the whip? As nervous as she normally would be, given the circumstances, she found herself remarkably calm. Whatever happened, she was resigned to the outcome. What use was it worrying now?

She chewed the jerky, with its odd taste and texture,

and looked around the dark cave to see how the other prisoners seemed. In Macie's cage, it was hard to avoid the sight of her two cage-mates still hooked up to their IVs, tubes protruding from their necks. Their colour seemed marginally better today, and even their eyes seemed slightly more alert than they had been a day ago. Macie was at the back of the cage getting to work on the coconut. *Good girl*, thought Geri.

Joe was eating a banana, staring blankly ahead of him. Leslie, in her cage further away, was doing much the same. Though they hadn't known each other long, Geri hoped that she'd be leaving with one of them. It would be nice to have someone to talk to, wherever they ended up. Kate was an alright cage-mate, but Geri suspected that she didn't like her. Geri wasn't a fan of her constant sarcasm and eye rolls, either. Mina seemed kind, though it was difficult to bond with someone who rarely spoke. Reflecting on this, Geri realized why she had so much trouble making friends back home. Nobody wants to talk to someone who won't contribute to the conversation.

Once breakfast was over, it was anybody's guess when the next step would begin, or what it would entail. There was palpable tension as everyone waited to see what would happen. Geri found the familiar pangs of anxiety returning. A shiver crept up her back, though the heat of the volcanic cave was as oppressive as ever. Her teeth chattered and her fingers trembled. She held her arms across her, hands hidden beneath her armpits as she rocked back and forth in a futile attempt to self-soothe. The anticipation of events to come grew with time.

Just as she wondered if her heart would suddenly stop, unable to sustain its quickening beat, something caught her attention at the entrance of the cave. A flutter of movement—people wearing colours other than the muted khaki of the guards.

They seemed disoriented, looking back and forth but not taking in much information. Many of them stumbled and looked as though they were just learning how to walk. They were surrounded by guards, who led them into cages.

Geri found herself looking forward to a new cage mate; she'd ask where they'd been and what they might know. Unfortunately, the new group was relatively small, and were assigned their temporary cells quickly. None found their way back to Geri's cage.

CHAPTER 18
NESTING

*L*isa pulled some of the vines and nestled herself among them, taking care to hide every inch of skin as much as she could. Though adrenaline had brought her to this point, it had since tapered off and she was again met with the exhaustion and disorientation that comes with dehydration and whatever metabolic cocktail she'd been given on the ship. Hidden among the greenery and the shade of her palm tree, she gave in to her body's demands for rest.

She jolted awake some time later and saw that the hulking ship had now left the island. It worried her that she hadn't heard anything while she was asleep. There was no way to know how close anyone had come to her, or if she'd been in any danger of being seen.

With no wristwatch or phone, Lisa had no idea what time it was. She looked skyward and saw that the sun didn't appear much lower, which she took as a good sign. She considered getting up to explore, but as she tried to stand, dizziness forced her back down. Her mouth was dry and she needed a drink, anything to soften the roughness at the back of her throat. But, she'd have to wait. For the time being, she returned to her previous position and rested her head back against the tree trunk.

The next time Lisa opened her eyes, the sun was beginning to set on the horizon. It was the most beautiful thing she'd seen in years. So beautiful, that she almost forgot the circumstances surrounding her picturesque vantage point.

Before attempting to get up again, she looked around thoughtfully. There were some small coconuts growing on the tree above her. They'd be easy to reach, but nowhere near ready for eating. The other trees around her were taller, and had fruit of varying stages of ripeness. She searched for a branch or anything that she could use to dislodge the coconuts growing at the tops of the trees. Unfortunately, it seemed that none of the trees around here had branches, though there were innumerable stray leaves littering the ground.

With a grunt of effort, Lisa got up on her trembling legs. She gathered as many large palm leaves as she could in her uninjured hand, and then returned to her tangle of vines. With close concentration, she tried to weave the thinnest vines around the sturdy leaves, her goal to tie them end-to-end to create a staff long enough to reach the high fruit.

The fingers on her injured hand were barely functional, and the pain was almost too much to bear. She would have cried if she wasn't so dehydrated. Instead, her face wrinkled into a grimace as she heaved empty sobs and threw everything to the ground.

She huffed in frustration before again rising to kick a nearby tree. She was hungry and thirsty and tired and weak. Her breath came in quick gasps of hopelessness. She had never been so alone or helpless before.

After allowing herself a few minutes of hysterics, Lisa focused on her breath, slowing it down and closing her eyes. She counted to four with each inhale and each exhale; one-two-three-four in… one-two-three-four out… Once she had calmed down, she again got to her feet and began searching the sandy ground for anything that might be edible.

After stumbling around for about 10 minutes, she came across a small coconut. Relieved, she hastily grabbed it up with one hand and brought it back to her previous location near the rocks. She used one of the large boulders to smash the armoured fruit against. After four tries, she got the husk open enough to begin to peel back. She sat on the ground, holding the fruit in place with her feet while using her one good hand to slowly peel the husk. She again smashed the coconut against the sharp edge of the boulder and was rewarded with a loud crack as juice spilled out over the stone and her hand. Lisa quickly turned the coconut over to prevent any further loss, and then put the opening to her dry lips and sucked down the remaining liquid from inside. It was warm, but she was grateful for the refreshment. Once she had drunk all she could, she cracked open the shell some more to reveal the meat inside, which she eagerly scooped out and ate with shaking fingers as she again held the coconut between her feet.

After she finished, she considered going back to look for another coconut when something caught her attention in the water. It was a boat. Smaller than the cruise ship, but quite large and expensive looking. A yacht, perhaps? Lisa had never seen one before, but she imagined this was what one looked like. It exuded high-class excess, and was probably worth more than any house in her neighbourhood back home.

Lisa watched curiously as the boat approached the shore, anchoring itself very close to where the cruise had docked earlier that day. At first, she couldn't see anyone aboard the boat. Soon enough, however, a number of people came into view. Their state of dress ranged from semi-formal to formal, with men wearing full suits alongside others wearing casual slacks and collared shirts. She even saw a woman on board in a bright yellow dress.

As much as Lisa wanted to seek out help, she wasn't sure who she could trust anymore. She knew she couldn't stay on this island forever, but she certainly didn't want to leave in a bodybag.

She decided to observe the group from a distance before directly approaching anyone. She watched as they carefully disembarked. A porter assisted each person as they were loaded onto a raft before being lowered into the water. Another uniformed worker scrambled to shore to pull the small craft onto the sand, and offered the woman in yellow an arm to steady her for the walk across the beach. She wore low-heeled yellow pumps. *An interesting choice for the locale*, Lisa thought to herself. None of the people from the boat had any luggage with them, suggesting that this was a day trip at most. *Why would anyone be so dressed up for this type of place?*

Lisa got closer, being careful to stay hidden in the brush. She followed them at a distance as they entered the forest. They made quite a bit of noise, talking and laughing loudly as they walked along a relatively clear trail. It made it much easier to follow them without detection as their own noise muffled Lisa's footsteps. Whatever they were doing here, it either wasn't a secret, or they didn't see any threat of anyone else finding out about it.

They walked for at least half an hour, and Lisa grew tired. She wished she'd found another coconut or something else to eat. Her legs felt like jelly and she quietly swatted at mosquitoes and other flies that hounded her. Eventually she pulled her injured hand into her shirt to protect it. It had mostly stopped bleeding but was horrific to look at and was starting to ooze. She wished she had something to wrap it in, but all she was wearing was a t-shirt and shorts and her undergarments, all of which were still damp from her earlier swim, and none of which could be considered clean.

After walking for what felt like hours, she could see the brush clearing and slowed down. There was a large rock wall ahead. As she got closer, she realized it was the mountain she'd spotted before.

"To the volcano!" declared the woman in yellow, followed by a resounding cheer from the rest of the group.

A volcano, thought Lisa. *That's interesting*.

She watched as the group began their ascent up a well-worn trail that spiralled up the volcano's side. She had no intention of following them from here, as the bare rock face was far too exposed to anyone passing by. She settled on watching from a hiding place among the trees and some bushes until they went up around a bend and out of sight.

What now?

She blankly looked around for some inspiration, and was shocked to find a full bunch of brown, on-the-brinkof-rotting bananas just 20 feet away on the ground. It was the best thing she'd seen all day.

CHAPTER 19
SOLD

*I*t was hours before anyone else entered the cave. This time, there was a crescendo of echoing voices before any person stepped inside. This group was obviously different than the other; they carried themselves confidently.

They came streaming in, loudly moving toward the centre of the cave. They all appeared to know each other. There were a number of scholarly-looking people wearing casual-yet-expensive looking clothes, including at least one carrying a stethoscope, while others wore formal business suits. Geri wondered how they could stand the heat wearing all those layers. She saw beads of sweat already forming on each person's brow. Others were more dressed-down in summer apparel, though still had an air of aristocracy about them. Most of the crowd were male, though Geri did hone in on one woman scanning the cages with an excited smile. Her bright yellow dress seemed best suited for an afternoon brunch, and was accessorized with gaudy pearls hanging from each ear, around her neck, and on her wrist. Each person had a file folder in one hand, and a glass of champagne in the other.

Geri noted that the guards smiled and engaged in small talk while leading people to different cages. It was the first time she'd seen them interact with others in a relaxed, human way.

At her own cage, the only people who paid Geri interest were the businessmen in suits. Similarly, "the nerds," as Geri saw them, visited other specified cages, including Leslie's, while the more casually-dressed visitors were led to still others, including Joe's. Different cages were meant for different buyers. Geri wondered what the distinctions were, and what each group intended to do with their respective purchases.

She made an effort not to look at the men who surveyed her. Instead, she kept her focus elsewhere, taking in the scene around her. She saw that the men in suits were also directed toward Macie's cage. The two other girls had their IVs removed earlier in the day, but they still appeared worryingly frail. Geri watched as a guard opened the cage door and dragged out one of the girls by the arm. She was prodded, turned over with the tips of shoes, and poked with the backs of pens.

"I think *she'd* be better suited for those guys," said a squat man in a suit as he gestured toward the nerds. "She won't do much for any of us, I doubt."

A few of the men from the adjoining group of buyers looked over, one chuckling as he replied, "We need healthy subjects to start with. Try them," he said, pointing toward the casually-dressed group. The woman in the yellow dress took a few steps forward, looking down her nose at the woman at her feet.

"Not for *my* customers," she sneered. "Not nearly enough meat on her, and she probably has worms," she added, looking even more disgusted. "I wouldn't take her for free. And the other one looks just as bad," she said, noticing the other severely underweight girl still sprawled on the cage floor.

"Can I see that one?" asked another man in a suit, pointing at Macie. In response, the guard ducked into the cage and roughly pulled her out for inspection. She was told to stand up straight with her arms out at her sides. As she stood, the man circled, taking in every inch of her body and occasionally feeling various parts.

Geri could see Macie shaking and holding back tears, shuddering with every breath. She wished she could reach out to comfort her, but knew that she'd be experiencing the same soon enough. As the man's hand traced Macie's back, it lingered over her buttocks and he gave it a squeeze. At this, Macie slapped him across the face. Every breath in the cave was held in the moments that followed. Macie's regret was immediately apparent as her eyes widened with fear. The man looked as bewildered as she, before his shock turned to fury. His fist collided with her temple, sending her reeling backward with a clang against the corner of the cage. The collective gasp could barely be heard over the bone-shattering impact.

"Bitch!" the man barked, his own cheek turning pink where she'd slapped him. He began to lift a leg to kick her before being stopped and held back by a guard.

"Hold up!" said the captain, stepping between the man and Macie. "She's still our property. Let our other guests decide what she's worth to them." She then looked from the man to the group behind him. "Let's get some bidding started before she's damaged any further. This is a healthy female about 25 years old, AB negative blood, no signs of illness. Starting bid, ten thousand!"

None of the men in suits raised their hands to bid. They each looked down at Macie, and uncomfortably back to the captain. One finally piped up.

"Some like a challenge," he said sheepishly, "but most of us prefer someone more...docile."

The others laughed, while the captain nodded. The man Macie slapped merely glared. "Understood," the captain responded. "How about you?" she asked, addressing the nerds.

"I'll give you ten," said a tall, wiry man in oversized glasses. "But I'll need to see her records," he added.

"All health records will be delivered before any money trades hands," the captain answered. "I have ten, do I hear fifteen?"

"Fifteen," responded another man.

"Eighteen," countered another immediately.

"Eighteen, do I hear twenty?" asked the captain. "Any bids for twenty?" she asked again.

"I'll give you twenty," said the female buyer coolly, looking over Macie with new interest.

"It just occurred to me that she'd make a lovely dancer, once her face heals," she smiled.

The captain smiled in return. "Okay, we have twenty. Do we have twenty-five?"

The other buyers looked at each other and shook their heads.

"Sold!"

In a moment, Macie's arms and legs were zip-tied together and she was dragged to an empty corner. Her buyer, the strangely sunny aristocratic woman, put a thin chain around her neck. Hanging from it was a tag that read, "C Group: 1"

The two women who had shared Macie's cage were laid out next to each other on the ground.

"These are a two-for-one special," the captain began. "I know they can't be used for much, but we'll let them go cheap. Any bids?"

"Are they sick?" asked one man in khakis and a polo. "Why are they so thin?"

"Hunger strike," said the captain quickly. "No worms or anything else. You'll get their papers too."

The buyers scrutinized the women closely before each shook their heads in decline of any sale.

"I would take them as a throw-in with another, legitimate purchase," said the man in the polo. "Could be an interesting project, but I wouldn't spend money on something that probably won't last the ride home."

"We don't give anything away for free," said the captain with a smile. "You're welcome to make another purchase, and you're welcome to use these girls as you wish, but you will have to pay for them."

"I had to try," he said with a smile. "I'm out, in that case."

"Okay, anybody else have any other offers for these two?" she asked. She scanned the room, but found no interested buyers. The captain then gestured to two nearby guards, who picked up and carried the seemingly-lifeless bodies to a small tunnel at the back of the cave that Geri hadn't noticed before. It was so narrow that it blended in with the rocks, especially in the dark. She wondered what was back there.

Before she had any more time to think about it, all eyes were on her own cage. Mina was pulled out first.

Like Macie, she saw immediate interest from one of the businessmen. Then from another, and another. As their hands roamed her body, Geri realized they'd likely find the phone when it was her turn. While all eyes were focused on Mina, Geri quickly transferred the phone to her underwear. She couldn't think of anyplace else to put it.

Mina stoically stood with her arms out at her sides, her hair cascading in water-like waves over her back. Unsurprisingly, the petite brunette sparked a bidding war, with a final sale of $32,000.

Geri was next.

As she was roughly pulled from the cage, her first thought was the phone in the waistband of her underwear. The other girls hadn't gotten a full pat-down, but nobody could predict where wandering hands would end up. She cursed herself for not thinking to get rid of it while all eyes were on Macie. She'd been too distracted by the debacle herself to think of anything else. She hoped it wouldn't fall out from her shorts in front of everyone.

She stood, as directed, with her arms held out at her sides. She was taller than Mina, but the few days locked in the cage already had her hunched over. She hadn't bathed or combed her hair since the morning of her capture, and could only imagine what she must look like now.

As the men closely surveyed her, she was acutely aware of her own odour. She knew they'd be used to the smell by now, and that the overall stench of the cave probably masked her own scent, but she couldn't help but feel utterly humiliated under their scrutiny.

She bit her lip as firm hands assessed her body. Though tears pricked the corners of her eyes, she did her best to keep them from falling. She stood as still as she could, forgetting to even breathe as she focused on a single rock in the wall ahead of her.

After agonizing minutes had passed, it was time to begin the bidding. She let out a deep breath, grateful that nobody had touched her waistband.

For the first time, Geri really looked at the men in front of her. Though they all had different features, they all looked much the same: Detached, arrogant, and cold. One was considerably older than the rest, and Geri almost hoped that he'd be her buyer. She expected an older man to be less capable of inflicting serious injury, and perhaps would have a softer demeanour overall. As she looked at him, he met her gaze. She quickly looked away before looking back. Maybe she could send a message with this brief contact. *Buy me. Help me.*

"Let's get started!" the captain boomed, causing Geri to flinch. "Let's start at ten!"

"Fifteen," said the man who hit Macie. Geri shuddered.

"Eighteen," said another man.

"Twenty," said the first man.

There was a pause. The captain piped in, "We have twenty, do I hear twenty-two? Twenty-two?"

Another pause. Geri could feel her heart thrumming and a fresh sweat breaking on her brow.

"Twenty-five," said the old man, much to Geri's relief.

"Twenty-five thousand," said the captain. "Do I hear twenty-seven? Twenty seven thousand dollars?"

The captain looked around at the men, making sure not to miss anything.

"Sold!"

Geri was brought to the wall where Mina now sat,

bound at the wrists and ankles. Geri was similarly zip-tied and forced to the ground, an identifying tag placed around her neck. She waited and watched as the rest of the auction went underway. Kate was sold next, and quickly went for $35,000. *More than Mina*, Geri thought to herself.

Kate was led over quickly and bound as they were on the ground.

"Guess the guys like blondes," she said with a smirk. Geri smiled back and saw that even Kate was trying to hide a tremble of fear. There was nothing to like about being kept in the cave, but nobody knew what was to come, either. The three were all sold to different men, so there was no telling if they'd ever see each other again. Or anyone from their past lives, for that matter. Friends and family, all gone in a matter of days.

Geri was about to check her waistband out of instinct but had forgotten that with her arms tied behind her, that was impossible. Mina must have had the same thought in that moment.

"You still have it?" Mina whispered.

"Have what?" Geri asked, trying not to sound confrontational or suspicious.

"The phone," Mina replied. So she *had* seen it that morning. Geri sighed, not wanting to answer. Another girl was now being brought to their corner, and Geri and Mina were both silent until the guards left.

"Yes," Geri said quietly. "But there's no signal here. I have no way to send anything."

"I know someone who can help us," said Mina.

Geri sighed again. "But I can't reach anyone out here," she said, agitated by the conversation. "And it's not like I have any way to write down a phone number for later, how would I even remember it?"

"It's an easy number," said Mina, before looking up and nodding in the direction of the incoming guards with yet another girl coming to join their group. They stayed quiet until the guards were out of range again.

"It's an easy number," continued Mina. "Just text 7266. Tell them everything you can, as soon as you can. They'll track us down. Tell them you're Ximena. They'll come."

"How would they know where to find us? We could be anywhere by the time they get the message," Geri asked.

"They have ways," said Mina. "They'll find us."

Geri thought on this. She didn't know who "they" were. She didn't know how they could possibly track everyone down. Were they FBI? Was Mina actually some federal agent in disguise? Was this some kind of sting? She had no idea what she was caught up in now, but she couldn't imagine it getting much worse as a result of the text message. She had to try. 7266. She repeated the number in her head so as not to forget it.

All the while, new girls joined their growing group in the corner, until there were nearly 20 huddled together, waiting for whatever came next.

Geri observed the ongoing auctions from her cramped position along the wall. She saw that they were now focusing on the cages with the men. They were of varied ages and sizes. One man in particular appeared to be in his mid-twenties and was physically fit and quite attractive. He set off a bidding war himself, bringing in a final bid of $28,000. He was the only man who joined Geri's group of young women in the corner. The rest were split between Macie's corner of the cave, and a new, third group. Geri was glad to see that at least Joe had joined

Macie where she was being held. She didn't like the idea of her being alone among so many strangers.

Once the men's cages were emptied, the older women's auctions began. Leslie ended up being sorted and sold into the third group, away from her brother and anyone else she'd met before. For the first time, Geri was able to count all of the captives. There were 114 people now sold and waiting.

"Alright!" beamed the captain. "That concludes today's auction! Thank you all and enjoy your purchases."

The captain looks genuinely happy, Geri thought. She hadn't thought the woman was capable of happiness, but here she was, showing a true smile thanks to the results of the auction.

"What do you say we celebrate?" said the woman in the yellow dress excitedly, clapping her hands together. She'd been one of the buyers for Macie and Joe's group. "How about a little show?"

"It's your stock now," said the captain, returning the woman's smile with an open palm facing up, inviting the woman to do as she wished.

"I tell you what," the woman began, "what if we use one of those two skinny girls? Might as well get some use from them!"

The captain thought for a moment, then nodded in agreement. "Alright," she said.

The woman in yellow again clapped her hands together.

"Do you have any salt?" she asked, still smiling with her hands clasped together.

"Of course," said the captain. "Follow me," she said, leading the woman through the cages and into the narrow corridor where they'd carried the two emaciated women.

Geri, along with the rest of the captives, all silently watched and waited to see what kind of celebration they'd soon be witnessing.

After a few minutes, the two women came back out, each carrying a canister of salt. Behind them, a guard was dragging one of the near-unconscious women out into the cavern.

"You're right, might as well," said the captain to the woman in yellow. "We weren't going to get much out of either of them anyway."

"Exactly," said the woman enthusiastically. "Might as well have some fun," she giggled.

Geri was afraid to see whatever they had planned, though like the others, she couldn't help but look on. She watched as the women directed the guard to drop the woman in the centre of the room. She landed on the bare rocky floor with a thud. Geri was sure she heard a bone crack beneath the woman's thin skin. A barely audible groan escaped her lips as her skeletal limbs slowly writhed in pain.

"Put her out of her misery," the captain ordered the guard.

Without a second's hesitation, he pulled out his gun and shot her square between the eyes. A collective gasp filled the air, punctuated by screams throughout the cave. Geri's hands went to her mouth, her eyes wide and unable to move away from their current focal point.

The woman on the ground was totally still now. Dead. Nobody even bothered to check her pulse. But they weren't finished with their spectacle.

The captain motioned over another guard.

"You two, make some cuts in her arms and legs," she instructed.

"Deep cuts, into the muscle," added the woman in yellow. "This will be fun, I promise," she said with a wry grin.

Geri couldn't believe what she was seeing as the men carved into the woman's lifeless body. She looked away at this point, though she saw most of the people around her were still watching, out of either shock or horror.

"Now for the fun part," said the woman in yellow. "Pour this into the wounds," she said, handing a guard the salt. The captain did the same for the other guard. They each poured the salt over the woman's limbs. In a moment, shouts of repulsion had Geri look back at the scene, in time to see the dead woman flailing as if brought back to life.

"Aha!" exclaimed the woman in yellow, clapping her hands over her laughing face. "Didn't I tell you this would be fun!"

"It's like the dancing squid from the videos!" exclaimed one of the guards.

"Exactly like the dancing squid!" replied the woman in yellow. "I always love combining dinner with a show!"

Geri sat, horrified at what was unfolding before her. She was paralyzed, unable to blink or shut her mouth, which hung open in shock. Nobody around her spoke. They were all similarly struck dumb from the scene. A person had been shot dead mere yards away. The body was then desecrated by guards, and seemingly brought back to life in a fit of convulsions thanks to some salt? Geri wondered what fresh nightmares awaited her—awaited all of them.

"Dance," a small voice said across the cave, barely more than a whisper.

"Dance," it said again, slightly louder now.

Geri found her eyes pulled by the sound, the only sound that could be heard over the peals of laughter at the centre of the cave. She looked across, her head slowly following the direction of her gaze. Sitting across from her, staring blankly ahead while occasionally repeating the single word, was Macie.

"Dance," she said again.

At first, Geri had no capacity to think beyond the body at the centre of the room, still twitching obscenely. She simply watched and heard. Then, her mind started turning the word and its context over in her head.

Dance. "*Just like the dancing squid*," the woman in yellow had said. Geri slowly accessed the files of her mind to find it, long since hidden away. A video taken in a restaurant. A squid arranged on a dish, dead and cold, but reanimated when soy sauce was poured over it. The dancing squid. She'd read the explanation online but couldn't remember the mechanics of the whole thing, although that didn't seem to matter now. It repulsed her when she first saw it, and it petrified her now.

And then she remembered.

"*She'd make a lovely dancer*," the woman in yellow had also said of Macie. Geri never could have dreamed that *this* was what the woman meant. She kept her focus on Macie, who was getting more visibly agitated and rocking back and forth, tears now streaming down her face.

Macie looked at the people in the centre of the cave, still talking. Then she looked to the other side, toward the tunnel they'd passed through to enter the cave days ago. There was a single guard with a gun stationed in front.

Macie began to move. She squirmed, her arms and legs still zip-tied together. She tried to get to her feet, but kept tipping over back to the ground. Finally, she began inching along like a caterpillar, writhing toward the cave's exit.

Geri looked away, afraid she would draw attention to Macie simply by watching. The people in Macie's corner of the cave couldn't help but watch. Joe tried to get her attention, whispering for her to stop and come back, shifting his gaze in a frenzy between Macie and the guards. His pleas went unheeded. She continued to squirm toward her only exit.

It wasn't long before she was spotted; she'd only made it a few feet away from where she'd started. The woman in yellow saw her first.

"Well, I guess the party's over," she said pointedly to the captain. She then turned to the rest of the buyers, who were still gathered around sipping their champagne.

"Bottoms up, time to go," she said forcefully.

"You there," she pointed to a guard. "Get some tranquilizers and take care of that one," she said, gesturing toward Macie.

The guard looked over and alerted another guard, who rushed to Macie and pulled her roughly away, back to the corner she'd come from. She screamed a guttural cry of frustration as he held her down. The first guard returned quickly with an injection. He pushed it into her shoulder, eliciting a jump and shriek of pain from Macie. Within seconds, her head slumped forward, followed by the rest of her body.

"Alright!" shouted the captain. "Time to get everyone loaded. Let's move!"

Guards appeared with knives held out in front of them. Geri's heart raced as they approached. She found herself gasping for air and closing her eyes until she heard the sound of a snap. The guards were cutting the zip-ties from the prisoners' ankles. Her own were cut free in under a second. They were told to stand, and everyone did as they were ordered, though it took a moment to find their balance with their arms still secured behind them.

The buyers filed leisurely out of the cave first, followed by four armed guards. Geri's group followed next, with another four guards behind. Next came Macie's group, four more guards, and then Leslie's group with another set of guards pulling up the rear.

Hundreds of people slowly bottlenecked from the cavern into the passageway. The tunnel they had to pass through was dark and narrow. Geri felt the scrape of bare rock against her body to the right. On her left was a woman she couldn't even see. The shaft was barely large enough for two people to go through at once.

Though there was dim lighting throughout the passage, Geri still felt herself stumbling along the rocky surface.

Finally, she could see light glowing ahead. As they rounded a corner, they were met with blinding sunshine. Geri reflexively closed her eyes and continued walking, trying to maintain her pace. Still, she felt herself walk into the person in front of her, and was reactively bumped into from behind. It seemed everyone had the same sensitivity to light after spending days to weeks in darkness.

The temperature had changed too. Geri was now shivering despite the warm climate of the island. She had somehow become accustomed to the sweltering heat of the cave without even realizing it. Her skin prickled in protest of the change.

They were led down the same steep and narrow path

they'd gone up previously. Geri wondered how many of her companions were considering jumping over the edge now, as Macie had almost done.

As if on cue, Geri looked up just in time to see a woman ahead of her break from her line and leap. There was no time to react or try to catch her. She plummeted silently down to the forest floor below. The only noise was when she fell through the treetops and landed with a far-away thud.

If anybody else had seen or heard what just happened, nobody made it known. Everyone continued on, following the people in front of them. Geri wondered when the buyers would notice the missing cargo.

Though she wasn't particularly religious, Geri said a silent prayer for the woman. She hoped her fall had been without pain, and that the ending was quick. Then she added a prayer for the rest of them, wishing that whatever was to come wouldn't be as bad as it seemed.

They continued down the narrow path. Geri could barely feel the strain in her leg muscles as they carried her downhill, her mind was so occupied with other thoughts.

Eventually they reached the base of the volcano. Next came the ambling walk through the forest. The guards spread out around the prisoners, making sure nobody tried to run. They had their guns loaded and brandished across their chests. Nobody would be making any kind of break from here.

No more neat lines of two, they were now spread out to cover more ground and get to the boat quicker. This meant walking through overgrowth and ducking to avoid errant vines and leaves. Only the buyers and a handful of prisoners were fortunate enough to walk along an actual trail. Geri lost a shoe while tripping over a root. She didn't even bother stopping to retrieve it. Up ahead, she could see that the cattle prods had returned and were being used on anyone who was too slow or looked the wrong way. She continued on, feeling the many sharp-edged palm leaves and roots littering the forest floor beneath her feet.

Geri wondered how Macie fared behind her. She didn't dare break stride or turn back to see, she just hoped that she was at least being carried rather than dragged. She then thought back to Billy. *Was he still on the island?* she wondered. She couldn't help but hope he'd come bursting through the trees at any moment with help to free them. Of course, she didn't actually expect that to happen, but that didn't stop her from replaying the unlikely scene in her head. She simply wished that he'd made it back to the cruise ship safely, and that he'd alerted whatever authorities could help.

Help, Geri thought. Mina mentioned people who could help—what was the number? 7266, she thought to herself.

7266. She repeated the number in her head as they continued their exodus through the trees. She had no idea when she'd be able to send any messages from the phone. *If* she'd be able to send any messages. Still, she couldn't allow herself to forget that number. It was a long shot, but it could be something. 7266.

CHAPTER 20
VOICES

*F*rom her small nest among the brush and leaves, Lisa could occasionally hear excited voices coming from the volcano above. She couldn't make out what they were saying, but tried to listen as well as she could. Eventually, she found herself dozing off. There had been no sign of anyone leaving the mountainside, and it seemed that hours had passed since that odd group of overdressed people went up.

She awoke with a start to a loud bang echoing from above. Aside from the resounding noise, she didn't hear anything else. No shouts, no running footsteps, nothing. *Maybe it was just a falling rock*, she thought.

She decided to stay alert. Even if it was a rock, a loose boulder could kill her in an instant. Lisa got up and began walking around, trying to see if a different angle offered more visibility into whatever was going on. She made sure to stay hidden behind the trees as she moved.

Soon, the unmistakable sound of a woman's laugh carried through the air. *Perhaps it was nothing too serious, then*, she thought. Still, she was suspicious of everything given her current situation. She decided to sit tight and wait to see what happened next.

After just a few more minutes, she was rewarded with the growing echo of voices. They got louder and clearer, and soon, Lisa could just make out the tops of peoples' heads as they followed the steep path along the mountainside.

A pulse of adrenaline sent Lisa back further into the trees. While a decent-sized group had gone up the mountain earlier, an enormous group was now descending. *Who were these other people, and how long had they been up there?* she wondered.

As she watched curiously, she saw something launch off the volcano's edge. It arced above her, over the trees, before falling heavily a short distance away. Hesitantly, she made her way over, even more wary about being seen now.

As she drew closer, Lisa saw a foot, and then realized she was looking at a pair of legs. She froze, taking in the sight of the woman's twisted body, long dark hair spilling out over a growing pool of dark blood that was slowly being sucked into the ground.

Lisa's breath came in deep huffs. There were no thoughts, no plans. Just shock. Her body tensed, unsure whether to run or hide. It was the sound of her own rasping breath that brought her back to her senses. Her wide eyes returned to the volcano and searched for the mass of people. They'd continued on their descent and must have rounded a curve, out of sight. But she listened, and could hear them when she focused.

She didn't know what was happening, and she didn't want to get any closer to these people, but she needed answers.

Lisa again followed whatever path they were taking ahead, this time keeping more space between herself and the others. She tried to keep her attention on the task at hand, but continued to return to the image of the woman tangled and broken on the forest floor. Did she fall, or did she jump? Was she pushed? The way her body careened through the air, she couldn't have fallen. And if she was pushed, she likely would have been fighting back, kicking and grabbing on her way down. But she wasn't fighting, and she didn't even scream. Her body simply moved with gravity. She must have jumped. But why?

As she walked along the base of the volcano, hidden by trees, Lisa saw that she was catching up to the group. She slowed a bit and tried to get a better view now that they were lower and closer to her level.

She was overwhelmed by an odour she hadn't noticed before. Looking at the mass of people, it was clear that most of them hadn't bathed or had a clean change of clothes in days, if not weeks. Aside from the armed guards, and the well-dressed people leading everyone, the majority of the group looked haggard and lost. They all walked as if on the verge of collapse; hunched over with feet dragging along the forest floor. One woman at the rear was either dead or unconscious, and she was being carried on a stretcher of canvas held up like a hammock by two men.

At this point, Lisa was sure that she didn't want to be seen. This was no rescue, and wherever these people were headed, it couldn't be good for anyone but the people in suits. Still, she didn't want to lose sight of anyone, either. She decided to stay close to keep an eye on things.

As she watched the people ahead of her, Lisa became aware of footsteps behind her. She turned quickly to find a bloodhound following her trail, closing the gap now that she'd stopped moving. She wasn't afraid of dogs, but she was cautious around ones she didn't know. On this island, a dog would only serve one purpose—tracking down people like herself.

Before she could formulate any kind of plan, the dog looked up at her and howled its guttural alert that it had found someone. It didn't seem aggressive but Lisa didn't bother running away. It could easily outrun her, and she'd already seen enough guards with guns to try anything risky around here. Her hand was damaged enough, she didn't want to risk any further mangling. Instead she sighed and closed her eyes.

As expected, two guards came barreling through the trees. One grabbed the dog by the collar, though it didn't seem to be going anywhere. The other guard grabbed Lisa by the arm.

"Where are your restraints?" he asked angrily.

"I don't have any," she answered truthfully.

"Where's your tag?" he continued.

"Don't have that either," she said.

He growled. "I can see that," he said, roughly leading her toward the larger group. Her heartbeat quickened and she suddenly felt hot with the realization that she was trapped. She stumbled over roots and leaves littering the forest floor before coming face-to-face with the mass of people she'd been quietly stalking.

"I got a runaway," the guard said, addressing the female captain as he quickly led Lisa toward her. She could feel hundreds of eyes watching.

"Where's her tag?" the captain asked. "And why aren't her wrists tied?"

"I don't know, she wouldn't tell me," the guard replied.

The captain looked at her closely. Lisa tried to avoid her gaze, but when she did look back, she realized that she recognized the woman in front of her. She'd seen her on the ship. Lisa quickly looked to the ground, hoping the woman wouldn't recognize her too.

"What happened to your hand?" the captain asked suspiciously.

"The dog got me," Lisa quickly answered. "After I got loose from him he started barking," she added, trying to cover her tracks.

"And I suppose he chewed through your zip-ties?" the captain asked sarcastically.

"I guess he did," Lisa answered flatly.

The captain sighed, clearly confused but wanting to take control of the situation.

"Does anyone remember who bought this one?" the captain asked, addressing the group of buyers who were now looking on curiously. They each looked to the other and shook their heads.

"I doubt she'd serve any of us well with that hand," said the woman in yellow, looking disgustedly at Lisa's gaping wound.

Lisa turned her attention to the larger group of harried wanderers. Incredibly, she found a face she recognized.

"Her!" Lisa shouted. "I'm with her!"

CHAPTER 21
REUNION

G eri's head jerked to attention as she did a double-take, seeing the spitting image of Lisa being dragged to the front of the group, straight to the captain. As the woman spoke, any doubt was cast aside. Here was Lisa, on the island.

When they locked eyes, Geri didn't know what to do. She didn't know if it would hurt either of them to admit they knew each other. But when Lisa said that she was with her, Geri immediately responded in affirmation.

"We had the same buyer," Geri said shakily as she slowly nodded, looking up the line toward the captain, and then to her own buyer, who she knew had only made one purchase.

He narrowed his eyes in thought, but didn't say anything to the contrary. Instead, after a moment's pause, he turned to the captain and said simply, "She's mine."

"Alright," said the captain through clenched teeth. "Get those two tied together so we don't lose track of this one again." She glared at Lisa as she was led toward Geri.

Lisa was relieved that they only zip-tied her uninjured hand to Geri, allowing her to keep her bloodied hand at least somewhat safe from insects and debris by hiding it under her shirt.

"What happened to you?" Geri whispered as the group began walking again, "I thought you were sick on the ship."

"I don't know what happened," Lisa whispered back. "I woke up in a dark room with a bunch of other people. We were all drugged or something. They woke us up to lead us off the ship, and I jumped into the water. I swam here and I've been hiding in the forest," she explained, looking to Geri, who broke her pitying gaze and looked down at the ground, shaking her head. Lisa paused and looked away. "Then that dog found me," she said with a sideways glance, finding the dog happily trotting alongside the group, occasionally stopping to sniff the ground.

"Did he do that to your hand?" Geri asked, alternating her gaze between the seemingly harmless dog and Lisa's hand, which was hidden under her stained shirt.

"No," Lisa whispered, lowering her voice more. "I got shot while I was in the water."

Geri gasped, then quickly shut her mouth to stifle any other outburst that might gain attention. She simply stared at Lisa, wide-eyed with shock, waiting for her to continue.

"That lady at the front was there," Lisa continued, nodding her head in the direction of the captain. "She didn't seem like she recognized me just now, but I don't see how that's possible. She was in charge of the group leading us off the ship this morning."

After a pause, Geri replied. "Maybe it's easier to

pretend you were one of our group from the start," she said.

"Maybe," Lisa replied. She sighed, "I guess it doesn't matter, does it? What about you? How did you end up here?"

Geri let out a slow breath. "It's a long story," she said. "Well, actually, I guess it isn't. I came to the island on a shore excursion, and haven't left."

"Did they take everyone who left the boat?" Lisa asked.

"I don't think so," Geri replied. "I left with a couple of other people, and two of the guys who were with us haven't been around since. I think they might have made it back to the boat, but there was a much bigger group that left the boat that day. I just don't know who else was there, I wasn't paying attention to anyone else at the time," she said, remembering how her main focus was on Billy.

"How did the other two get away?" Lisa continued.

"It was a big mess." Geri sighed again, trying to remember all that happened. "We left the main group to go exploring—which was a really stupid idea—and we came across a hand in the dirt. Things started getting crazy from there. One guy disappeared at that point, and then we were caught in a net, but the other guy was outside the net so he said he'd go looking for help. I haven't seen him since."

"Huh," was all Lisa could say.

They continued in silence after that, walking unsteadily through the tangle of forest foliage. Eventually the tree line thinned and they could hear the water lapping at the shore. In a moment, they could see the large, luxury yacht floating in the surf. A narrow wooden dock met a small metal staircase that led up to the deck.

"Do you think we're getting on that?" Geri asked incredulously.

"I guess we'll find out soon," said Lisa.

As they approached, the group of buyers walked ahead onto the dock. They leisurely boarded the vessel while the group of captives were held back on the beach by guards. Once the last buyer had made it safely onboard, crew members pulled the small staircase up after them, leaving no way to get from the dock to the ship. *Maybe we won't be leaving here just yet*, Geri thought.

Her musing was interrupted by the guard captain's shout.

"Okay everyone, listen up!" she ordered. "You're all going to walk single-file, through the water, to that boat," she said, pointing to the yacht. "Once you get to the side, the team will lower down a harness. There will be two men in the water to strap you in, and the guys onboard will pull you up. Follow their directions once you're aboard."

"We're walking through the water? Not on the dock?" a male captive asked.

"Through the water," the captain confirmed. "You all stink and need the bath. Think of it as a refreshing dip," she said with a wry smile.

"I can't swim," a woman said, and Geri was grateful that she wasn't the only one in that predicament.

"The water's just about five feet deep, you'll be fine," the captain said, judging the woman to be about five-foot-six.

"And if anyone tries anything stupid," she added, looking directly at Lisa as she pulled a handgun from her waistband and fired into the air, causing everyone to jump in surprise. "Remember, I'll only make you *wish* you were dead." Lisa sarcastically grinned in response.

Again, Geri felt the familiar panic rising in her chest. She was afraid of open water, which was one of the reasons going on the cruise was so stressful to begin with. Now she'd have to wade through the ocean with her hands tied behind her back. There was no way out. The gunshot only amplified her terror, sending a shock of adrenaline through her already electrified system. She wanted to run, yet her legs were cemented in place.

"Calm down," said Lisa, seeing right through her. "Slow down your breathing. It's okay, I'm right here."

Geri found herself mute, but shakily nodded her head as she became aware of her breath, which came in deep gasps. She hadn't even realized her mouth was agape until that point. She closed it promptly, and tried to breathe slowly through her nose. She felt like she might suffocate, as if there was no way enough air would reach her lungs if she didn't keep her mouth open. Still, she struggled, and she focused on her breathing as they made their way into a single-file line—all except herself and Lisa, who had no choice but to go together as a result of their joint restraints. Geri was grateful they'd been tied together at that moment.

One small step at a time, they followed those in front of them along the sand. Soon, water crept up to their toes before quickly retreating. It was warm, and Geri was grateful for that too. The tide continued to tease, offering a moment's taste followed by gritty sand that pulled seaward. Eventually, the water was constant under the soles of their feet, and then around their ankles, then their shins, then their thighs. As it approached their hips, Geri couldn't hold back her terror. She was hyperventilating again, and could barely hear Lisa's reassurances over her own panic. Still, she was pushed forward by those behind her, while simultaneously being gently pulled by Lisa.

"I can't do this!" she cried, tears beginning to fall down her cheeks.

"It's okay, we're almost there," said Lisa. "Look, nobody's gone underwater ahead of us," she added, nodding her chin toward the others who were now chest-deep. "It's okay, you'll be okay."

Lisa didn't wait for a response, she simply continued pulling Geri forward. Geri staggered, her feet spread wide apart to maintain her balance as the water lapped around them. Each time a foot left the sand, she felt like she was struggling against the lack of gravity to bring it back down.

Soon, the water was above her waist, and a few moments later it had reached her armpits. She was now gasping for breath as the weight of the water squeezed against her chest while they continued walking.

"Look, we're here," Lisa said gently as the water throttled their necks. There were just three people ahead of them now, being harnessed and pulled up one by one.

Geri exhaled deeply. "Okay...okay..." she repeated while holding her head as high as she could.

When it was their turn, the men in the water weren't sure how to harness them. They only had the equipment to hoist one person at a time.

"Just put the harness on her," suggested Lisa. "I have a free arm. I can hook my arm around her. Just tie another rope around us for more support since I can't grip anything," she said, showing them her gnarled hand. They winced, but did as she suggested.

Lisa wrapped her arm around Geri's shoulders as they tied them together. Geri turned her head away to avoid looking at Lisa's damaged hand. As they began to lift off the ground, Lisa braced herself, holding all her weight on one arm, and wrapping her legs around Geri. She immediately regretted suggesting that they be hooked up in this way, but she couldn't think of any other options.

Geri's collarbone and shoulders felt like they could snap under the added weight of her friend. She struggled not to shout in pain, instead grimacing and waiting for it to be over. It was just seconds before they were brought on deck.

Both women collapsed in gasping breaths of relief once they reached the solid floor, before quickly being pulled to their feet to be unharnessed, though still bound to each other by the wrist.

A man with a clipboard checked the soggy tag around Geri's neck and made a quick note on the papers in front of him.

"Deck two, room three!" he called out to another man behind him, who quickly took Geri's arm to lead them down a narrow set of stairs. Geri and Lisa struggled not to trip over each other's feet on the way down. Their legs might as well have been saddled with lead weights after walking through the water. It didn't help that they were now shivering in their sodden clothes. At the staircase landing, they were led through a heavy door to a large utility room. In it were many of the women who'd been in Geri's group of captives during the auction. She spotted Kate and shakily sat with her, Lisa having no choice but to follow.

"H-h-hi, K-kate, this is L-l-lisa," said Geri through

chattering teeth, both from cold and nervousness.

"Hi Lisa," Kate nodded her chin, still soaking wet like the others, but seemingly unaffected otherwise. "Quite the introduction you made today."

"I like to make an entrance," Lisa smiled. She trembled a bit from cold, but mirrored Kate's calmness.

Kate laughed. "I'm sure you do, I don't know why you'd want to enter this mess though."

"Caught between a rock and a hard place," Lisa replied. "It was this mess," she said, looking around her, "or downing."

Kate sighed. "Honestly, drowning probably wouldn't be such a bad way to go... who knows what we're in for now."

They were all silent now, staring ahead of them and wondering what was to come. In a few moments, Mina was brought in and knelt to sit with them.

"Do you still have it?" she asked Geri.

Geri stared at her blankly for a moment, unsure of what she was talking about until Mina diverted her gaze to Geri's waistband. The phone! Geri gasped and tried to reach for where the phone had been before remembering that her hands were still tied behind her back.

"I don't know," said Geri quickly, frustrated that she couldn't check herself.

"What's going on?" Lisa asked, as she and Kate looked on, both confused.

Geri looked around to make sure no guards were nearby. None were in the room at the moment. She whispered, "I had a phone."

"And you didn't think to use it?" Kate reflexively shouted. Mina kicked her leg and told her to hush, looking toward the door to remind Kate that anyone could be walking by. Kate just huffed in response.

"I tried, there was no service on the island," Geri quietly explained. "I wrote a message to my mom but it couldn't go through. I was going to try again once we got somewhere with coverage."

"There might be coverage on this boat..." said Lisa, looking around at the metal-reinforced room they were in and doubting they'd have any luck specifically here.

"The phone was in my underwear," Geri cut off Lisa before she could finish her thought. "I don't feel it there now, and even if it is still there, it was in the ocean... the phone's gone either way."

Geri couldn't look at any of them, she was angry at herself for forgetting about it before they went in the water, and angry at the situation since there wasn't much she could have done about it, even if she'd remembered.

"Anybody have some rice?" Kate joked. Lisa scoffed. The others remained silent.

Kate sighed. "Ugh, whatever, it doesn't even make a difference." After a pause, she added, "I'm hungry."

Even over all of the muted chatter of the dozens of people locked in the room with them, each woman could hear her own stomach writhing in hunger. The events of the day had distracted them, but now they were all aware of how long it had been since they'd been given anything to eat or drink. Geri regretted not eating a banana that morning.

As two more women were led to the room, the guard who brought them turned around. "That's everyone?" he asked someone behind him.

"That's it," came the reply.

"Alright, good night ladies," the guard said as he clicked off the light. The room went completely dark, with no windows for any hint of sunlight. They all listened as the heavy door creaked closed and the locking mechanism was put in place.

"I guess we're not getting dinner, huh?" asked Kate, to nobody in particular. No one responded. They all sat in the quiet darkness, listening as the boat's engines revved to life, wondering where they were headed, and how long it would take to get there.

CHAPTER 22
SUSPICIONS

*T*hough Geri's parents never worried much about their daughter living away from home, they realized that she'd never otherwise travelled on her own before. They weren't nervous people generally, but over the years had found that Geri's own anxiety often rubbed off on them.

For two days, they'd waited for an update. She'd promised to call and let them know how she was doing on the cruise. They purposely stayed home those days to make sure they were available to answer her call as soon as the phone rang. While they each had cell phones, Geri always called the landline first, where they were most likely to answer. For two days, they'd been answering every solicitation with a bright "Hello," followed by a disappointed "oh."

Geri's mother sat at the kitchen table sipping her decaf coffee, still in her cozy bathrobe and slippers. Geri's father was dressed in his standard button-down shirt and khakis and was buttering toast for them both to share with some scrambled eggs he'd made minutes earlier.

"Do you think we should call her?" her mother asked, hands clutching the warm mug.

"I'm sure she's fine," answered her father without looking up from the toast. "Wouldn't want to bother her."

"I know, I just want to make sure everything's okay. She should have called by now." Her face wrinkled with worry.

"Well, let's have some breakfast and then you can put her on the speakerphone, how's that?" Geri's father suggested as he turned around with the prepared dishes.

"Thank you," she smiled, kissing him on the cheek as he bent to set down the plates.

They ate quietly, if not altogether leisurely. While Geri's father casually read his morning paper between bites, her mother quickly ate what was on her plate and finished off her cup of coffee. She noisily pushed her plate away, and then clanked her coffee mug on top of it. Her husband looked at her over his paper.

"Alright," he huffed dramatically. "Give her a call now. I can talk, eat, and read all at once."

"Great!" she beamed, jumping up to retrieve the phone from the living room.

She dialled the number from memory and put the phone on speaker. They listened to the dial tone, excitement building, then deflating as it went to voicemail. They heard Geri's familiar voicemail greeting, and decided to leave a quick message after the beep.

"Hi honey!" her mother said, smiling. "Just wanted to say hi and see how things are going. Call us back when you can. Hope you're having fun!"

"Talk to you soon," added her father.

Her mother finished the message with a quick "Love you, bye."

She pushed the button to end the message, then looked to her husband as the smile she'd worn for the recording faded.

"What time is it?" she asked.

He looked at the watch on his wrist. "8:40."

"She's usually up by now," her mother said.

"She's usually not on vacation," her father countered.

"That's true…" she replied, thinking of the possibilities. "I'm going to send her a text."

She returned the landline to its designated spot by the sofa and rummaged through her purse for the cellphone she hardly used. As she picked it up, she secretly hoped there would already be a message from Geri on the screen. There wasn't. She brought the phone back to the kitchen table, where her husband was already reading his newspaper again.

At first, she stared at the blank text screen, unsure of how to begin. She started typing.

Hi honey. Tried calling but got your voicemail.
Hope you're having fun! Talk to you soon.

She placed the phone on the table in front of her and looked out the window. A moment later, she was startled by a loud buzzing against the table. Her husband put down the paper as she checked her phone.

"It's Geri!" she exclaimed. "She says, 'No cell service. Can't talk. I'm good. I'll call when I can.'" Her mother paused after reading this aloud, studying the message in front of her. "She didn't write this," she said matter-of-factly.

"What do you mean?" her husband asked. "How could you know that?"

"Look at it," she said, handing the phone to him to read. He squinted at the screen.

"What am I looking at?" he asked.

"Look at the way she wrote it," she said impatiently. "Look at that text, and then look at every other text above it." She waited as he scrolled up to past messages.

no cell service cant talk. Im good ill call when i can.

"She's a *writer*," she said emphatically. "She capitalizes letters and uses apostrophes and proper punctuation. She doesn't say 'I'm *good*,' she says, 'I'm doing *well*.'"

He sighed across the table, still looking down at the phone.

"Look, it's early, we don't even know what time it is where she is—" he began, before being cut off.

"Where she is—we don't even know where she is!" her mother howled.

Her father again sighed, and put the phone back on the table. He looked across at his wife, who was breathing heavily and staring at him, waiting for a response.

Quietly, he said, "Okay. We'll call the cruise line and see how she's doing, how's that?"

She let out a heavy breath. "Okay."

"I'll look it up and see if I can get a phone number from their website. We'll find out where exactly they are, and we'll ask if they can get Geri on one of the ship's phones."

"Okay," she said, calming down.

"Okay."

He looked out the window for a moment, then got up and went straight to the upstairs office. As she listened to his footsteps on the stairs, Geri's mother sat alone at the table, staring straight ahead. When she heard him open the door to the office, she got up, gathered his dishes from the table and rinsed them quickly before leaving them in the sink for later. She took the newspaper and absently threw it into the recycling bin, then walked through the living room and up the stairs to join her husband in the office.

She walked in and found him at the computer, browsing through Google results.

"What was it called again, the ship?" he asked, turning to face her, his face a map of perplexed concentration. "Fall something? Fall Bounty, maybe? No... Harvest...it was the Harvest Cruise, right?"

"I think so," she answered quietly.

"I think I found it," he said, rolling his chair to the side to make room for her next to him. "Here's a phone number, looks like it's just for bookings though."

Geri's mother bent over and read through the webpage, leaning on the back of the computer chair.

"Here, I'll give them a call and they can direct us to the right department," her husband said reassuringly.

She nodded but said nothing. He dialled the number and put the phone on speaker. The phone rang and rang, until they were both agitated at the sound.

"Good morning!" beamed a sudden, bubbly voice. "I'm Sandra with Harvest Cruise, how can I assist you today?" Geri's parents both jumped at the energetic answer.

"Yes, uh, hello," her father stumbled. "My daughter

is on your cruise right now, and uh, we'd like to speak with her."

"Alright, that shouldn't be a problem! What's your daughter's name?" she asked.

"Margorie Collins," answered her father, "M-as-in-Mary—A-R-G-O-R-I-E, Collins."

"Okay, just a moment, sir," she replied, audibly typing into her own keyboard.

"Alright! I've got her itinerary pulled up and it looks like she registered for a shore excursion today. She's probably on the beach right now, so I'll have our staff leave a message for her in her room to give you a call when she returns."

"Okay, thanks," said Geri's father.

"Wait!" interjected Geri's mother. "Her phone didn't have service. Is there a phone on the ship she can use?"

"Of course," Sandra assured her. "We'll mention that in the note and instruct her to come to the ship's main desk to give you a call. Is there a particular number that would be best to reach you?"

"Just tell her to call home," her mother said.

"Okay, no problem. Is there anything else that I can help you with today?"

"No, that should cover it," said her father. "Thanks for your help."

"My pleasure! Have a beautiful day."

They hung up the phone, and Geri's father looked up to her mother, who was still standing above him.

"Well, I think that went well," he said.

"Yes," she said noncommittally.

"It was good how we didn't have to get transferred to a dozen different departments," he added.

"Yes, that was interesting," she said.

CHAPTER 23
ON THE BOAT

*A*side from the brief walk through the jungle, not much had changed since the passengers' time in the cave. They were still locked in a dark space with no way to tell how much time had passed. They were still hungry. They were still dehydrated. And they were still hot.

The only difference now was that half the women suffered from seasickness, resulting in a cacophony of dry heaving. Nobody had eaten in hours, which was a small blessing in that at least the floor wasn't covered in vomit. However, it also served to make everyone's nausea worse. Geri couldn't help but think back to all of the Dramamine she'd left in her cabin on the cruise. Not that she could have brought it here—but still, it seemed such a waste to have just left it there in the room she'd never return to.

She and Lisa sat with their knees up at their chests. As their eyes adjusted to the darkness, they could see that most of their compatriots were curled up in fetal positions on the hard, wet, floor. They had no idea how long they'd be here, but Geri was certain there'd be plenty of time for sleep. In the meantime, she focused on her breathing and tried not to think about her alternating hunger and nausea. *At least the water's calm*, she thought.

A loud sound jerked everyone upright and turned all attention toward the door, which was creaking open. Light streamed in and momentarily blinded everyone on the floor.

"Let's take a look at that hand," said a familiar voice. They could hear multiple sets of heavy boots entering the room.

Someone leaned over Geri and Lisa. Geri strained to see against the light, and was surprised to find her buyer standing above them. He took Lisa's free arm, and inspected the ghastly injury

He winced, but didn't pull away. Instead, he looked to the guards.

"Get her some antibiotics, I don't want her getting sick on me now," he said authoritatively. He turned back to Geri and Lisa and gave the faintest sad smile, almost an apology.

A guard behind him unzipped a pouch at his belt and pulled out a fresh syringe and a small vial. He opened the syringe with his teeth before pulling the liquid into it. Without a word or warning, he stuck Lisa in the arm and injected. She grunted, more from surprise than pain, and then looked up at their new owner.

"Thank you," she said genuinely.

Without a word, he nodded and left. The guard put the discarded syringe back in his belt after capping the needle. He then pulled out some gauze and hastily wrapped Lisa's hand before leaving. Just as suddenly as the door had opened, it was closed. They were once more submerged in darkness. Nobody could see Lisa's smile.

"How many people did he buy?" Lisa asked Geri.

"Just me," answered Geri. "And now you, kinda," she added.

"I think we'll be okay," Lisa said, still smiling.

"I hope so," Geri replied.

CHAPTER 24
BREAK IN

*G*eri's parents hadn't spoken much since their call to the cruise line earlier that morning. Her father appeared in good spirits as he breezed through his crossword puzzle and then got to work on the dishes left in the sink, humming as he worked.

Her mother, on the other hand, still hadn't changed out of her bathrobe. She stared at her open closet for about 15 minutes, looking for some inspiration for the day's outfit before giving up and deciding she wouldn't leave the house today, anyway. She was waiting for a phone call, and she wouldn't leave until she got it.

She sat at the kitchen table, not really reading the home and garden magazine in front of her as her husband energetically scrubbed and rinsed the dishes and mugs. Though she wasn't in any mood to talk—with anyone but Geri, at least—she didn't want to be completely alone with her thoughts either.

Over the next few hours, the television was turned

on, then off. Curtains were opened, then closed. Another trip to the closet produced a pair of lounge pants and a tent-like t-shirt. She kept on her slippers.

Her husband had returned to the upstairs office to play Solitaire. She sat on the sofa with her magazine, still unread yet creased from handling. She absently turned on the TV again and flipped to the cooking channel just to have some background noise as she blankly stared at the pages in front of her.

Every 20 minutes or so, she glanced up at the clock to see how much time had passed since their call earlier that morning. By 4:32 p.m. she'd had enough. *Geri should have returned to the ship by now*, she told herself. She got up from her cushioned refuge and walked across the room to retrieve her cell phone from her purse. She checked to see if she'd gotten any messages. She hadn't. She returned to the text exchange between herself and Geri, and decided to send another text.

Hi honey, are you back on the ship?

She kept the text screen open, and could see that Geri was typing a reply, then deleting it, then not typing, and then typing again. After a long moment, her phone buzzed with a response.

Yes. Got ur message but phones are down n i still dont have srvice. Tried calling but didnt go thru. Love n miss u. Say hi to dad.

Geri's mother stood frozen to the ground, her grip tight on the phone as she scanned over every word. Her lips pinched together, and she breathed heavily through her nose. Finally, she stomped across the floor and up the stairs to meet her husband at the computer. He was already turned around in his chair to face her, having heard her leaden footsteps approach. Without a word, she handed him the phone.

He read, and re-read, the text. He loudly sighed, opening his mouth to speak, and then closing it again.

"What do you want to do?" he eventually asked.

"I don't know," she answered tightly. "Can we call the police?"

"I really don't know," he said. "I think you're supposed to wait 24 hours to file a missing person report, and we don't actually know that she's missing."

"Somebody has possession of her phone that isn't her," she seethed through her teeth. "At the very least, her phone has been stolen. At the worst… " she began, before choking on the sob caught in her throat. She inhaled quickly, trying to stop the tears that were already pooling at the corners of her eyes.

Her father stood up and hugged his wife tightly, his eyes shut so firmly that the crows feet which were otherwise unnoticeable now stood out at the sides of his face.

"Her phone was stolen," he said quietly, loosening his grip around her. "We'll call the police and we'll report it."

He took his wife's hand and together they descended the stairs. For the second time that day, they brought their land-line into the kitchen. Geri's mother had a magnet with public phone numbers on the fridge door. She'd never needed it before, but retrieved it now. She gave it to her husband, who used it to dial the local non-emergency number for their local police station as they sat together at the kitchen table.

They listened to the dial-tone for two beats before a dispatcher picked up on the other line. As she answered, Geri's father found himself flustered and suddenly unsure of what to say.

"Yes, uh, hi, uh… we have a situation with our daughter," he began.

"Yes, sir, what's the problem?" the voice on the other line responded.

"Well, uh, we have reason to think that her phone has been stolen."

"Okay, and what leads you to believe that? Is your daughter there with you? How old is she?" she inquired quickly.

"She's not with us, she's on a cruise right now," he said haltingly. "She's, what is she now? She's 28 years old," he said, looking to his wife for confirmation, who nodded silently.

They could hear a clear sigh on the other end of the line.

"Alright, sir, and why do you believe her phone has been stolen?" she asked.

"Well, she hasn't been answering her calls, and she hasn't called us back," he said, aware of how ridiculous he sounded talking about his adult daughter not calling her parents while on vacation.

"She didn't write the texts!" her mother exclaimed.

"Right!" her father exclaimed, "the texts! She also replied to some texts, but she obviously didn't write them," he added.

There was a pause. "So, you are receiving texts from your daughter's phone, but you don't believe that she wrote them. What leads you to think that?"

At this, her mother again piped up to respond over

the speakerphone. "Our daughter is a professional writer," she said emphatically. "She speaks and writes with perfect grammar, always. These texts from today were written in broken English at best. She did NOT write them."

"And she isn't responding to calls," her father repeated. "We haven't heard her voice, only gotten those texts."

"I see," said the dispatcher simply. "Well, we can't find the phone if it's still on the cruise ship. Wherever it is, it's outside of our jurisdiction. My advice is to contact the cruise line and explain the situation. They'll be able to assist you better than we can in this situation."

"I see," her father said, looking across to his wife under furrowed brows.

He hung up as the dispatcher asked if there was anything else she could help them with today.

The two sat silently at the kitchen table, both looking down at the phone between them.

"Well, calling the cruise line will get us nowhere," her mother said, slapping her hand against the table. She wished she had a coffee mug in front of her to grip, she needed to hold onto something.

"We can still try," said her father, unsure of what else to do.

Neither of them said anything after that. They both stared at the phone on the table, as if willing it to ring.

Instead, they both looked up at each other as they heard what sounded like someone knocking at the front door. Neither moved from their seat until they both heard the knock again, louder this time.

They both got up together.

"Don't worry, I'll get it," said Geri's father,

motioning to his wife to sit back down. She followed him through the living room, looking out the front window as he approached the door.

"I don't see anyone," she said, pulling back the curtains slightly. He looked through the peephole and didn't see anyone either. He opened the door cautiously, looked around and then cracked open the screen door. Looking down, he saw a box at the doorstep.

"We got a delivery," he said, bending to pick up the package.

"I don't remember ordering anything," replied his wife.

He brought in the box and shut the door as he read the label. "It's from Geri!" he shouted, holding up the box with an excited smile. In that instant, the sliding glass door in the kitchen opened, and five masked men wearing camouflage rushed into the room.

Before anyone could say anything, five handguns were aimed at the bewildered homeowners. Geri's father put both hands over his head instinctively, one still holding the box he'd just picked up. Her mother just stood, staring at the man closest to her as if she could see him through his mask. Without hesitation, the man pulled the trigger and struck her between the eyes. A spray of blood showered the curtain behind her as she fell backward onto the couch.

"Miranda!" shouted her husband, dropping the box and attempting to run to her. He was grabbed by the man at his side and dragged so that he faced her body directly. He fell to his knees in deep sobs.

"She just had surgery," he cried. "She just had surgery!"

He didn't notice the gun as it was put into his hand.

He didn't feel the weight of another hand closing in around his. He didn't fight as the fingers squeezed the trigger against his own skull. His sobs were silenced as he thudded heavily to the floor.

The masked men made sure both were dead. They made sure there was just one set of fingerprints on the gun that killed both of Geri's parents in less than a minute. They watched their footsteps to make sure they didn't track blood through the house. This would be an obvious murder-suicide, with no evidence of a break-in. The men quietly exited through the unlocked sliding glass door of the mountain-side home, where the biggest threat had always been bears.

The men left as quickly as they'd come. They walked through the woods, their all-terrain vehicles parked miles away in the forest. After the first mile, they removed their masks. They looked like any other group of hunters one might encounter here.

The lead man, who'd twice pulled the trigger, took out a disposable phone and dialled.

"It's done."

CHAPTER 25
FIRST STOP

*E*very time the boat rocked, Geri told herself that it was just like a baby being rocked to sleep in its cradle. It didn't stop the sudden dropping feeling in the pit of her stomach, or the intrusive thought of a storm capsizing them. Not for the first time, she wished she'd learned how to swim.

Just as it seemed she'd finally nodded off, Geri was awoken by the loud door creaking to life, and the flood of outside light entering the room. She'd forgotten where she was—thinking she was back on the cruise ship and wondering who opened the door to her room. As she thought of moving the hair from her face, the cuffs around her wrists reminded her of her reality, and what had happened since her brief time on the ship.

"Alright, everyone up!" a guard shouted

Groggily and with effort, everyone got to their feet. Just as Geri and Lisa stood, the boat tipped a bit and sent them both crashing into the wall behind them. Others fell backward onto them. Again, they got up and took a wide stance to keep their balance.

"Move out!" the guard shouted, gesturing behind them toward the door. They shakily followed another guard through the hall and toward a small door that led outside. One-by-one, they exited down a narrow staircase and into the glowing sunset of another tropical island.

"Wow," Lisa said as it was their turn to exit. "Under different circumstances, this would be really beautiful."

"It is beautiful," Geri said.

The stairs led to a large wooden dock that brought them onto land. Geri was grateful not to have to get into the water this time. Once on the beach, they were ushered over to their buyer, who greeted them with a small smile. A Jeep pulled up, and their buyer opened the back door and gestured for them to get inside. Once they were settled, he closed the door and took the front passenger seat.

"So, where are we headed now?" Lisa asked, seeming much more at ease than Geri felt.

"The airport," the older man answered personably. "This island has a small air strip, so a lot of the buyers use private planes to bring their people wherever they're going back to. A few stay by the dock and have their own boats ferry them back. It's all a matter of preference and convenience."

As much as Geri hated the boat, she didn't like the thought of getting on a small plane either. Like everything else, however, she kept this to herself and let Lisa guide the conversation.

"So, where are we flying?" Lisa continued.

"That is private, I'm afraid," he answered.

"Well, are we staying with you, or are you some kind of broker?" she asked.

"No, you'll be staying with me," he said.

"Well, then I'm sure we'll be fine wherever we end up," she replied.

Geri looked over at her friend, surprised by that response. The man did seem softer than the others, but there was still no way of knowing his intentions. Either way, he'd come to a secluded island specifically to buy a living human—*good people don't do that,* she reminded herself.

After a few minutes of driving along a narrow but well-worn path through the trees, they came upon an expansive clearing where the single air strip was visible, along with a handful of small planes. The Jeep stopped alongside a red one.

Their buyer exited the vehicle and opened the back door for the women. As they got out, a pair of guards appeared and blindfolded them, startling them both.

"I'm sorry for this, it's not my choice," the old man said. Then the women each felt a needle pierce their arms. A moment later, the world faded away as they collapsed into the guards' arms.

CHAPTER 26
SOUP FOR TWO

*M*ary had been lounging in bed scrolling through her social media feeds on a lazy Sunday morning. She knew that Lisa would be coming home that afternoon, and planned to have her over for an early dinner to welcome her back.

She decided to text her sister to get an idea of what she might be interested in eating, and she hoped that whatever it was, it was something she already had available to cook at home. She had no intention of leaving her cozy bed to go shopping anytime soon.

Hey, hope you had a great trip! Are we still on for tonight? What are you thinking for dinner?

As she went back to her Facebook feed, her phone buzzed with a response.

Hey! Super tired, I think I'll pass tonight. Thanks anyway.

Mary frowned as she read the message. She'd been looking forward to seeing pictures from the trip and hearing about how the week went. Though she'd have liked to have gone with Lisa on the cruise, she was genuinely happy that her sister finally had a chance to take a real vacation.

> Okay, let me know when you want to hang out. I want to hear allll the details!

Her reply sounded much more upbeat than she felt. She held the phone out in front of her as she sat upright in the bed. She stared at it, waiting for a reply.

"Hmf," she sighed, surprised that Lisa hadn't responded.

Two days passed. Mary had just finished transcribing an interview she'd recorded the previous afternoon. She sat at her cubicle desk, headphones still on, her fingers hovering over the keyboard as she thought about how she was going to structure her article. It was a feature story on a local woman who'd just celebrated her 103rd birthday. She smiled as she thought of the woman, obviously old but still so full of life. She'd told Mary that the secret to longevity was keeping a full schedule so that you always have something to look forward to.

Mary looked up at the calendar hanging next to her on the grey wall. It was already Tuesday, and there was absolutely nothing on her calendar to look forward to this week. Or this month, for that matter.

She picked up her phone, which had been sitting on the messy stack of spiral notebooks and colourful two-pocket folders next to her. She stared at it for a moment before beginning her text to Lisa.

> Hey, want to hang out Friday or this weekend?

A speedy reply came through.

> No thanks, got a bad cold.

Mary slammed the phone against the notebooks, which muffled much of the thump. She looked sideways at the phone, her mouth a thin line of contempt. Lisa had never brushed her off this way before. They didn't see each other every week, but close enough to it, and they spoke on the phone every few days. But now, ever since Lisa had stepped aboard that ship, she'd been brushing Mary off at every turn. She didn't pick up her calls, or call her back. She'd only been responding to texts, and clearly didn't want to see her. Mary wasn't sure what had changed on that cruise, but she didn't like it.

She looked back at her computer screen, fingers tensely perched above the keyboard, before picking the phone up again. She scrolled through her contacts, finding a cousin who lived nearby that she hardly spoke to.

> Hey, I know it's been a while, but do you want to catch up sometime? I'm free all weekend and down for whatever.

She took a deep breath, re-read the text four times to make sure everything was spelled correctly and coherent, and finally pressed "Send."

She put the phone down delicately in its place next to her, wondering why her cousin would want to see her anyway. They only got together during major holidays or other family events, despite only living a few towns away. A buzz at her side brought Mary out of her reverie.

Hey, I'd love to catch up! Want to do Sunday brunch?

Mary smiled, excited to see her cousin outside the confines of a relative's house. As she thought about it, she couldn't even remember the last real conversation they'd had that didn't involve asking for a recipe or complimenting a holiday-themed outfit.

They decided on a café mid-way between where they each lived, and agreed to meet there at 11:30 a.m. that Sunday.

The rest of the week flew by as Mary wrote up her feature story, got it published with almost no edits, and went to work researching her next assignments. She'd continued reaching out to Lisa, but couldn't even leave any more voice messages since her voicemail was full. While she started out angry at her sister's flippant behaviour, she was beginning to get concerned. By Friday afternoon, she decided she'd drop by Lisa's apartment the next morning with some soup and magazines to help her feel better and see what was going on.

She spent Friday night looking up soup recipes, and then scouring her cabinets to see what ingredients she actually had on hand. She had a few cans of tomato sauce, and an almost-empty box of instant rice. Tomato soup it was.

Mary was up early Saturday morning to begin preparing the soup, something she'd never made before. Her smartphone was there to guide her through the minimal steps. She tasted her creation on the stove, burning her tongue on the metal spoon with a wince. She took another sample, carefully blowing for a full minute before bringing it to her lips again. It was good! Feeling confident in her newfound cooking skills, she found some bread and American cheese and added a grilled cheese sandwich to the day's menu. She forgot to butter the pan, so it was quite a bit drier than she expected, but overall she was happy with the results of her efforts, and couldn't wait to deliver the homemade meal to Lisa.

She looked through her cabinet of mismatched Tupperware until she found a container and lid that fit. She packed up the soup, and wrapped the toasted cheese sandwiches in foil. By pure luck, she spotted a clean-enough brown paper bag in her drawer full of plastic bags. *Something about a brown paper bag just makes it seem more like an official food delivery*, Mary thought.

She put on a pair of comfy moccasins, grabbed her keys and jacket, and headed for the door before hastily turning back to retrieve the food from the counter. Brown bag in hand, she set off for Lisa's apartment.

CHAPTER 27
COMING "HOME"

*G*eri awoke in an unfamiliar bed. She didn't know where she was, but wasn't startled by that fact, as she normally would be. She recognized the comfort of a mattress, blanket, and pillow, and decided to hold on to her peaceful ignorance for a few moments longer.

Within seconds, she heard a tired exhalation of breath somewhere else in the otherwise quiet room. She opened her eyes and lifted her head to get a sense of things. As her eyes focused, Geri recognized Lisa slowly waking up in her own bed across the very large, ornate bedroom they currently occupied.

The walls were a dusty rose colour, and the vaulted ceiling looked at least 15 feet high. The furniture was a rich cherry wood. There was a vanity with a delicate mirror and sitting stool, two large dressers, and other pieces Geri didn't even know the names of. The beds were both large, with matching pink upholstered headboards and footboards. It was as if she'd woken up in a life-size doll house.

"Where are we?" Lisa asked with a mystified grimace, now surveying the room too.

"I don't know," Geri answered, still caught up in the delicate details all around them.

Lisa looked at her arm, which was severely bruised where an IV had previously been placed. She then looked to her injured hand, which was expertly wrapped in clean medical gauze.

"Do you know how we got here?" Lisa asked, still looking at her hand and trying unsuccessfully to flex her fingers.

"No idea," said Geri. "I don't even know how long we've been here. All I remember is being at that tiny airport, if you can call it that."

"Same," said Lisa.

A soft knock came at the door. Neither one of them had even considered the door up until that moment. Now they each silently reprimanded themselves for not investigating further while they had the chance.

"Come in?" said Lisa hesitantly, looking to Geri, who shrugged her shoulders in response.

The large, solid wood door opened to reveal a young woman, perhaps still a teenager, wearing a modest maid's uniform.

"Good evening," she began formally with a small curtsy. "I hope you've found your room satisfactory. I've come to offer you dinner, if you're hungry."

Neither woman had eaten an actual meal in days, and the mention of food quickly reminded them of that fact.

"Yes, please," answered Lisa hurriedly. "We'll eat anything."

"Very well," she replied with a shy smile. She turned

around and retrieved a rolling cart from the hall behind her. It had already been laid with two bowls of clear broth, and two biscuits with pats of butter on the side.

"The Master felt it best to start slowly so you don't get sick," the girl explained. Geri looked at her as her thin arms pushed the heavy cart. What was she doing here? What year of school should she be in?

Lisa thanked her and immediately dove into the bowl of broth, not bothering with the spoon. She burned her lips on the hot liquid, but continued drinking after a few quick blows to cool it down. It still burned, but she couldn't help herself

The girl who'd brought the cart poured two glasses of water from a pitcher, then lightly bowed to the two women before leaving the room, shutting the door behind her.

"Do you trust this?" Geri asked Lisa in a whisper.

"At this point, I really don't care. Drink your soup, it's good."

As Geri cautiously sniffed the broth, she found herself ravenous. Unlike Lisa, she picked up the spoon and blew on each mouthful before slurping it up. After a few spoonfuls, she noticed the biscuit and tore off a bit to taste. She ate the rest in three large bites, and washed it down with the rest of the broth, which she was now drinking straight from the bowl as Lisa had.

They both finished their meals quickly. Then they looked to the butter. Neither one had taken the time to add it to their bread. They'd both been starving for days, and didn't blink at eating the butter on its own, as if it were an after-dinner mint. They were grateful for the additional sustenance.

"What do we do now?" asked Geri, sitting cross-legged on the bed, looking at the empty dishes and bowls on the cart.

"We find an opening to get out of here," Lisa said. "I doubt we'll be treated like honoured guests here forever. We need to find out as much as we can about this place and figure out a way to escape. For now, we play nice, gain their trust, and stick together."

About five minutes later, the young girl returned with a tentative knock to collect the dishes and the cart.

"We figured you'd be done quick," she said with a smile.

"Thank you for everything," Geri said. "We hadn't eaten in a while."

"I know, I got here the same way you did," the girl, still smiling, replied as she stacked the bowls.

"You did?" Geri asked, her eyes wide, looking up to Lisa, who was closely following the conversation. "How long have you been here? Where are we? What's going on?"

"It's okay, it's okay," said the girl, her arms out as she tried to calm Geri. "I've been here about a year now. The Master will explain everything to you, but you're in a good place here. You'll be okay. Don't worry about anything, he'll explain everything." She reviewed the cart to make sure she had everything in its place before she turned to leave. "I have to go back to work now, but we'll be seeing each other a lot. There are books in that cabinet over there you can read in the meantime," she said, pointing. "I'll be back tomorrow morning. Have a good night!"

"Good night," the two women replied quietly. They listened as the door locked from the outside.

"I forgot to ask her name," Geri said.

"I forgot to ask what day it is," Lisa said with a smirk. "But it sounds like we'll get another chance tomorrow. In the meantime, let's look around."

Lisa got up and crossed the room to the bedroom door. She tested it, just to confirm that it was in fact locked, before checking the other doors in the room. One opened into a large walk-in closet, and the other provided access to a small en-suite bathroom. Like the bedroom, it was a muted shade of pink, complete with a matching pink toilet and sink. On the counter were two toothbrushes and a tube of toothpaste.

The small shower stall had a caddy that contained a few types of shampoos and conditioners, body wash and bar soap, and two luffas.

Under the sink, Lisa found extra rolls of toilet paper, toothbrushes, and neatly rolled up bath towels. There were no windows in the bathroom or the bedroom.

"Well, it's not much, but I guess it's home for now," Lisa said as she surveyed the space, which seemed smaller now than it did when they initially woke.

CHAPTER 28
GOOD TO KNOW

*M*ary caught a bus that dropped her off a few blocks from Lisa's apartment. She walked at a brisk pace, excited to see her sister and proud to show off her culinary accomplishments. As she reached the front door, she buzzed Lisa's apartment number to be let in. After getting no response, she buzzed twice more. Still nothing.

Lisa lived on the ground floor of her building, so Mary approached a window and rapped her knuckles against it. She peeked in, and was surprised to find the apartment clean, but empty.

Where could she be? Mary wondered. She placed the bag of food on Lisa's stoop and took out her phone to text her.

Hey, where are you? I wanted to surprise you with some soup.

I'm at the doctor, came the reply, followed by another

telling Mary to go home, since she'd be a while.

There were many things Mary wanted to say to her sister in that moment, but none could be effectively conveyed over a text message. She picked up the soup, and dropped it with a heavy thunk into a nearby trash bin. It didn't occur to her until the bus ride home that she could have saved the Tupperware. Or had at least two more meals to tide herself over until brunch.

She got home, changed into her pajamas, and cried in her bed. She spent the rest of her day watching a Harry Potter marathon on TV, and eating cold cereal and ice cream. She regretted not bringing home the soup and eating it herself. She briefly considered making another grilled cheese sandwich, but found the pull of her warm blanket stronger than that of the stove. *It's a self-pity kind of day anyway*, she thought.

She scrolled through her phone, and more than once thought of canceling brunch with her cousin, Ally. The only reason she didn't was that she couldn't think of a good excuse, and wasn't one to lie. So, she comforted herself with cat videos while spells were performed in the background.

"What's wrong? Is everything okay?" Ally asked as she hugged Mary hello. Somehow she always had a sixth sense about how people were feeling.

"I'm fine, I'm just... I don't know how to describe it," Mary said, looking away as they each sat across from each other at a small table at the outdoor café.

"What's up?" Ally pressed.

Mary sighed, hesitating before answering. "I don't want to seem paranoid, but I think Lisa's been avoiding me. She went on a cruise two weeks ago. Didn't talk to me while she was away, and won't talk to me now that she's back. She says she's sick, but she refuses to get on the phone, she only replies to texts."

"That's odd… had she been acting differently before the cruise?"

"No! That's what's so weird, this is all so sudden," Mary exclaimed, then looked around sheepishly at the other diners, who were quietly enjoying brunch. A waiter caught her eye and came over to take their orders.

Blushing, Mary ordered a Mimosa and french toast. Ally ordered the same. After the waiter left, Ally looked back at Mary.

"You haven't seen Lisa since the trip then?" she asked.

"No, she won't let me. I even stopped by with soup yesterday since she said she was sick, but she wasn't there. She said she was at the doctor's," Mary explained.

Ally scrunched her lips. "Look, it could be a lot of things. Maybe something happened while she was away that she's not ready to talk about. Maybe she met someone and wants 'privacy'… who knows? It's probably not about you though."

Mary rolled her eyes. "I don't mean to think it's all about me, but I'm just… I don't get it." She ran her fingers roughly through her hair and rested her chin in her palm, her elbow perched against the side of the table. The waiter arrived with their drinks, causing Mary to bump her elbow against the table as she quickly withdrew it to make room.

The waiter asked if they needed anything else, and then left the two women stirring their drinks quietly. "I'll be honest," Ally started, "it raises a red flag that Lisa's only talking to you through text."

"Yeah, that's really been bothering me too," Mary agreed.

"Do you want my brother to look into it? He can scope things out and see what's up, just to make sure everything is okay," she added reassuringly.

"I hadn't even thought of that. Tom's a cop, right?" Mary asked.

"Kind of… to be honest I'm not even sure what he does exactly, but I'm sure he could do a quick check during the week or something."

"Yes," Mary said emphatically, locking eyes with Ally. "Let's see what he can find out."

CHAPTER 29
FAMILY

*G*ood morning," said a grandfatherly voice as he slowly opened the bedroom door. Geri and Lisa had already awoken and were both sitting up in bed, considering what the day might bring.

"Good morning," they both answered tentatively.

The Master, as the other girl had called him, stepped slowly into the room, looking around in the dim light. He was the older man who'd purchased Geri and saved Lisa on the island.

"I'm sorry that it's so dark in here, this is one of the few rooms in the house with no windows. This light is dimmable though, so you can adjust it as you like," he said, turning the dial near the door to slowly brighten the room. He wore khakis with a patchy vest over a simple button-down shirt. His white hair had been slicked back.

"I don't want you to get the wrong impression of me," he said after a pause. "I'm not some monster who just goes around buying women for pleasure… it's a bit more complicated than that."

Neither Geri nor Lisa moved. They both sat stiffly on their beds, watching and listening as the Master moved pensively around the room. He seemed almost as nervous as they were.

"I want to help you," he said. "That's why I go to the auctions, to help people. If I didn't buy them, somebody else would. I know what happens to the others, but I can't help everyone. So, every so often, I go, and I pick out one person to help. This time, it was you," he said, looking to Geri. "And then, you came in and of course I couldn't say no," he said, looking to Lisa. "I knew what would have become of you, and I couldn't just let that happen."

"What would have happened to me?" Lisa interjected. "What do you mean?"

"Well, it's hard to say exactly, since there are a few different possibilities. You may have noticed there were different groups who came to the auction," he said, looking to Geri, who nodded.

"That's because there are three main uses they've found for people like you. The first group, *your* group," he said to Geri, "is for prostitution, as I'm sure you guessed. You probably would have ended up in that group too, if not for your hand," he said to Lisa, gesturing to her bandages.

"The second group is much darker," he said, scowling at the floor. "That woman—the one in yellow—she's heartless, as you saw, but they're all just like her. They see people as livestock. They take the healthy ones, and sometimes the fat ones, and they host dinner parties…" he said, pausing. "Their customers pay a premium to eat human meat. There's an entire class of rich bastards who have more money than they know what to do with, and this is the latest fashion," he spat out.

"There's a waiting list for the dinners. It's disgusting."

Geri and Lisa just sat wide-eyed, afraid to look anywhere but forward.

The Master sighed. "And the third group buys people for medical experiments and organ harvesting, whichever has a higher price tag at the moment. That's why they run so many tests on you while you're in the cave, to pass along that information to the harvesters. There's a big black market for organs and body parts. It's sad, but it's the way of the world. At least their patients are sedated for surgery. The cannibals like to eat people alive half the time; they paralyze them. It's horrible."

He sighed again. "I don't mean to disturb you, but I do want you to know what you've escaped from by being here. I'm here to help you, and in return, you'll be helping me. I've had a sad life, and I just want some sense of normalcy. I just want things to be the way they were..." he said sadly, his eyes becoming glossy with unshed tears. He sniffed, then stiffened upright. "Well, I think that's enough for now. Clarissa will be in with your breakfast soon. I'll see you again in the afternoon," he said over his shoulder as he left, closing the door behind him.

After the door closed, Geri and Lisa sat motionless for a few seconds before turning to each other.

"What did we walk into?" Lisa asked.

"I really don't know what to make of any of this," Geri said quietly. She wrapped the covers around her, shaking though she wasn't cold.

A moment later, the young woman from the day before came in with the breakfast cart.

"Good morning!" she said brightly.

"Hello. Clarissa, is it?" Lisa asked.

"Yes, that's me," she smiled. "I have your breakfasts ready. Hard boiled eggs and some toast with butter. Hope that's okay?"

"That's fine," answered Lisa simply.

"Good, we're still keeping you on a bland diet for now, but we'll start adding more fun stuff in a few days," she said cheerily.

"Thank you," said Geri as Clarissa brought her a tray to eat her breakfast in bed. She then delivered Lisa's tray to her, and poured some tea into two small teacups.

"There's sugar, honey, and some milk on this shelf," she said, pointing to the cart. "Take your tea however you like it. I'll be back for the cart in an hour. Take your time, enjoy your breakfast!" she said as she smiled and left the room, closing the door again.

"I wanted to ask her about what he said before, but I guess it doesn't really matter, does it?" asked Lisa.

"Probably not," concurred Geri, who wrapped herself tightly and didn't touch her food.

"You should eat," said Lisa, taking a bite of her own buttered toast. "We need to be strong if we're going to get out of here."

Geri looked at her blankly. "Do you think we *can* get out of here? We don't even know where 'here' is."

"That's what we're going to find out. But you need to eat first, and act normal. There are a lot of questions that we need answers to. And they'll take some time to figure out. Now eat your breakfast."

CHAPTER 30
ON THE CASE

"Hey Tom, it's your cousin, Mary. Ally said I should talk to you about something. Call me back when you can. Thanks!" Mary ended her voicemail but didn't want to put down the phone just yet. She'd just gotten back from her brunch with Ally and was energized to do something to figure out what was going on with Lisa.

She opened up her texts to start a new message.

Hi Tom, just left you a voicemail. Hope you're doing well, sorry to bother you! Was hoping to talk to you about something. Hope to hear from you soon.

She re-read the message a few times to make sure it didn't come across as too demanding, or too urgent. She didn't want to alarm anyone, but she was worried and wanted reassurance. She and Tom had never spoken much, so she also felt awkward asking for help out of the blue.

To her surprise, she received a quick text in response.

Hey Mary, can't talk now, but I'll give you a call
a little later. Hope everything is okay.

She held her breath while reading the message, and exhaled slowly once it was finished. It was still an early Sunday afternoon, and she didn't know what to do with the rest of her day. Normally, she'd be doing laundry and catching up on dishwashing. Today, she found herself unmotivated to do either.

She sat on her plush bed and looked at the remote, but didn't feel like watching TV. She needed to be *doing* something, but what? She looked across the room to her jacket slumped against a chair and grabbed it without another thought. She picked up her purse on her way out and slammed the door closed behind her.

Almost an hour later, she was once again standing outside Lisa's apartment, having walked the whole way from her own home. She rang the buzzer, and wasn't surprised when there was no answer. She peeked into the window and saw no signs of anything being different. Everything looked exactly as it had the day before; as if nobody had been home all this time.

She began hyperventilating, her chest heaving with gasping breaths as tears streamed down her face. Her heart was already working hard from the brisk walk, and now felt like it could burst through her sternum.

She sat on the stoop and cried, her head in her hands, elbows on knees. If anyone walked by, she didn't see them. If anybody asked her if she was okay, she didn't hear them. She didn't even hear her own sobs over the thoughts of what could have happened to her sister.

A vibration in her pocket was the only thing that got her attention. She clumsily pulled out the phone and saw that Tom was calling her back. She immediately picked up, still sobbing into the phone.

"Shhh... Sh... She's g-g-gone!" she cried.

On the other end of the line, Tom tried to understand what he was hearing.

"What? Who's gone?" he asked, unable to make out anything else Mary was saying as she cried and sniffled.

"Okay Mary," he said softly. "I need you to take a deep breath. Take a deep breath, don't try to say anything. Just breathe for 10 seconds."

She did as instructed, trying not to sob every time she exhaled. After a few more seconds, he could hear her quieting down on the other end of the line.

"Okay, that's good. Now try to explain what's going on," he said.

She took another deep breath. "Lisa's gone," she said in a raspy but intelligible voice. "I don't think she ever came back from the cruise," she said, quietly crying again.

"The cruise? What cruise? When did she go?" he asked.

"She went on a cruise about two weeks ago, and she was supposed to come back a few days ago, but I haven't seen her since before she left," she explained.

"Okay, and have you spoken to her at all?"

"No," she began. "She's only been responding to texts, she won't answer any calls or call me back. And she keeps brushing me off every time I try to see her."

"Have you been to her apartment at all to see if she's home?" he asked.

"I'm outside it now, it doesn't look like anyone's

been here in weeks."

"Okay, and did she go on the cruise with anyone else, do you know?" he asked.

"Yes!" Mary exclaimed, feeling like she'd just stumbled on a puzzle piece she didn't realize she was missing. "She went with her friend... oh, what's her name?... Geri! Her friend Geri, from work."

"Oh." Tom paused. "Alright, I'll check in with her and see what I can find out."

"I don't have her number," Mary replied sadly.

"I do," he said simply.

"Oh."

"I'll do some digging and see what I can find. Do you know what cruise line they went on? I can check the records from that too," he said.

"It was the Harvest Cruise," she said. She had looked up their upcoming departures days before, hoping to plan another trip for Lisa and herself in the coming year. Now, she wasn't sure if that would ever happen.

Tom assured her that he'd make this a priority and figure out what he could. He told her it was probably just a misunderstanding, and he'd call her back once he had an update. They said their goodbyes and hung up.

Mary looked up at the sky. There were streaks of pink and orange slicing through the pale blue, and she had a long walk home. She got up on wobbly legs, and began her slow trek, grateful for the breeze that helped lift the heaviness from her mind.

In a fog of exhaustion, she reached her apartment. She didn't even remember the walk there, though somehow, she was back at her own front door. She dropped her bag on the floor, along with the jacket she didn't remember taking off, slunk to her bed, and collapsed into the blankets.

Hours later, she awoke briefly to text her boss that she'd be out sick the next morning.

CHAPTER 31
PLANS

*O*ver the next few days, Lisa and Geri read through just about every book on their bookshelves. Though they tried to find out as much as they could about their surroundings, there simply weren't enough opportunities to do so. Their days so far had mostly been spent locked in their windowless bedroom. So, they occupied their afternoons by discussing the books they'd both read, as well as the overall revelations of the day, which were few.

Clarissa had been dutifully bringing them meals three times per day, but rarely stayed long enough to chat. The Master only popped in to check on them every other day or so.

When Clarissa came to deliver their lunch on this day —a rare treat of roasted duck and vegetables—Lisa asked her to stay for a bit and talk to them.

"Only for a bit," Clarissa conceded. "I'm a little bit behind on my chores for the week."

"What are your other chores, aside from feeding us?"

Lisa asked.

"I prepare and cook all the food, plan out the next day's meals, keep the place clean, do laundry... pretty much everything around here," she laughed without a hint of resentment.

"Nobody else works here with you?" Lisa asked incredulously.

"Well, there's Andrew. He works in the garden and does our shopping," Clarissa said. "I'll bring you around for introductions in a few days."

"Oh, so how many people live here other than us? Not many?" Lisa asked.

"There's me, Andrew, the Master, and Tabitha, the Master's partner."

"His partner, like a girlfriend?" Lisa asked. Geri sat listening, asking the same questions in her mind, and grateful Lisa was there to ask them aloud.

"Kind of," Clarissa began, trying to think of the right way to describe the situation. She twirled her hair and looked up at the ceiling. "Tabitha is like us, she was saved from an auction years ago. They're practically a married couple, except that they can't *actually* get married since nobody knows she's here. It's a secret, like the rest of us." Clarissa looked at Geri and Lisa, but couldn't read the look on both their faces. "They really are in love though, I think," she said quickly. "You'll see soon, and you can talk to her. She's like our mother here. I'm sure she'll love meeting you." She smiled. "I really have to get back to my chores though, I have to clean up the dishes and do the laundry. Speaking of, I'll be back with fresh bed linens this afternoon, and with fresh clothes. If there's anything you'd like washed, just put it in the hamper and I'll take care of it."

"Thanks, Clarissa," said Lisa.

"You're welcome," she said with a nod and a smile. "Enjoy your lunch. I'll see you later!"

After the door was closed, Geri began eating her own meal.

"Well that was insightful," Lisa said. Geri couldn't tell if she was being sarcastic or not.

"We forgot to ask for more books," Geri said.

"Ah, yeah, I knew I was forgetting something. That girl has a way of making me forget everything I wanted to know. She always seems so perky and I have no idea why."

"Well, we now know that there are more people here, and at least one of them works outside," Geri replied.

"That's true," Lisa answered. "That could be helpful later. It means there's a chance we'll be able to go outside at some point too."

They both quietly finished their meals, while each thinking about what the outside world might look like around them. Based on the room they currently occupied, they imagined a palatial mansion outside their bedroom door, with marble floors and sunlight flooding in through 20-foot windows. They had no idea what country, or even what continent they were on, but they pictured a perfectly landscaped outdoor oasis with manicured trees and winding stone paths.

After lunch, they were surprised by a visit from the Master himself.

"Hello, I understand you've been chatting with Clarissa today," he said brightly.

"Yes, I hope we didn't keep her from her work too long," Lisa answered. Geri felt her pulse quicken.

"Not at all." He laughed. "I'm glad you're making

friends. I want everyone here to be friendly, we're all in the same boat, after all."

"I don't know about that," Lisa replied coolly.

"Oh?" he asked, his face a mask of confusion rather than malice.

"Well, I don't mean any disrespect, after all, you did save us. But you're here because you want to be, whereas we're not," she said.

"I see," he nodded, truly seeming to understand. "It's true, you were brought here, whereas I chose to come here. But we are all victims of circumstance. I'd rather not get into it now, but you should know that things have happened in my life that I never thought I'd recover from. I still haven't, to be honest. But as I'm helping you, you'll also be helping me. We all help each other here. We're all family."

"You say that you just wanted to help us, but I can't help but wonder about the people getting eaten alive. Why not help them?" Lisa said, trying to be as non-confrontational as possible, but still coming off brusquely.

The Master looked down at the floor, focusing on a scuff mark as he quietly answered. "Tabitha was one of those people. So was Andrew," he said with a sad smile. "I can't help everyone, but I can help a few. I have to be a bit selective, which is much more difficult for me than you'd know. At the end of the day, I choose the people who I think will fit in best here. This is a large house, and we all have our jobs to do."

"And what will our jobs be?" Lisa asked tentatively, her eyes narrowing. Geri could feel herself sweating through her thin shirt and hoped nobody noticed the hot flush creeping up her chest and neck.

"For now, I just want you to be happy here. I'm old enough to be your father, and I'd like you to think of me that way. I have help around the house, but to be frank, I just want what I had before. I want my family back. I want to spoil you and give you everything I couldn't give my own children. Please just let me do that," he said softly, his eyes beginning to water.

Neither woman answered. Geri looked down at her blankets, while Lisa continued to watch his face.

"I'll be going now. I'll introduce you to everyone soon," he said, closing the door gently behind him.

"I believe him," Lisa said without looking at Geri.

"I feel weird about this whole thing," Geri said, crossing her arms across her torso, hugging herself tightly.

"Me too, but I believe him."

CHAPTER 32
INTRODUCTIONS

*B*y Tuesday, Mary was still on edge, but functional enough to return to work. She conducted a few interviews over the phone and began outlining the stories she'd meant to write up the previous day. By 1 p.m., she was on her third cup of coffee and still hadn't eaten anything.

She was entrenched in her keyboard when she smelled cologne and suddenly noticed a figure standing over her desk. She jumped, causing her coffee to spill.

"Sorry to startle you," the stranger laughed.

"Sorry, I didn't see you standing there," she said, pulling napkins from a desk drawer to mop up the spill while forcing a polite smile.

"Are you Mary McDaniels?" he asked.

She stopped wiping the desk without looking up. "Yes…" she replied cautiously.

"Is there a quiet place we can talk? It's about your sister, Lisa," he said.

Mary felt as if her head suddenly weighed 50 pounds

and was about to fall from her shoulders. She felt hot and the office began to spin. She gripped the arms of her chair for stability.

"Who are you?" she asked once the room stopped spinning, afraid to look up in case the sensation came back.

"I was on the cruise with Lisa and Geri, and I haven't been able to get in touch with either of them since. I was hoping you could tell me if they're okay," he said calmly.

Her mind whirled with this information and what it could mean. She shakily led him to a small conference room and shut the door. He sat down in a nearby chair, tapping his foot softly on the carpet as she stood at the door, still holding the knob and not looking at him.

"Who are you?" she again asked.

"I was on the ship with your sister and Geri—"

"No, I know that, but who are *you*?" she cut him off.

"I'm Billy."

Mary and Billy went to a coffee shop around the corner to discuss what each of them had experienced since the cruise returned. Mary sat with a fourth cup of coffee in front of her, along with a scone that remained untouched. Billy had ordered an iced tea with a turkey wrap, which he'd been eating leisurely throughout the conversation.

"So you'd been... seeing Geri? On the cruise?" Mary was trying to understand the relationship.

"Yes, we'd gotten very close," he said between bites. "We exchanged phone numbers and had been talking and seeing each other every day. We were going to keep in touch after, but I haven't heard from her since we docked. At first I thought she was ghosting me, but when I texted Lisa to ask, I got these weird answers that didn't sound like her at all," he explained.

"Yeah, I know the feeling," Mary answered, rolling her eyes.

"It just wasn't sitting right with me, so when I saw your name in the paper I was hoping you might be related, based on the last name. I did stalk your Facebook a bit." He smiled sheepishly. "It looked like you were Lisa's sister. I know this must sound creepy, and I hope I'm not crossing any weird boundaries, but I'm just worried about them," he said.

Mary sat quietly, hovering over her still-full cup of coffee, warming her hands against the paper cup and inhaling the fragrant steam.

"Have you been able to reach either of them?" he continued.

"No, I haven't," she answered.

"What do you think we should do? Have you called the police?" he asked urgently.

She sighed. "Not exactly, but I have a guy working on it."

His eyes widened. "Who?" he asked.

"A friend," she said, looking up at him now.

"I'd like to talk to them, tell them what I know," he said, leaning into the table.

Mary leaned back in her chair. "I'll talk to him and see what he says. What's your number? I'll give it to him so he can call you if he needs anything."

"Actually, why don't you give me his number? My phone isn't always reliable and I work crazy hours, might be better if I can call him." He smiled reassuringly.

"You know, I had his business card on me earlier, but I lost it, must be at home," she said, patting her pockets. "Give me your number, and I'll pass it along," she said. "Don't worry, I won't spam you," she added with a laugh.

He laughed with her. "Okay, no problem. I'm sure we'll figure something out." He told her the phone number and she typed it into her phone.

Back at her desk, Mary typed the phone number into her search bar. A pizzeria in Brooklyn popped up as the result.

Hmmph.

She wasn't surprised. Something about the guy, Billy, seemed off. She regretted not getting a last name. Although, who knew if his name was really even Billy? She tapped a pen against her desk, wondering what to do next, finally deciding to give Tom a call.

"Hello?" he answered. She was surprised he picked up on the first ring.

"Hey, Tom, I just had a really weird experience," she started. "Is now a good time to talk?"

She recounted the events of the day, describing how Billy showed up at her desk, what he'd said about how he knew Geri and Lisa, and his demeanour in the coffee shop.

"For someone who was worried about someone else, he had a pretty good appetite. He seemed more interested in hearing about you than anything else," she remembered.

"Did you tell him my name or give him any information?" Tom asked cautiously.

"No, I didn't trust him. I took his number, but he gave me the number to some pizza place in Brooklyn."

"That's interesting…" he said. "And he was specifically asking about Lisa and Geri, you never mentioned them first?"

"No." She was sure. "He brought them up on his own, he said that's why he came to find me."

Tom thought for a moment. "It was very bold of him to just show up at your office like that. I don't think you should have gone anywhere with him, but it's good you're back at the office now. Tell your building's security to keep a lookout for him."

For the first time, Mary realized how vulnerable she'd been.

CHAPTER 33
MEET THE FAMILY

*T*he next morning, Clarissa was beaming as she brought Geri and Lisa their breakfasts. Today, they got a special treat of blueberry pancakes with whipped cream.

"Good morning! We're celebrating today; you're going to get a tour of the place!" she exclaimed. "Eat up and get dressed. Once you're ready, I'll bring you downstairs to meet Tabitha and Andrew."

Geri and Lisa both feigned excitement and politely smiled as Clarissa delivered the happy news and drizzled melted butter and syrup over their pancakes. She left them to their meals and set out their outfits for the day, chosen by the Master himself for the occasion.

Once they'd eaten their fill, they looked at the clothing that had been carefully folded and left at the foot of each bed. They each held up their outfits for the day; matching purple corduroy dresses. They were sleeveless, but long-sleeved white shirts with lace trim were apparently meant to be worn underneath the dresses, along with bright white tights and shiny black Mary Jane shoes.

"Well this is… something," said Lisa, holding up the purple dress with a face stuck between confusion and disgust.

"Very… old fashioned?" Geri suggested, not sure how else to describe the outfit.

"Mary Janes?" Lisa exclaimed. "What are we, 5? What kind of clothes are these? And when's the last time you wore tights?" she asked, holding up the stretchy white material. "Ugh, I'm not wearing this," she said definitively, throwing the tights back on the bed, where they softly landed in a delicate heap. "I don't want to wear any of this," she said.

"We shouldn't cause trouble…" Geri said quietly. "I think you should just put it on, we'll go meet everyone, and then you can get changed after."

Lisa snorted and rolled her eyes. "This is ridiculous."

They put on their outfits, which were stiff but otherwise fit well. Lisa avoided the white tights, while Geri obediently put on each piece as intended. They buckled their shoes, which fit remarkably well considering neither remembered telling anyone her shoe size.

"Look, we have pockets!" Geri laughed as she put her hands in the pockets of her dress.

"Great!" Lisa said. "I'll have a place to put my phone and wallet… oh wait…" she laughed sarcastically while holding out her empty hands.

Geri gave her a jokingly admonishing look. The comicality of it all made her smile every time she looked in the mirror. They looked like overgrown children, and it put her in the best mood she'd been in since her days of flirting on the cruise. It seemed so long ago since she'd last smiled for real. Yet here she was, held hostage in a rich man's palace, wearing a dainty outfit meant for a child, and preparing to meet the other happy hostages in the house. It was so absurd it was funny, and now she even began to laugh.

"Don't laugh," Lisa said, beginning to laugh herself. "Oh god, soon we'll be having a pillow fight, I just know it," she scoffed.

Clarissa returned a moment later, stifling a giggle as she saw the women in their outfits. "My, much more… colourful than I realized."

"Don't even start," said Lisa. "Why do you get to wear a normal grey uniform and we have to be dressed as sugarplum fairies?"

At this, Clarissa couldn't contain her laughter. "Your job is to make the Master happy, I guess this makes him happy," she giggled, holding up her arms in a *don't ask me*, gesture. She took a moment to catch her breath, and tried her hardest to minimize her smile.

"Alright, ladies, serious faces now," she said, still fighting the smile. "Come, follow me." She turned around to lead them outside the room.

As they walked through the door, the air seemed to get lighter. It was certainly brighter out in the hall, where the walls were a soft grey with white wainscoting along the lower half. The floors were polished marble, and there were paintings all around them. Bright meadows and colourful flowers surrounded them as their shoes clicked along the floor. The hall even smelled like flowers, which was likely from the fresh bouquets neatly displayed along tables spaced every few feet.

At the end of the hall was an elegant, sweeping staircase with curved iron railings. Geri and Lisa walked slowly behind Clarissa, who smiled back at them knowingly as they took in their extravagant surroundings.

"Careful on the stairs, it might be slippery in your new shoes," she gently reminded them.

The bottom of the staircase opened into the largest room either had ever seen. Was it the entrance to the house? A ballroom? Neither was sure. The cathedral ceilings put the vaulted ceiling in their own bedroom to shame. This truly was a palace, thought Geri, who's own house seemed like a hovel in comparison.

Clarissa led them back behind the stairwell, along another hall that brought them into the kitchen. As they got closer, they could smell the lingering aroma of the blueberry pancakes they'd eaten just before. Geri had expected to step into servant's quarters with a cramped kitchenette. Instead, they walked into an impressive gourmet kitchen with a double wall oven, the largest eight-burner stove she'd ever seen, and more cabinets than she'd know what to do with. Like the bedroom, the woodwork was a rich cherry wood, accented by black onyx counters flecked with gold. It went well with the double sink, which had gold basins and a matching faucet.

"If you're ever hungry or thirsty, help yourself to whatever's in the fridge," Clarissa said, pulling open what appeared to be a large pantry, but was in fact the door to the oversized refrigerator, hidden among the cabinetry. Inside the fridge were covered glass trays with what appeared to be leftovers, all neatly labeled with the types of food and when they were prepared. There were also loose fruits and vegetables, as well as bottled water, juices, iced tea, and at least three different types of dairy-free milk.

"Is the Master lactose intolerant?" Lisa joked.

"He seems to think so," she said, looking around and getting closer before whispering, "but that doesn't stop him from having a bowl of ice cream every night!" She winked and they all laughed lightly. She opened another cabinet door to reveal at least 10 different cartons of ice cream in the hidden freezer.

"Wow!" Lisa said, scanning the many flavours. "No meat, though?"

"Meat is delivered fresh every day. If Master is in the mood for something, we order it straight from town," Clarissa explained.

"Oh, you have a delivery service?" Lisa asked casually.

"Andrew usually takes care of that," she answered. "I put in the order and he goes to pick it up. Speaking of Andrew," she said, "he's just outside in the garden. We can go through the back door here to meet him," she suggested. She led Geri and Lisa across the kitchen to the door.

Walking through the doorway, Geri inhaled the warm air deeply, taking in all the greenery. She brushed her fingers against the hedges as they walked, grateful to be outside in the sunshine.

They followed a brick pathway framed by fragrant lavender, colourful rose blooms, and other flowers and shrubs all around. Ahead of them they could see a small yellow cottage.

"This is where Andrew stays," Clarissa explained. She approached the door and knocked. Almost immediately, the door opened to reveal a richly tanned, well-built figure who could have come straight from the cover of a romance novel.

"Good morning, Andrew! These are the newest

members of our household, Geri and Lisa," Clarissa explained, gesturing to each in turn.

"Good morning," he said, smiling to each of them.

"Hellooo Andrew!" Lisa said dramatically, caught off guard by his looks. He laughed in reply before returning her greeting.

"Wow, we get two this time," he said, looking at them both. Geri felt herself blushing under his attention, the sun feeling hotter against her skin. Lisa, meanwhile, stood tall with a confident grin.

"We were a two-for-one special, who could pass that up?" she said. They all laughed lightheartedly, and Geri was grateful for the distraction from her own flushed cheeks.

"Alright, well, we'll all have plenty of time to get to know each other better soon enough, in the meantime, let's go see Tabitha," Clarissa suggested.

"Do we have to go so soon?" Lisa joked.

"Don't worry, you'll be seeing more of Andrew," Clarissa laughed.

"How much more are we talking about?" Lisa teased, winking at Andrew, who again laughed in return.

"You'll have to wait and see," he said, his smile wide.

"Alright, come on now, Tabitha's waiting," Clarissa reminded them, gently pulling Lisa away.

They retraced their steps over the brick walkway back towards the house. When they were some distance away, Clarissa turned to Lisa.

"Just so you know," she said in a whisper, "Andrew's gay."

Lisa and Geri looked to each other in surprise. "Ugh, honestly, it figures, all the good ones are," Lisa replied jokingly.

"Yeah, naturally the only guy any of us would be

interested in here, isn't interested in us," Clarissa agreed.

"I wonder if that was planned," Lisa mused. "Less competition for Master…"

"More like, less distraction for us. Master has Tabitha, he doesn't need or want anyone else," Clarissa answered. "All he wants from us is whatever he wants from us," she laughed, still unsure of what exactly he did want from the two newcomers.

She led them back the way they had come through the house, but instead of going upstairs, they continued past the other side of the staircase.

"My room is down that hall," she said, inclining her head toward a hall behind the stairs, adjacent to the kitchen. "It's the door on the right."

They continued on and reached a set of French doors, which Clarissa opened to reveal a formal living space. "These are Tabitha's quarters," Clarissa explained. They walked through the room to another door, which Clarissa knocked on. "Come in," came a pleasant voice from the other side. Clarissa opened the door to reveal a woman who appeared to be in her early-fifties, and very well groomed. The woman smiled warmly at them as they entered. She was sitting on a built-in bench in front of a large bay window with a grey cat in her lap and a book in her hand. Her hair appeared to be a natural brown with silver streaks throughout, styled in such a way that she could easily have passed for a 50s pin-up girl. Her skin had a natural glow, and her clothing was old-fashioned, but in the most fashionable way.

She gently picked up the cat on her lap and placed it on the floor, before it scurried away under the bed. She rose and held out her hands to greet them.

"So glad to meet you, I'm Tabitha," she said, taking

each by the hand one at a time. And from the look in her eyes, she truly did seem glad to meet them.

CHAPTER 34
ABLAZE

*T*he next few days found Mary and Tom speaking more frequently. He couldn't find any information about Billy, but he did make some headway researching the Harvest Cruise.

"Geri never came back either," Tom said in a hushed tone. Mary had invited him over to chat about his findings in person. She was tired of the back and forth texts and phone calls, and frankly, she was feeling more and more paranoid lately. The two sat at her tiny dinette table. A teapot whistled on the stove, but neither one seemed to notice.

"How do you know she didn't come back?" Mary asked, even though she already assumed the answer.

"I tried calling and got nowhere, like how you did with Lisa," he began. "Then I tried texting, and she was brushing me off, but in an aggressive way. I've only met her once, but I could tell it's not in her nature to be confrontational like that, so I didn't believe that she was the one texting me back. I took a trip to her house and a few things stuck out," he continued.

"First, the lawn hadn't been mowed in at least a few weeks. I'd been to her house before and saw her yard, it was gorgeous. She would *not* let the lawn go like that, and especially not the weeds that have been popping up too. But that's just the tip of the iceberg," he said, pausing. "I checked her mailbox, and it was empty. Weird, right?" he asked. Mary nodded.

"So I knocked on the neighbour's door and flashed my badge. Sweet old lady. She said Geri asked her to pick up her mail before her trip, and that she'd been doing it for a week before the mail stopped coming."

Mary raised an eyebrow, unsure of what this could mean. What happened to the mail?

"I hid a security camera in one of the bushes behind her mailbox. I checked the footage for a few days and got nothing. Nobody was taking the mail—the mail wasn't coming. I checked the postal records, and her address wasn't changed, so there's no reason for her not to be getting mail. Something's going on here."

Mary let out a long breath. "This is big," she said.

"Yes, I really think it is," he agreed.

They were both silent. Mary looked up at the teapot on the stove, finally realizing that it was screaming for attention. She snapped up and removed it from the stove, holding the handle in one hand and looking for a trivet with the other. She set it down on the counter once she found one.

For a moment she just stared at the teapot before turning around to ask Tom if he wanted any. He gently declined. She found she wasn't in the mood for tea either and returned to the table empty handed.

"What do we do now?" she asked, fidgeting with the

cheap rings she always wore.

"I'm going to track down Geri's family and see if they've heard from her at all," he said. "Then I want to see who else might be missing from the ship. There were thousands of passengers, so this could take a while. I've already gotten the passenger list, I just have to find each person's information and see if they made it home."

"Is there anything I can do?" Mary asked, feeling useless in the process.

"No," he replied, "I've got resources and can handle it."

"Should we call the police?" she asked.

"This is above the police. I have a team working on it with me," he replied as he stood up from his chair, not giving any further details. Mary didn't ask for any.

"I gotta get going, thanks for having me over," he said, retrieving his jacket from the coat rack.

"Yeah, of course," she said.

After he left, she locked the door behind him and pulled the deadbolt that she'd installed the previous day. She poured the full teapot of scalding water down the kitchen sink, creating a plume of rising steam. She closed her eyes and inhaled the warm air, deciding to take a quick shower to help relax before getting ready for bed. Lately, she'd been going to bed earlier and earlier, and finding it increasingly difficult to wake up for work each morning.

In the shower, she found herself preoccupied with the possibilities behind her sister's disappearance. Everything was still a mystery, and each new day brought more questions than anything else. She imagined an accident on the ship that had been covered up by the cruise line. She imagined that Lisa didn't actually like her—that she'd secretly hated her and decided to start a new life without telling her. She imagined that Lisa and Geri were secretly in love and ran away together to avoid judgement. In her mind, this was the best case scenario, since at least Lisa would be safe and might eventually come back.

As Mary lathered her hair and considered the possibilities, she thought she heard a sound from outside. She wasn't sure what it was, but reassured herself that it was probably a tree branch brushing up against a window. She continued scrubbing, but kept her ears open for any other sounds. It was hard to hear anything over the pounding shower, but she heard something now that made her freeze.

Creaking floorboards.

In her small apartment, it wasn't uncommon to hear the goings-on of her neighbours on all sides. But Mary was used to every sound, and in the shower, she'd never heard much of anything. She considered turning off the water to listen better, but didn't want to alert anyone that she'd heard anything out of place. She quickly stepped out from the shower stall, still dripping wet with soapy lather falling from her hair. She tiptoed across the slippery bathroom floor to quietly lock the door. Now what?

She pressed her ear to the door. She was sure there was somebody in the apartment now. There were shuffling sounds coming from the kitchen.

She grabbed a towel and patted herself dry, then re-dressed in the clothes she'd been wearing before, forcing herself back into her jeans, which tugged against her still-damp skin. If her bathroom had a window, she would have jumped out. Instead, all she had was a tiny vent in the ceiling; not nearly large enough for her to escape through. She went back to the door, listening. She could smell smoke, and the door felt warm against her cheek. As if on cue, her smoke alarm began screaming in the next room, causing her to jump.

She couldn't hear anything now over the alarm and the shower. She shut off the water and closed her eyes. Her heart pounded with adrenaline and fear. She had to get out. Now.

She steeled herself as she planned to leave the bathroom and run for the front door. She wished she'd brought her shoes in with her; there'd be no time to retrieve them from wherever she left them. She took the wet towel from the floor and soaked it further in the water that remained at the bottom of the shower before covering the lower half of her face with it. She took two deep breaths, in… and out… in...and out… before bursting through the door.

A wall of dark smoke greeted her, stinging her eyes and burning her throat despite the towel. She could vaguely see the flames shooting upward in the kitchen, but most of her vision was occluded by darkness. If anyone was still in the apartment with her, she couldn't see them, and it was doubtful they'd see her. She clumsily crawled across the floor, one hand still pressing the towel to her face while the other was used as support as she made her way toward the door.

She finally made it to the threshold and stood up to unlock the deadbolt, which was swollen from heat and difficult to move. Once she got it free, she turned the hot doorknob and threw open the door. Blindly, she ran straight into the large figure who'd been standing just outside.

CHAPTER 35
PAMPERED INTO BOREDOM

*G*eri and Lisa returned to their room to decompress before dinner, which they were expected to join promptly at 6:30 that night. They undressed and returned to the usual leisurewear that their dressers were stocked with. Before she left, Clarissa informed them of the formal attire they'd be expected to wear to dinner, and that they could find suitable options hanging in the closet.

Once they were comfortable, they decided to pick out their outfits for the night. While they'd searched through the closet on their first day, they weren't interested in clothes then; they'd been looking for hidden cameras or evidence of anything particularly suspicious. They'd found nothing. Now, looking at the wardrobe they'd been provided, they were surprised by their findings: formal floor length gowns, Cinderella-inspired ball gowns, short sparkly party dresses, elegant jumpsuits, and just about every other kind of formal attire one could think of.

What kind of dinner would this be? they both wondered. For a moment, Geri's mind flashed to the cannibals, and she wondered if the Master was indeed one of them. Thinking back on their conversations with him, however, she pushed the thought from her mind.

They still had hours before dinner, and decided to go back downstairs to find Clarissa and ask what to expect. They headed straight for the kitchen, where they found her working on the night's spread—which by the look of things, was to include at least three ducks, which were buttered and seasoned and about to go into the oven, and lots of fresh vegetables that were in the process of being peeled and chopped.

"Lisa, Geri! Is everything okay? What can I get for you?" Clarissa asked, putting down her peeler and the carrot she was working on and wiping her hands against her apron.

"No, no, nothing at all!" Lisa assured her. "We were just wondering what to expect at this dinner, who else will be there, that sort of thing."

"The clothes in our closet are very formal," Geri added. "We just wanted to make sure we're ready."

"Oh!" Clarissa laughed. "Yes," she began, "I should have explained. The dinners are very formal, but it's just us. Every night, we dress up and basically pretend we're living another life. It's like living hundreds of years ago, where everyone got dressed up and just enjoyed dinner together. Feel free to wear whatever you like from the closet, nothing is too fancy," Clarissa assured them. "This is your chance to be a princess," she added with a smile and curtsey, "and we get to do this every night!"

Geri and Lisa smiled at each other, unsure of what else to do. The oddness of this place continued to confound them. Not in any rush to leave, Lisa decided to redirect the conversation.

"Wow, what a magical place. How can we help with dinner tonight? I'd feel terrible playing dress up all afternoon while you're busy down here doing all the work."

"Nonsense," the girl said, brushing away the offer with her hand. "Your place here isn't in the kitchen. Your job is just to be happy. Go, enjoy your afternoon," she said warmly.

"Well, that's the thing, we don't really know what else to do here," Lisa said. "What do you do for fun around here?"

"Well…" Clarissa began. "I guess this is what I do, I have fun cooking. I'm just not sure what else there is for *you* to do during the day. Your days will be much different than mine… maybe you should talk to Tabitha. I'm sure she can give you some suggestions," she smiled.

"That's a good idea," Lisa replied brightly. "Maybe the Master will have some ideas too. Where can we usually find him?"

"Oh, he's usually out and about during the day," Clarissa answered dismissively. "Who knows where he goes half the time." She laughed. "Talk to Tabitha, you can always find her in her quarters."

Geri and Lisa thanked her and set off down the hall toward Tabitha's rooms. When they reached the set of French doors, they weren't sure whether to knock first or simply enter; the doors were mostly glass, so they provided little in the way of privacy, anyway. Geri looked to Lisa, who in turn lifted her good hand to gently knock on the door.

"Hello?" a small voice answered.

"Hi, it's Lisa and Geri," Lisa replied loudly.

"Come in!" the voice replied.

Lisa opened the door and she and Geri entered the salon area, where they were met by another cat, an orange tabby. Geri knelt to say hello to the cat and give it a scratch behind its ears. It rewarded her by arching its back and brushing against her leg. Reluctantly, she got up to follow Lisa into the next room, Tabitha's bedroom. She hoped the cat would follow her in, but it jumped up into a nearby chair instead.

Entering Tabitha's room, they found her exactly where she'd been earlier, in the window seat with a cat on her lap and a book in her hand. This time, the cat was black. The grey cat from earlier was now curled against a pillow on the otherwise empty bed.

"How many cats do you have?" Geri asked, surprised each time she saw another one.

Tabitha laughed, "There are four that I keep here, and a few that visit the garden. This one is Onyx," she said, stroking the black cat on her lap. "That's Blue on the bed, and Tux is probably hiding under the bed, he's a black and white tuxedo boy, and Sunny is an orange tabby, though I'm not sure where he is now," she said, looking around the room.

"He's out in the next room," Geri answered.

Tabitha smiled. "So, what can I do for you ladies?" she asked.

"Well, we seem to have a lot of spare time," Lisa began, "and we're not really sure what to do with it all. We were hoping you could give us something to do, or advice in general on living here."

"I see," Tabitha said, still smiling, and looking out the window. "Well, that's why I have all these cats, I guess.

They keep me busy and entertained," she said, playfully tugging Onyx's tail, resulting in a quick swat and play-bite from the cat. "Master is kind, but he's also very old fashioned, as I'm sure you've noticed, so you won't find a TV or any other sort of electronics here. It's a bit like living like the royalty of past centuries I guess, pampered into boredom," she said wistfully. After a pause, she added, "You can ask Andrew to pick up books for you during his trips to market. And you're more than welcome to have a small pet of your own in your room. Just no dogs, unfortunately, Master's allergic. But I'm sure anything else is fine. You see my personal preference," she said, now picking Onyx up to snuggle her face.

Lisa and Geri thanked Tabitha for her time and suggestions. She told them that she looked forward to seeing them at dinner, and they left to return to their own room. Once there, they shut the door to talk.

"I was thinking," Geri started, "there are a lot of flowers and plants in the garden that I've never seen before. If we ask Andrew for a plant book, we might be able to get an idea of where we are." With her own knowledge of plants and gardening, she was sure she'd be able to find some clues to help.

"That's a great idea," Lisa said. "I've been looking for a phone since we've been here, but the only one I've seen is in the kitchen. If you still remember that phone number from the island, we might be able to do something with that."

Geri looked at her wide-eyed. *What was the number?!* She closed her eyes tightly, trying to remember. 72-something… 72-something…

"Seven-two… six six! 7266!" she shouted triumphantly.

"Wait, we'd have to text it though, a regular phone won't work," she said, her spirits immediately dampening.

Lisa sighed. "Why would anything be easy?" she asked nobody in particular. Neither said anything for a moment, they were both deep in thought, trying to think of their next move.

"You know," Geri said quietly, "the Master might have his own phone."

Lisa didn't reply at first, still thinking. "He might," she finally conceded, "but we have no idea where he'd keep it, if he has one at all. We don't even know where he is now, or where his room is." While they'd had a brief tour of the house, they'd only visited a few rooms. Most of the estate was still a mystery.

"Well, we still have some time before dinner, and I think we're allowed to roam the halls throughout the day…" Geri said conspiratorially.

Lisa scoffed. "And everyone thinks you're so innocent, just 'cause you don't talk in public." She laughed, then sighed and groaned. "I'm worried about keeping everyone's trust right now, but I guess it's no harm to just walk the halls." Geri smiled, while Lisa continued. "We won't open any closed doors, or walk into any bedrooms or offices. We're just going to get the overall layout, okay?"

"Okay," Geri agreed.

CHAPTER 36
PLAYING WITH FIRE

*T*wo strong hands gripped Mary by the upper arms and held her as she fell into the hall.

"No! Stop! Help!" she screamed and thrashed, hoping a neighbour would come to her aid as she struggled to get away from the blaze behind her and the dark figure blocking her path.

"It's me!" came a familiar voice. "It's Tom! C'mon!" he said, steadying her on her wobbly feet and leading her down the hall and out of the building. As they deeply inhaled the fresh air outside, they could already hear sirens approaching.

As Tom looked at Mary, he noticed the steam rising from her still-wet-yet-singed hair.

"What happened, exactly?" he asked, afraid he already knew the answer.

"Somebody was in my apartment," she croaked breathlessly. "I went into the shower after you left, and I heard somebody walking around the apartment. I locked the door, and then I smelled smoke," she said in between gasping breaths.

Tom took a deep breath. He didn't have to say anything, they both knew what was going on. The question was, what were they going to do about it?

"What should we tell the police?" Mary asked.

"The police won't get too involved unless it seems like arson," Tom explained. "If this guy was any good, it won't seem like arson. It'll seem like you were careless and let something burn on the stove while you were in the shower."

Mary thought on this, unsure of how to feel. Would it be better for the police to get involved at this point? Or would they just complicate Tom's work. She still didn't know exactly where he worked or what he did, but got the feeling that it was something he'd rather keep to himself and not get the local police tangled up in.

"So, should I let them believe it was an accident, if that's what they think?" she asked, as much as she hated the idea of it.

Tom sighed. "I don't know if there's a right answer here, but I think that's best for now. If they do think it was in any way suspicious, we might have to tell them what we know."

Outwardly, he seemed relatively calm. Inwardly, his anxious thoughts threatened to bubble to the surface, spewing all of his hidden fears surrounding this case. If local authorities did get involved, the case would likely go public. This would complicate things as any guilty parties would be working twice as hard to cover their tracks, making it that much harder to gather evidence.

As it was, Tom wanted to be the first one back in the apartment once the fire was put out to see what he could find. That would be difficult to accomplish with so many eyes around.

The firefighters arrived and were firing a water canon directly through Mary's window, which had broken in the blaze. Dark, billowing smoke continued to rise from the building as more and more residents fled to the safety of the sidewalk clutching small dogs, blankets, backpacks, and whatever else they thought to grab on the way out. All Mary had was the clothing she'd hastily thrown on in the bathroom, and the burnt towel that had helped her breathe through the thick haze.

Tom stood by quietly, wrapping his jacket around Mary's shoulders, though she was too dazed to notice. They were each trying to formulate a plan around what to tell people.

Ambulances arrived on the scene to treat any burns and smoke inhalation. Mary looked to Tom, who told her to go and get herself checked out. He felt that a trip to the hospital might give her some time before any questioning began, and it would allow him some time to talk his way into the apartment.

Mary walked to the back of an ambulance and was promptly loaded onto a stretcher and given oxygen. Tom waved to her as she was wheeled into the ambulance and sent on her way.

As the flames receded and steam began to replace the smoke billowing from the window, Tom took his opportunity to approach the fire chief, who was on the scene. He flashed his badge, explaining that he'd like to take a look at things seeing that his cousin's apartment was involved. Wordlessly, the chief stepped aside.

Tom used the collar of his shirt to cover his face and quickly followed the path up the stairs and back into the apartment, which was now black with ash and completely flooded. Immediately he could see the source of the fire —the garbage can had been moved near the stove, which had the burnt remnants of what appeared to have once been a towel laid across the electric elements, with the tea kettle perched on top. While it appeared that a careless Mary left a towel on the stove, which promptly set ablaze the garbage pail, he knew that the fire was intentionally set in the pail and then staged. He just hoped the police and fire department fell for the trick, as the assailant intended.

He poked around a bit longer, checking for any other possible evidence, then bounded down the stairs and thanked the chief for letting him inside.

"Looks like she was just careless with her cooking," he said with a good-humoured smile. "Glad nobody was hurt. I'll go check on her now and tell her to be more careful next time she wants a warm drink," he winked.

"Maybe have her stay out of the kitchen for a while," the chief joked back.

Tom drove straight to the nearest hospital, where he found Mary set up in the Emergency Room, still breathing through her oxygen mask but looking slightly less frazzled. Her forearms and hands were bandaged, but overall she looked okay.

"Hey," he said, pulling up a chair next to her cot. "I got back in and checked it out. From the looks of it, you burned a towel on the stove, which was conveniently hanging over the garbage can."

"The garbage can?" she asked incredulously. "That was across the room… and I don't even have any towels in the kitchen!"

"I know, I remember where everything was before I

left," he assured her. "Somebody was there, and they set it up. I don't know if they meant to kill you, or just scare you, but we need to figure out what to do with you now."

Neither knew what to say. Mary had no place else to go; normally she'd just stay with Lisa. The closest people she had now were her cousins, Ally and Tom, but she didn't want to impose on either of them.

They both sighed in unison. Tom was the first to speak.

"I think we need to get you a new identity and have you lay low for a while," he said, staring straight ahead.

"Okay…?" she replied, her trepidation given away by the fast-beeping monitor tracking her pulse.

CHAPTER 37
GARDEN SECRETS

*O*ver the next few days, the novelty of extravagant sit-down dinners had worn off. Geri and Lisa had become accustomed to their colourful wardrobes and realized that Tabitha's traditional sense of style probably wasn't her own, either; they were all part of their Master's fantasy life.

Fortunately, it only really mattered at night when he joined everyone for dinner. Aside from that, he was often out of sight. Nobody discussed what the Master did for a living, or how he was able to afford their lifestyle of luxury. Geri and Lisa knew better than to ask. They were still working to solidify everyone's trust in them and thought it best to avoid most questions. Instead, they spent their days reading, talking, and planning. And caring for their new rabbits, Harley and Davidson.

"Look at him jump!" Geri squealed as Davidson ran across the room and flicked his heels. Harley stood against her cage bars, trying to get out to join him. Since neither rabbit had been spayed or neutered, the women thought it best to keep them separated during playtime. Being that their days were long and otherwise unscheduled, they had plenty of time to spare for entertaining the energetic duo.

"Yes, he's very cute," Lisa said flatly. "I still would have preferred something a little less... furry." She pulled some stray hairs from her shirt and blanket.

"Well, Andrew said there weren't too many options," Geri replied. "And we can always see lizards and snakes in the garden anyway." In addition to their new indoor companions, Lisa and Geri had been taking daily walks in the manicured yard to get some fresh air and keep from going stir-crazy. The outdoor area was beautifully landscaped and harboured many different small animals that could come and go as they pleased over and under the high brick wall that enclosed them.

"Speaking of the garden," Lisa remembered, "have you had any luck with the plants?"

Geri scrunched the corner of her mouth. "Not yet. All Andrew's been able to get me is old *Better Homes & Gardens* magazines. Nothing too helpful there. All I can tell is that we're not in Kansas," she said with an eye roll.

Lisa thought for a moment. "What about the lizards and snakes? What if we could figure out what they are and where they're from?"

Geri perked up at this idea. "That's a possibility. We can see if Andrew can find any reptile books or magazines. I'll ask for those along with some rabbit stuff," she said. "I'll say I was thinking about bringing a lizard inside or something. I don't think that would be a problem."

Geri took a small treat from a bag on her shelf and showed it to Davidson before tossing it in his cage. As he hopped in after it, she shut the wire door so they could head downstairs to find Andrew and make their requests.

As expected, Andrew was out in the garden, lounging in a hammock under the shade of a large tree. Geri hesitated approaching him, but Lisa pressed on ahead.

"Hey, Andrew!" she said loudly, startling him enough that he was nearly tossed from the hammock.

"Sorry to scare you, I was wondering if you could get us some rabbit books or magazines the next time you go into town. We want to make sure we're doing everything right for them," she said.

"Yes, I'll take a look." He smiled, still breathing heavily from being shocked awake.

Geri delicately approached. "Also, if you find any reptile books," she started. "I was thinking about maybe catching one of the lizards in the garden, but I'd like to learn more about them first," she said shyly. In reality, she liked lizards anyway, so it wasn't a far-fetched notion. If it took her a while to identify the creature, at least it gave her another distraction to pass the days.

"Well, we have plenty to choose from," he laughed, gesturing around and watching at least one lizard scurry under a rock. "I'll see what I can do. Any other types of books you want?"

"Romance novels would be great," Lisa quickly answered. "Thanks." She smiled over her shoulder as they turned to walk back toward the house.

"Romance novels?" Geri asked pointedly after they'd returned to the privacy of their room.

"Just so he doesn't get suspicious," Lisa answered coolly. "But don't judge me when I start reading them," she added. They both laughed as Geri let Harley out of her cage for a turn at playtime.

Later that afternoon, their requests were answered as a stack of magazines and small paperbacks were delivered to their door. There were two rabbit magazines, one reptile book that appeared to be from the 1970s, another issue of *Better Homes & Gardens*, and three well-read romance novels that were close to disintegrating.

"These *must* be good," Lisa said, holding up one of the battered novels as a page fell out. "Clearly they've gotten a lot of love over the years," she said wryly. As they looked over their haul, Harley hopped over to nibble at the pages closest to her.

"No!" Lisa shouted, gathering all the books and magazines in her arms and dumping them on the bed. Geri started reading the reptile book, while Lisa began leafing through *Better Homes & Gardens* on the minimal hope that something there would look familiar.

After about 20 minutes of silent reading, Geri suddenly gasped and jumped, causing Harley to bolt back into her cage and thump her foot in alarm.

"This one!" Geri breathed, pointing to a picture in the book, and holding it out to Lisa. "Look at this one!"

Lisa leaned over and looked at the picture, which showed a shiny brown lizard with faded stripes.

"Yes!" Lisa agreed. "I've seen that over by the pond."

"It's a Bermuda Skink," Geri said excitedly. "It's endangered—and only found in Bermuda! We're in Bermuda!"

Neither Geri nor Lisa were the hugging type, but without any thought or hesitation, Lisa reached out her hands and pulled Geri into a tight embrace. The two were giddy and couldn't help but jump with joy at the revelation.

"This is big," said Lisa softly. Pulling back to look

Geri in the face. "This is really big. We can use this. We're in a big house in Bermuda. A big white mansion with a blue tile roof and a giant brick wall fence. This could work for us."

"But how do we get the word out?" Geri asked, coming back down from her initial elation.

Lisa sighed. "There has to be a phone somewhere, I'm sure the Master has one. All this," she said, gesturing to everything around them in their ornate room, "costs money."

The two were silent again. "I have an idea," Lisa finally said. "But I'm not going to tell you what it is. If I get found out, I don't want you to know anything if anyone asks any questions."

"I don't like the sound of that…" Geri said truthfully, suspicious about what her friend might be planning.

"I won't do anything today, or in the next few days. We'll pretend like everything is the same for a little while, okay? Nothing to worry about," Lisa assured her. Geri nodded, but was discomforted with whatever Lisa was suggesting.

They went about the rest of their day as usual and didn't speak on it any further. During dinner, they laughed with everyone else as the Master told a long-winded joke, and at night, they went to bed as usual.

Geri tried to sleep, but was kept awake by her many thoughts about whatever Lisa might be planning, and by the realization of where they were. In the middle of the night, she heard Lisa get up slowly from bed. One of the rabbits thumped its foot, prompting the other to do the same.

Lisa froze, listening to see if Geri stirred, and then left the dark room. Geri pretended to sleep, her heart racing and her breath coming in quick gasps. She felt like she could suffocate. It took some time before she was able to calm herself, but she stayed awake through the rest of the night.

Sometime around dawn, Lisa stealthily returned to the bedroom. Geri's heart pounded once more as the door creaked open, but still, she pretended to sleep. Lisa fell asleep in minutes. They both slept in until mid-morning, and neither one mentioned anything out of the ordinary upon waking up.

CHAPTER 38
STARTING OVER

*M*ary had stayed in the hospital overnight while they monitored her oxygen levels and gave her intravenous antibiotics to prevent infection. Fortunately, her injuries were minor, mostly first and second degree burns that stung whenever she moved, but were little more than an inconvenience.

Two of her fingers had deeper burns that required more care. She shut her eyes tightly as the nurses cleaned the wounds and peeled away the blackened skin. She hoped that she'd pass out from shock, but instead had to suffer through the pain in full consciousness. Once they were finished and the fingers bandaged, it still took her some time to catch her breath.

While this was happening, Tom worked with her insurance company to file for short term disability—it would be difficult to type with two heavily bandaged fingers, he reasoned. More importantly, he'd be able to keep a better eye on her if she wasn't going to work each day. Unbeknownst to Mary, Tom had also secured her a new apartment just down the hall from his own. He'd already chosen a new name and ID card for her.

When it was time to check out from the hospital, Mary collected her belongings in their respective Ziplock bags and was surprised to find a new wallet in place of her old one.

"I think *I* better hold onto this one for now," Tom said, holding the wallet she'd been using for the past three years.

Mary unzipped the bag that held the new wallet, and looked through the bill-fold. It contained all the money she'd had before—$57—as well as her new ID.

"What about my credit cards?" she asked, quickly noting their absence.

"No credit cards right now," he said quietly as he wheeled her down the hall toward the exit. "You'll need to use cash for a while."

Mary sighed. "I had a lot of points on one of those cards," she lamented, immediately feeling silly for saying so aloud. "Never mind. I'm sorry, you're right."

"I'm also holding on to your insurance card, just so people don't find it attached to you. But you'll still have access to that if you need it. I'm having another one sent to you, but it might take a few days to get here," he said. "If you do need to go to the doctor or a hospital in the meantime, we'll try to get you into one that's further away just to add some layer of protection, okay?" he said.

"I guess," she said hesitantly, trying to make sure she understood everything. "You said another card will be sent to me, but where exactly is it being sent? Where am I going?" she asked, suddenly realizing that she probably wasn't going back to her own apartment.

"I got you a new apartment in my building. We'll be

neighbours!" he said brightly. For the first time all day, Mary laughed.

After a pause, she asked, "So what happens now? What's next?"

Tom explained that for her, nothing much would happen if all went well. She was to stay in the apartment as much as possible, and call him if she needed anything, even groceries.

"Here's a new phone too," he said, almost forgetting the simple flip-phone in his pocket. "I'm going to keep your old phone at my office. I'll see if anyone texts or calls and I'll let you know. Don't give anyone your new phone number, understand?" he added seriously.

"What about Ally?" she asked. Though they weren't best friends, Mary fretted the thought of not being able to talk to *anyone* except Tom.

Tom thought for a moment, then decided that Ally would be okay. "I'll give her the number," he said.

They approached the hospital exit, at which point Mary was able to get out of the wheelchair and stand on her own. Tom carried her things and led her to his black sedan. The drive to her new apartment was quiet. Tom didn't turn on the radio, and neither did she. Though she had too many questions to count racing through her mind, she found herself unable to voice any of them. Instead, she tried to focus on her breathing and stop feeling the quick thumping in her chest, which only got faster the closer they got to the building. Pulling into the parking lot, she could feel sweat beginning to pool in her collarbone, which was hot to the touch. *It's okay*, she told herself. *You made it through fire, you can get used to new living arrangements.*

Tom's parking spot was fortunately near the entrance

of the building, which had a doorman for added security; Mary was relieved to see that upon entering. Tom introduced her as an old friend from college, and used her new name, Alice.

"Pleasure to meet you, Alice," the man said warmly. "Everything okay?" he said, looking at the bandages creeping up her arms.

"Alice just got back from a hiking trip up in New York," Tom said smoothly. "That poison ivy is no joke!" he added.

"Yes," Mary agreed with a smile, feeling herself flush under the attention. "I'll never go near unfamiliar plants again." She laughed nervously.

"Aw, well that's a good rule to live by." The doorman laughed. "I'm Jim, by the way, and you just let me know if you need anything."

Alice thanked him and Tom led her toward the elevator, which brought them up to the fifth floor where both of their apartments were located. He led her to her new home, unlocked the door, and handed her the keys. There wasn't much to tour in the small studio, but Tom showed her the narrow door that led to the bathroom and the small cubby that was the kitchen. He pulled down the full-size Murphy bed from the main room's wall and opened the fridge to show her that it was already stocked with milk, fruits, and vegetables, and the pantry filled with canned goods, boxes of cereal, and small pots and pans.

"I tried to remember everything you had in your old apartment," he said. "But then I remembered that there wasn't too much there to begin with." He chuckled. "Hope this is stuff you'll eat."

"It's great," she said. "Really, thank you so much for

all of this." Even in the bathroom, the shelves were already stocked with shampoo and other toiletries.

"It's no problem," he said. "And Ally actually helped a lot. I asked her to go shopping for whatever else you might need, and she filled up your closet over there," he said as he pointed to the built-in unit. "She didn't know your shoe size, so she got you a pair of sneakers in at least five different sizes to be safe. She'll be over tomorrow to help with whatever else you might need, and to return at least four pairs of shoes."

Mary could feel the tears prickling at the corners of her eyes. "Thank you so much," she said, trying to stop herself from sobbing. Tom put his hand on her shoulder, not sure if he was supposed to hug her or not. Their family was never known for physical affection.

"Thank you, I'm okay," she said, clearly sensing his discomfort with an emotional cousin.

"Okay," he said with a sigh. "I'm right down the hall and my number's in that phone. Let me know if you need anything."

"I will," she said.

CHAPTER 39
LISA'S NIGHT

*L*isa knew they needed access to a phone to escape. She also knew that a phone would not be easy to come by. With each day that passed, she worried that they were slipping dangerously closer to comfortable complacency with their situation.

They'd been drugged, kidnapped, caged, and sold like animals. Compared to their time in tortured captivity, their new surroundings were considerably more agreeable. It would be all too easy to give in to the call of simplistic luxury—clearly the other residents had. But nothing here was really their own; even their lives now belonged to the Master.

Every day, it seemed that Geri got more and more enmeshed in the fantasy. Lisa worried that in a few weeks, she'd be reluctant to leave. Lisa herself had wondered about the harm in just staying here indefinitely. Would it really be so terrible to shrug off all sense of responsibility and just start fresh? Albeit at the whims of an old man who nobody seemed to know much about.

When Geri figured out where in the world they were, Lisa took it as a sign that they were meant to leave. The mysterious paradise was no longer a mystery. Time to go home.

She didn't tell Geri what her plan was, but she'd been musing on it for a few days now. If anyone had a cellphone here, it would be the Master. If he indeed had one, he'd likely keep it on him, probably in a pants pocket. She'd need to get close to access his pockets… Very close.

They went to bed as usual, and Lisa waited until it sounded like Geri had fallen asleep. As silently as she could, she slipped out of bed and tiptoed across the cool wooden floor. Of course, there's no sneaking past a prey animal at night. The rabbits sounded the alarm with resounding thumps.

Lisa froze mid-step and held her breath. No other sounds were heard. Geri hadn't rolled over or stirred. Lisa continued on out the door, closing it slowly and softly behind her.

With each step toward the Master's door, her chest felt tighter. The hall was dark, but she could see a slight glow peeking out from under his bedroom door. That was a welcome surprise, at least—she wouldn't have to wake him up.

She stood in front of the door, wondering what to do next. Should she knock, or just turn the knob? She didn't want to attract any outside attention with too much noise, but felt that it would be a bad idea to just enter. She held her fist up to the door, braced herself, and quietly rapped at the wood with her knuckles.

She didn't dare breathe.

Nothing happened.

She knocked again, slightly louder this time. A confused voice responded, "Is someone there?"

"It's me," she said, trying to find the right pitch to be heard by him, without being heard by anyone else. "It's Lisa. Can I come in?"

From the other side of the door she could hear the faint click of a television being turned off, and then bed springs creaking under his shifting weight before hearing his footsteps approaching the door. She then heard a deadbolt slide over before the handle turned and the door crept open a few inches, revealing the Master in satin pajamas.

"Everything alright?" he asked through the gap in the doorway.

"My hand hurts," she said, holding up the still-bandaged appendage. "I was wondering if you could take a look at it, make sure it's okay," she said quietly.

His face softened, and he opened the door and ushered her in, closing the door behind them. He gestured her toward an upholstered bench at the foot of his bed. While she sat, he went to his private bathroom to retrieve scissors, ointment, and a fresh roll of gauze.

"I happen to keep these things here, just in case of an emergency," he said. "It looks like you haven't changed the bandage in a few days," he said as he held up her hand to inspect it. "There's a first-aid kit downstairs by the kitchen. Clarissa should have showed it to you at some point."

"Oh, she did," Lisa said quickly. "I just forgot about the bandage, to be honest. I kept meaning to do it before bed, and then I just kept forgetting. I'm sorry to bother you like this, it's just been so painful tonight," she said, her words spilling out quickly. She winced as he cut away at the discoloured gauze.

"Well, it's good you came when you did, while I was still up," he said. "I try to avoid modern electronics, but I like to have an idea of what's going on in the world," he said, explaining away the television, which wasn't allowed anywhere in the house except this very room.

He removed the bandages, revealing the still-raw wound beneath that carried the less-than-healthy scent of old meat. Lisa was both concerned and a bit embarrassed.

"It doesn't *look* infected, which is good," he said politely. "But let's get it cleaned up just to make sure." He led her to the bathroom and poured some peroxide into a glass he'd filled with warm water. He held her hand over the sink, and slowly poured the mixture over her hand, flipping it over to get both sides. Lisa sharply inhaled as her face scrunched up in pain.

"I know, I'm sorry," he said softly, his own face wrinkled with sympathy. Once the glass was empty he took a small hand towel and dabbed the rest of her hand and wrist dry, before leading her back to the bench. She whimpered as he delicately applied the ointment to her hand. He looked up at her briefly, and she met his gaze with glassy eyes before he looked back down again.

He knelt in front of her as he wordlessly wrapped each layer of gauze. She considered what she might say next; she was running out of time as he finished the bandages. She took her other hand and grazed it through his sparse hair. His body tensed. She felt like she could vomit. *Did she have to do this? She had to do this. Couldn't she just go back to bed? No... no...*

She swallowed hard, and held his cheek against her good palm, stroking his skin with her thumb. She took a deep breath to steady herself as he waited, frozen in suspense. She leaned forward, aware of the gaping neckline of her nightshirt, and kissed the top of his head, holding back the gastric juices that threatened to spill out all over him.

Her injured hand rested limply in his, wrapped in its fresh white fabric. She didn't move. She waited to see what his response would be. As much as she wanted to run and hide in revulsion, she stayed the course and hoped that whatever happened next would be over soon.

At first, he continued looking blankly at her hand in his. Then, his eyes rose up to meet hers.

"What are you really doing here?" he asked gently.

"My hand hurt, and I knew you could make it better," she answered. He looked away, but neither one of them dared to pull back, their hands still very much aware of the heat of the other. She knew she had to keep things moving, but didn't know what else to do. What to say?

"I want you to know," she began slowly, softly, "that I appreciate all that you've done for us. You saved my life. You've given me life." The tears she shed were real, though she wasn't sure exactly what prompted them: disgust, or genuine gratitude? Normally, she'd refrain from crying in front of anyone. Tonight, she knew it was best to let it flow.

As she expected, the tears immediately had an effect.

"Oh, my dear," he said, leaning in to kiss her forehead while pulling her into an embrace. She was thankful to be crying, as it hid the disdain from her face. Still, she had committed to what came next, and went through the motions for the next 10 minutes. She was thankful he didn't last any longer. He was fast asleep almost immediately after, holding her tightly against his white-haired chest.

She felt like she could die of heat stroke, suffocation, and shame right there in his bed. After some time, she rolled over to see how deeply he slept. Instinctively his arms pulled away and he rolled over to the other side, still asleep. She waited some minutes more before she began the very slow, gradual process of leaving the bed. She took advantage of this time by surveying every inch of the room within her line of sight, guided by the faint light peeking out from the bathroom door, which remained partially ajar. She saw the previous day's outfit neatly folded on his dresser, and decided she'd start there.

As her feet touched the floor, she used her good hand to distribute her weight gently on the bed as she rose from it. She held her breath with each creak of the mattress springs, but so far, the Master seemed to remain asleep.

She crossed over to the dresser and rifled through the folds of fabric, finding the pockets empty. She stepped across the floor, looking for any sign of a phone. She thought she saw it on the nightstand, and lightly treaded over to it, picking it up in her hand before finding it was the TV remote. She continued to look back at the sleeping figure to make sure that he was, in fact, still asleep.

Lisa looked closer at the nightstand and saw it had a small drawer. Carefully, she pulled at the drawer to open it, but it was stuck. She pulled a bit harder, and then harder. Finally it budged with a groan. She heard the Master move beneath the covers. She stayed where she was and didn't breathe as her heart pounded in her throat.

Fortunately, he didn't wake up. He merely shifted and continued his deep sleep. She reached her hand into the dark drawer and was rewarded with something small and metallic at her fingertips. She gripped it and pulled it out —a small flip-phone that appeared to be from the early 2000s. It would have to do.

She retreated to the other side of the room, where the blue glow from the screen would be masked by the light from the bathroom. She had to remember how to type out a text without a QWERTY keyboard.

Crouched low in the corner, she composed a message to whoever was at the other end of 7266, the number Geri had remembered from the island.

Dont reply. Kidnapped frm cruise. Ximena said 2 contact u. in Bermuda. Big white house blu roof. 10ft brick wall around. Send help.

She then sent a similar text to her sister, hoping she'd follow her instruction not to reply. After she sent both messages, she deleted the text threads to avoid the Master finding them. She held the phone in her hot, sweaty palm as she silently crouched on aching calves for at least an hour, hoping that nobody would text back.

When she felt enough time had passed, she stood up from her hunched position. Her legs were on fire but she quietly made it back to the nightstand next to the Master, still comfortably in his bed. Silently, she returned the phone to its place in the drawer.

Closing the drawer took more effort. The old wood strained and creaked with every movement. She spent the better part of the night slowly pushing it back into place, millimetre by millimetre until close to dawn. Eventually it was closed, and she once again crept across the floor, this time heading for the door.

She turned the knob, slowly still, but less concerned

with being heard now. It was perfectly understandable that she'd want to return to her own bed in the morning. She stiffly walked down the hall and melted under the covers back in the room she shared with Geri. Finally, she allowed herself to sleep.

CHAPTER 40
RESIGNATIONS

*I*t didn't take long for Tom to track down Geri's parents; a quick search brought up their obituaries.

A snippet from their local paper described a quiet couple who'd isolated themselves in the mountains of Virginia. The wife had been recovering from a recent heart attack when her husband was believed to have shot her once in the head. He then "turned the gun on himself," ending two lives in a matter of seconds.

According to the paper, they were survived by their daughter, Margorie Collins.

Tom wondered if that was still true.

He searched for any other relatives that he could reach out to, but couldn't find any. Geri's mother had one sister who'd died in a car crash when she was just 19 years old, and Geri's father was an only child. Both sets of grandparents were deceased, except for one grandmother. Geri's maternal grandmother was alive, but records showed that she'd been living in a long-term care facility for people with advanced dementia. He didn't think it necessary to disturb the poor woman with such traumatic news.

Next to look into was the office where Geri and Lisa both worked. He called the reception desk and introduced himself, explaining that he'd received a request for a wellness check on two employees. He kept his tone light to avoid causing panic.

The receptionist listened and seemed concerned. Without a word she transferred him to the Human Resources department. An upbeat, high-pitched voice answered.

"Hello! I understand that you have some personnel questions?"

"Yes, hello, I was asked to check on two employees of yours, Geri Collins and Lisa McDaniels," he calmly explained.

"Oh!" she sounded genuinely surprised. "They no longer work here."

"Oh?" and now it was his turn to sound surprised.

"They both resigned last week," she said.

"I see…" he replied. "Did they come into the office to resign in person?" he asked.

"No, they each emailed their resignations to us. I wanted to bring them in for exit interviews but they said they were out of the country. I tried calling but never got a response, just those emails," she said. After a pause, she asked, "Are they in trouble?"

"Oh, I'm sure they're fine," he said brightly. "You said they were out of the country. I'm sure they just forgot to tell someone they were leaving. Having too much of a good time, I guess," he chuckled humourlessly.

"Yeah," she laughed nervously. "I guess so."

He thanked her for her time and hung up, hoping she wouldn't get concerned enough to start digging on her own. The more people involved in this, the harder it would be to solve anything.

He was about to call Mary to let her know he'd be over later to discuss what he'd learned today, when something beeped loudly in his desk drawer. He jumped in surprise, trying to identify the source of the sound. Pulling out the top drawer of his file cabinet, he realized that Mary's personal phone, which he'd commandeered, was alerting him to a text.

He read the text, which came from an unknown number. His skin prickled as a shiver worked its way down his body.

Was this really Lisa?

Immediately, he searched the number in his database to see if an identity was attached. It was unlisted, probably belonging to a prepaid phone. However, he could verify that the area code was Bermudan, as the text mentioned. That was something, at least.

It could be a trap, or Lisa may have really found a way to reach out for help. There was no way to know for sure, but he had to take a chance. He called Mary's own prepaid burner phone and was going to come over straight away to deliver the news and discuss what came next.

He dialled the number and waited. The dial-tone continued until her voicemail picked up the call. He ended the call and tried again five minutes later, getting the same result. This time, he left a message.

"Hi, uh, Alice, I was wondering if I could come over later. Go over some things. Call me back."

———————

Mary had spent her morning absentmindedly watching cooking shows on TV. Normally, she'd be browsing social media during the commercial breaks. Without her phone, she felt restless and agitated. She didn't even have a computer in this apartment. She thought back to her own laptop, left behind in all the confusion of the fire.

It was probably ruined now. Even if the fire didn't make it into the bedroom, the firefighters' hoses probably left the whole place drenched. Still, maybe the laptop was intact? She'd kept it tucked away in a desk drawer, so it might have survived untouched.

She'd decided that she would ask Tom to take a look later, if it wouldn't be too much trouble for him.

As she blankly watched TV for the next half-hour, she had no idea who was cooking what on the screen. She thought of all that Tom had already done for her, and she didn't want to ask him to add something so trivial on top of everything else. She didn't really *need* the laptop. But she was bored. And she had absolutely nothing to do alone in the apartment all day. Maybe she could take a quick trip herself?

Even though she knew she wasn't supposed to leave, she grabbed one of the large jackets Ally had gotten her and walked out the door, keys in hand.

CHAPTER 41
AN AWKWARD DINNER

*L*isa felt dirtier than she'd ever been. She hadn't showered in the days following her capture on the cruise ship, and yet her skin was crawling now in a way that it never had before. She slept in past breakfast and waited for Geri to leave the room before she dared to move. She didn't want to be seen by anyone until she had scrubbed last night from her body. As it was, she couldn't help but wonder if Geri had noticed when she returned to the room. The stink of shame would be on her for weeks.

As she got up from the bed, she glanced at the rabbits, which looked back at her curiously. She was sure they knew exactly what had happened, and felt repulsed again by the thought of it. Animals had a sense for these things, didn't they?

"Ugh, don't look at me," she said disgustedly. She then turned back to the bed and stripped it of its blankets and sheets. The whole thing was contaminated, as far as she was concerned, just by having been in contact with her own skin. She left the bedding in a heap for Clarissa, wishing she could just wash everything herself without anyone drawing suspicion.

She picked out fresh clothes and quickly made her way to the shower, where she proceeded to scrape every inch of flesh until it was raw. She went through about half a bar of soap, and just as much shampoo. By the time she stepped out of the shower stall, the entire bathroom was foggy and the undersides of her fingernails were caked with suds.

Roughly, she towel dried herself and twisted her hair into a wet bun before getting dressed and venturing downstairs for food.

At the kitchen island she found Geri finishing up some scrambled eggs and sipping from a cup of tea.

"Good morning!" Clarissa chimed. "Or, afternoon... you really slept in today, huh?" she added lightheartedly.

"Yeah, couldn't sleep last night, wasn't feeling well," Lisa said without making eye contact. "I was in the bathroom all night. Do you have some plain toast with butter to settle my stomach?"

"Oh no, hope you feel better soon! Of course, I'll make you some toast. We have chamomile tea too, which should help," Clarissa offered. She set about slicing the bread and getting it into the oven, then looked through the cupboard for the tea. Within seconds, Lisa had the hot beverage in her hands as she waited for the bread to toast.

"Hope you're okay. Are you feeling any better this morning?" Geri asked.

"Better now, just want to keep things bland for today," Lisa assured her. She hated lying to people, especially her friends, but in this case, it was the best she could come up with. And last night's encounter really did turn her stomach. She wasn't even hungry now, but felt she should make an appearance for appearances' sake.

Geri slowly sipped her tea and waited for Lisa to finish her meagre breakfast. Once she was done, they headed out for a walk in the sunshine.

Andrew had gone to town not long before, leaving the garden to themselves. Geri casually led the way to a stone bench in the shade of a large tree.

"So, were you really sick last night?" Geri asked cautiously.

"Yes. Why?" Lisa retorted a little too quickly.

"Just curious," Geri answered quietly. After a pause, she added, "It really isn't too bad here, all things considered."

Lisa sighed and looked up at the sky. She saw this coming, and frankly, she didn't have a good argument otherwise. It really *wasn't* too bad here. They weren't being eaten alive or used for organ harvesting or medical experiments. They weren't sold into prostitution or drug rings. Again, Lisa waged an internal debate on the merits of staying versus leaving; but now, it was out of her hands. If anyone got her messages, they might be getting out of here soon enough. If not, she decided not to press the issue of leaving unless anything major changed in their situation.

They sat for a few minutes longer in silence, taking in the warm breeze. Lisa had her eyes closed against the mottled sunlight while Geri's gaze followed the many small creatures scurrying around them.

"I'm going to head inside and let the rabbits out for playtime," Geri finally said.

"Okay, I'm going to stay out here for a while," Lisa

said, smiling.

Once Geri got back into the house, Lisa laid down across the bench on her back, crossed her arms over her eyes, and ran through the possibilities of what might happen next.

A nearby crunch of leaves startled her to alertness.

"Sorry! Just me," said Andrew, returning through the gate with bags full of fresh produce and what smelled like fish. He also had a bag filled with something else. "See what I was able to get you today?" he said playfully, walking over with his arm extended for her to take the bag. Looking inside, she could see a handful of books and magazines.

"Thank you," she said with a genuine smile. "I'll bring these up to the room."

Lisa took the gift and brought it inside. She carefully cracked the bedroom door open to make sure the coast was clear of roaming rabbits. Geri looked up from her spot on the floor.

"Don't worry, Harley's just chewing up a magazine she found under the bed," she said as she saw the door creak open.

"Great," said Lisa as she quickly came in and shut the door behind her. "I just got some more from Andrew."

They spent the rest of the afternoon silently reading in the company of the rabbits, occasionally remarking on something interesting in a book or magazine. When it was almost time for dinner, they dressed up as usual and headed downstairs. Today, Lisa wore the most modest outfit in the closet; a long, flowy gown with billowing sleeves and a high collar that could almost be considered a turtleneck. It suited her better than she'd hoped, but she wanted to cover as much skin as possible.

The smell of cooked fish greeted them as they left the

bedroom, getting stronger as they made their way down to the dining room.

"Ugh, and I just washed my hair this morning," Lisa lamented as she rolled her eyes. "Now it'll smell like fish, along with everything else," she said, looking down at her dress.

As they approached the dining room table, Clarissa was just finishing up doling out each person's portion on their plates. At the head of the table, the Master's place setting was missing.

"Is the Master not joining us tonight?" Geri asked politely.

Tabitha, seated at the other end of the table, answered, "No, he had some late appointments today. It seems he got a late start this morning and had some catching up to do," she said with a cool smile, looking directly at Lisa.

Lisa looked away. "That's too bad," she said.

"Yes, it seems that something was keeping him up late last night. He didn't seem to sleep very well," Tabitha continued.

"Maybe something upset his stomach too," Lisa answered.

"Oh, were you not feeling well last night?" Tabitha asked sweetly as Clarissa finished setting everyone's dishes and sat down.

Lisa tried to stop herself from flushing, but of course there was no stopping the heat radiating up her neck and face. "No, last night I felt sick, but so far today I'm feeling better," she said.

"I'm glad to hear that. Hopefully it wasn't anything catchy," Tabitha replied.

They continued an awkwardly quiet dinner after that.

Lisa mostly pushed the food around her plate, occasionally nibbling at a piece of fish or steamed carrot. The only part of her meal that she finished was the rice, since she felt that would support her sick stomach claim.

Andrew, Geri, and Clarissa merely exchanged confused glances and looked back and forth between Lisa and Tabitha. Lisa, refusing to meet anyone's gaze, was a stark contrast to Tabitha, who seemed almost giddy.

Once dinner was finished, Geri and Lisa returned quietly to their room. As soon as Geri shut the door behind them, she snapped to Lisa.

"What's going on?" she asked, her brows furrowed with frustration.

"What do you mean?" Lisa tried to ask nonchalantly.

"You know what I mean," Geri seethed through her teeth. "Something's going on, and I don't know what, but you know something."

"Nothing's going on," Lisa assured her. "I was sick last night, I haven't been feeling great today, and Tabitha's being weird. I can't help that."

Geri sighed out of frustration. She looked to the rabbit cages, and decided they should be cleaned. She took a garbage bag from her supply drawer, picked up a scooper, and got to work on Davidson's cage. The rabbit thumped his foot in protest, clearly unhappy with the intrusion into his personal space. Geri continued to work, gritting her teeth as she did so. The rabbit lunged for the scooper and knocked it out of her grasp.

"Ugh!" Geri grunted, wrestling the utensil out of the cage and throwing it to the ground. She roughly closed the cage door and sat cross-legged, staring angrily at the offending rabbit, which simply turned its back to her in disapproval.

"God, this whole thing gets more ridiculous by the day," Lisa scoffed with an eye roll. "Even the rabbit has an attitude now."

A moment later, both women were startled by a knock at the door. "It's Clarissa," said the voice on the other side.

"Come in," Lisa said as neutrally as she could, though she was sure the girl had heard them bickering.

Hesitantly, Clarissa opened the door just enough to let Lisa know that Tabitha had requested her presence in her quarters.

"Of course," Lisa said to herself.

She followed Clarissa down the stairs, but made her way to Tabitha's rooms by herself as Clarissa returned to the kitchen to finish cleaning up from dinner.

She didn't bother to knock as she got to the imposing double doors, she simply opened them, and then walked through the salon to the next door, which she didn't knock on either. As soon as she entered, a cat pranced over and brushed against her leg. Tabitha was waiting in her chair by the window, no book in hand this time.

"Clarissa said that you wanted to see me," Lisa said by way of greeting.

"Yes," Tabitha smiled. "I think we have some things to discuss."

CHAPTER 42
WATER DAMAGE

*M*ary called a cab to take her to her apartment, but had the driver drop her off two blocks away to avoid drawing attention to herself or the building. She should have waited until she had a chance to dye her hair, she realized. *Too late now*, she thought, hoping she wouldn't run into anyone she knew. It was just a quick recovery mission; get in, find laptop, get out.

She felt her pulse racing as she approached the building, even more so as she saw the blackened outline of her apartment window.

She exhaled deeply through pursed lips, then steeled herself and walked inside. Though she'd lived here for over a year now, she felt somehow out of place in the familiar hallway, as if she were trespassing in her own home. She kept her head down as she walked through the corridor and bounded up the stairs, wishing she'd at least thought to bring a hat or scarf to hide her face.

Once she got to her floor, the smell of smoke and

char almost made her turn around and run back outside for fresh air—almost. Though her breathing was quick and shallow, she forced herself onward with clenched fists. As she reached her door, caution tape again made her instinctively pull back. After a moment's pause, she took her key from her pocket and inserted it into the lock. She turned it slowly, took a deep breath, and pushed the door open, ducking under the yellow tape.

The door had been warped from the heat, making it difficult to close behind her again. It finally shut with a bang, and she hoped none of the neighbours were home to hear it. She quickly crossed the dark, slippery floor, hoping it wouldn't collapse under her light tread.

In her bedroom, she was relieved to see that aside from obvious flooding, the damage from the actual fire was minimal. Most of the fire damage was isolated to the kitchen.

She quickly pulled out the drawer containing her laptop. The wooden dresser was still damp, but the inside of the drawer didn't appear too wet. She grabbed the laptop and its charger and held them under her less-burned arm. She should get a bag, she thought to herself, again admonishing herself for not thinking to bring one with her.

Mary put the laptop back into the open drawer and went into the kitchen to rummage through the cabinets. She found her bag full of other plastic bags under the sink and took two of them to double up. Returning to the bedroom she deposited the laptop and charger inside, making sure the bags were sturdy enough for the weight.

She took the cargo, left the room, and crossed the floor back through the living room. She made it halfway to the front door before a damp towel was thrown over her face and pressed to her nose from behind. Within seconds, the bag containing the laptop clanged to the floor, followed by Mary's limp body.

CHAPTER 43
AN UNDERSTANDING

"Sit down," Tabitha said softly, gesturing to the plush bench at the end of her bed, uncomfortably similar to the one Lisa had become too acquainted with the night before, in the Master's bedroom. Lisa did her best not to show any sign of revulsion at the thought, and sat down as instructed.

At first, Tabitha said nothing, simply smiling curiously as Lisa unsuccessfully tried to avoid her gaze.

"I know what you're doing, and I understand why you're doing it," the older woman finally said.

"I'm not doing anything," Lisa said as calmly as she could.

"You want to get out of here, and I don't blame you." Lisa was about to interject when Tabitha held up her hand to continue. "Nobody will ever know of this conversation, it never happened. I tried to get out once too, and this is what it got me," she said, holding up her arms to show the room around her. "It got me house arrest. And cats. The

Master never beat me, or even yelled. He just locked me in this room. It only opens from the outside," she explained. "People can come in, but I can't go out. Clarissa comes and escorts me to dinner, and that's the extent of my excitement for the day."

"I'm sorry to hear that," Lisa said, and she truly was sorry, though she was still hesitant to admit her own plans despite the disclosure.

"I've gotten used to it," Tabitha continued. "At first I went a little crazy. I destroyed most of the bedroom the first week, but eventually I got used to it. He isn't a cruel man, you know, he gave me these cats to keep me company, and he visits as often as he can... But things have to be his way," she said seriously.

"Looking at you, you seem like someone who's used to being in control of things, is that right?" Tabitha asked.

"Yes, that's right," Lisa answered.

"You're probably a manager, or somebody high up at work, right?" she asked.

"Yes, I am."

"I thought so. But Geri isn't like you, is she?" Tabitha observed.

"No, she's certainly not," Lisa conceded.

Tabitha sighed, not taking her eyes off Lisa, who still looked everywhere else but back at Tabitha.

"I understand why you want to leave. It's boring here, it's safe. You're used to controlling your own life. You're a go-getter, a doer..." she said, pausing before adding, "but Geri isn't."

"What are you trying to say?" Lisa asked pointedly, finally looking the other woman in the eyes.

"I'm trying to tell you that I won't stop you from leaving. I'll be happy to see you go, because I know that's what you want, and it's what I wanted for myself years ago. But I don't know if you should take Geri." At this, Lisa stood, prepared to fight, but Tabitha calmly gestured for her to sit back down. Lisa continued standing.

"Let me finish," she said. "All I want for everybody here is to be happy. I don't know you or Geri very well, but I am a good judge of people. Geri doesn't like crowds, and she doesn't like meeting new people. If she could lock herself away with a journal and some books, I think she'd be perfectly happy. This place is a prison for you. It's a prison for me. But to *her*, I really think it might be perfect."

Lisa huffed but didn't say anything.

"I'm sorry it's not what you want to hear. And I know that you don't want to leave your friend behind—if you can leave at all—but I just want you to give it some thought. Okay?"

Lisa didn't answer. Instead, she got up to leave.

"Wait!" Tabitha insisted. "Before you go, I'm pretending to be mad at you for last night. Clarissa overheard… things. She told me. Frankly, I couldn't care less, but we can't let other people know that, especially the Master. So I'm pretending to be mad at you, and you're going to pretend that I'm mad at you, got it?"

At this, Lisa couldn't help but crack a brief smile. "Got it."

CHAPTER 44
BRIGHT LIGHTS

*M*ary slowly opened her eyes, then shut them tight against the bright light. Her cheek was cold, and her bandaged arm throbbed. After a moment, she realized that she was laying flat on a cold floor. She squinted her eyes again to get a sense of where she was.

"Hi Mary," said a familiar voice. All she could do was softly groan in response.

"I don't know what to do with you," the voice continued. "I don't know who you've spoken to, and I don't know how much it matters, yet."

Billy.

"I wanted to kill you and get it over with," he said. "But I'm told it'll create too many loose ends... So, here we are."

Mary saw that they were in some kind of grey room. Her whole body prickled with pain, and her arm felt like it was on fire. She hadn't taken any pain meds since that morning, and her burns seared beneath the bandages.

"Where... is... here...?" she croaked, her throat feeling as if she'd spent a week in the desert with nothing to drink.

"It doesn't matter," he said. "We could be anywhere and it wouldn't matter. The question, is how long you'll be here, and what we'll have to do with you. In the meantime, I need you to make a call, but it has to sound natural," he said. Then he crossed the room to a water cooler Mary hadn't seen from her angle. She heard the water pouring into a cup, and the glorping sound of bubbles rising to the surface of the large container.

He walked back to her and crouched in front of her face, his arm outstretched with the cup.

"Drink this. I'll be back in 20 minutes," he said. He again walked across the room, this time creaking open a door and slamming it shut behind him. As far as she could tell, she was alone.

Though her head was heavy and the room spun around her, she forced herself up. She used her less-injured arm as support to bring herself to an almost-sitting position. If she'd been against a wall, it would have been easier. Instead, she'd been dropped in the middle of the room with nothing to lean on for stability. She looked to her left to find the wall about five feet away from her. She placed the cup of water closer to the wall with a shaky hand, then scooted herself in that direction. She repeated the process until she could finally lean back against the wall and slowly drink in a more upright position.

True to his word, Billy returned 20 minutes later with a phone in hand. Her phone, in fact; the one Tom had given her.

"Tom seems worried about you. He keeps calling,"

Billy explained. "I'm going to return his call, and you're going to answer. You're going to tell him that you went for a walk to clear your head, and you'll be back later."

"*Will* I be back later?" she asked, her head still spinning and her eyes squinting against the too-bright lighting of the room.

"I don't know yet," he said, pressing the button to call back Tom, and setting it to speakerphone. Tom picked up on the first ring.

"Alice?" Tom asked, using her new name.

"Hi Tom, sorry I missed you. I went out for a walk to clear my head and lost track of time. Don't worry, I'm fine," she lied, her throat still dry and leaving her voice raspy.

"Good, I'm glad to hear that. I was worried about you," he said.

"Don't worry, I'll be back later," she said, trying to sound as convincing as possible, and knowing she was failing. Somehow, Tom still appeared to be calm despite her unexpected departure.

"See you later," he said, ending the call.

The room went silent again as Billy held out the phone in front of him.

"Alice…?" was all he asked, a sly grin on his face.

"It's a nickname, my middle name," Mary tried to explain.

"Well, I know for a fact that it's *not* your middle name. And I don't see why it would be a nickname. But it doesn't really matter, does it?" he asked nobody in particular. "The question is, what to do now? You're a liability whether you're alive or dead now. Too many people are involved."

He continued debating aloud while pacing the small

room, not paying much attention to Mary. She, on the other hand, looked all around to get a sense of where she was. It was a nondescript concrete room, maybe a converted garage? There were no windows, and just one steel door that appeared to be the only way in or out. There didn't even seem to be heating or cooling vents anywhere around her. There was no furniture or anything else to wield against her captor—all she had was that plastic cup he'd given her, which she turned over in her hand.

She was lost in thought when she realized Billy was watching her.

"Whatever you're thinking, it makes no difference," he said. "Make yourself comfortable, you might be here a while."

He walked to the door and took a key from his pocket. As he turned it in the lock, the door suddenly flung open, sending Billy flying across the floor and landing in a heap.

"FBI! Don't move!" shouted an armoured man with a very large gun as a flood of boots, guns, and voices entered the room.

"Hey, told you I'd see you later!" said Tom by way of greeting.

"Hey," Mary answered with a weak wave. "Where are we?"

"Brooklyn."

On the long drive back to Boston, Tom explained everything he'd uncovered before Mary went missing. As it turned out, she'd been gone longer than she'd realized. What she'd thought was mere hours, turned out to be more than a day.

He told her what had happened to Geri's parents, and how the suicide of Geri's father appeared staged. From the research he'd done with the passenger list, it seemed that dozens of people had never returned from the cruise. Most of them had no family to report them missing, and all of them had lived alone. He made calls to each workplace, and was told each time that the employee had resigned via email and hadn't been heard from since.

Mary sat in the passenger seat looking out the window as she took in all of this information. She wasn't sure if she was still under the effects of the sedative, or if she was just too stunned to contribute to the conversation.

"There's something else that came out yesterday," Tom said. "Something about Lisa, maybe."

Mary perked to attention and turned her head toward Tom, who kept his eyes on the road.

"I got a text yesterday. Actually, you got the text, on your phone," he began. "It was from an unlisted phone number. The person claimed to be Lisa, and said that she and Geri were in some kind of mansion in Bermuda."

Mary still said nothing, staring into him and urging him on without saying a word.

"We looked into satellite images and there are a few houses that meet the general description, but only two that also have tall brick walls around them, which she mentioned in the text."

"So you think you found her?" Mary breathlessly interjected.

"Maybe."

CHAPTER 45
BREAKING DOWN WALLS

*T*he next few days at the mansion passed like all the others, but for the addition of increasingly awkward dinners. While Tabitha and Lisa had an understanding to dramatically avoid each other in the presence of the others, there was still the Master to contend with. When he did finally join them for dinner again, he would blush throughout the night while continuously dabbing his perspiring brow with a napkin. Mostly, his dinner conversation stuck to the quality of the food, which always received high marks, and asking Andrew about the goings-on at the market.

Fortunately, everyone enjoyed listening to Andrew talk about the market. None of the others had ever been allowed to venture beyond the high brick walls of the property, so hearing about the outside world was a welcome respite in which they could imagine something beyond the palatial abode they called home.

After dinner, things were mostly back to normal. Geri

still felt that Lisa was hiding things from her—which she was—but they continued to spend most of their time together either in their room or out in the garden.

Today was a rare day in that the Master had stayed at home rather than head out for whatever business he often attended to. He practically barricaded himself in his study, and everyone thought it best to give him space; poor moods were infrequent, but they were catchy among such a small group. When the Master was stressed or sullen, he had a way of bringing down whoever else happened to be around him. So, Lisa and Geri stayed outside in the garden most of the day, alternating between walking the grounds, picking flowers, counting fish in the pond, and sitting lazily on their concrete bench, each with a well-read book in hand.

"You know, I'm not sure if I'd want to go, even if we did get a chance to get out of here," Geri said suddenly, putting down her book.

Lisa didn't answer. She waited for Geri to continue, and pretended to keep reading as Geri stared ahead, seeming to struggle to find what to say next.

"I don't mind it here," Geri explained. "I always felt stressed and worried about everything back home... deadlines at work, bills, fixing the house, my parents—I wonder how they're doing now," she said. She hadn't thought of them much lately, or anything from her old life. It all seemed so distant now.

"But since we've been here, I haven't had anything to worry about. I'm not responsible for anything here. I don't have to pay bills or think of meals or go shopping. I can read and write and be in nature as much as I want. It's everything I've ever wanted here," Geri said, her arms extended out toward the trees around her.

"I know," Lisa finally said quietly.

"I don't want you to go either…" Geri said tentatively.

Lisa sighed, "I know."

"So, what do we do?"

"I don't know."

They sat quietly then, neither looking down at their books or at each other. Neither knowing what to say next.

The silence was broken by hushed voices and rustling coming from the other side of the wall behind them. Then a scraping sound against the wall itself. Geri and Lisa looked at each other wide-eyed, neither daring to say anything. Lisa pointed her chin toward the house, and they both bolted toward the door. They clambered through the doorway and fumbled to get it shut and locked behind them.

Clarissa had been staring into the refrigerator, planning the night's dinner. She looked at the two of them as they struggled with the deadbolt.

"What's going on?" she asked, clearly caught off guard by the outburst of activity.

"Someone's sneaking around by the wall," Lisa said in a huff.

"We heard whispers and it sounded like people are trying to get over," Geri added.

"Are you sure?" Clarissa asked, mirroring their sense of alarm. Movement outside the kitchen window suddenly got her attention. She froze, and Lisa followed her gaze to find a group of men wearing all black with bulletproof vests traversing the garden and approaching the house.

"Run," Lisa said, grabbing Geri by the arm and elbowing Clarissa to knock her out of her trance. Clarissa immediately ran for the front door to make sure it was locked, then followed the other women upstairs. It went against all better judgement to barricade themselves inside, but there was no way of escape for them outside. Unless… *how were the intruders planning to get out?* Geri thought.

Just as they were about to reach the Master's study, Geri pulled back.

"Wait!"

Lisa just looked at her while Clarissa charged between them to alert the Master. Geri pulled Lisa aside.

"How were they planning to get back out?" Geri asked. "They might have left equipment in the backyard."

Lisa followed her train of thought, but didn't want to risk running into whoever was ramming against the kitchen door as they spoke. At the sound of shattering glass, Lisa ran down the hall, dragging Geri behind her.

"The observatory! There's a balcony, we'll be able to see," Geri shouted. Lisa didn't answer but headed toward the room.

They reached the observatory, which was largely neglected from disuse. The large glass windows were opaque with a thick layer of dust, and the many telescopes that littered the floor looked like they hadn't been used in decades. It was a room that was open to all, but used by nobody in the house—until now.

They locked the door behind themselves and tried to barricade it with a heavy bookshelf, but were unable to move it more than a few inches as it screeched loudly against the floor. Lisa's injured hand was still largely unusable, and like every other piece of furniture in the house, this one was old and solidly built, making it very, very heavy.

They looked around the room and settled on moving the heaviest telescopes they could find into place against the door. They hoped it would buy them at least some time to come up with a plan.

Downstairs, they heard shouts and footsteps. They crept across the room and knelt low in front of the cloudy windows, each using an elbow to remove some of the dust to make it easier to see outside. There in the garden, two masked men with guns stood in stark contrast to the bright green all around them. There was no way to know if anyone was standing guard at the front of the house, but it was a strong probability. There would be little chance of escaping outside, then.

From their crouched position, they listened as each door along the hall got broken down in succession. Clarissa's scream signified that they'd made it to the Master's office.

"Where's Ximena? Where's the coke?" a voice boomed.

"I- I- I don't know," they heard the Master answer shakily.

"Where's the coke?" the voice again asked, louder this time.

"I don't deal with coke, I'm a doctor," the Master pleaded.

Now they heard Clarissa scream again.

"I'll kill her! Where's Ximena?"

"I don't know a Ximena!"

"She was on the boat and never came back. Where is she!" the voice screamed as Clarissa whimpered and sobbed.

"The boat? The ship? She was on the cruise?" the Master asked, finally starting to understand a little of what, and who, they were here for.

"Oh, so now you know her?" the voice teased.

"No, I don't know her, but I do know where she was taken from. I know that she would have been on another Caribbean island, but that she probably got sold and taken somewhere else. I don't know where she'd be now," he answered honestly. "I can show you the island on a map if you promise not to hurt anyone here."

"I don't make no promises. And I don't need to know where she been, I need to know where my shit is!"

"I don't know, she could be anywh—"

A loud bang interrupted the Master's appeal, followed by his own cry.

"Clarissa!... why? You didn't have to..."

Another bang silenced the Master. Geri and Lisa had both been listening in horror. Geri began hyperventilating, her breathing getting louder and more laboured by the second.

"We have to do something," she whispered too loudly.

"Shhh."

"We can't just wait for them to shoot us," Geri was adamant now. She started heading for the door. Lisa followed to cut her off, afraid to say anything to attract attention. Geri took one of the telescopes by the door and pulled it aside, knocking it over with a crash and a plume of dust.

"We're here!" Geri yelled madly. "Help us!"

"What are you doing?" Lisa desperately croaked.

"Saving us."

CHAPTER 46
SOMETHING'S MISSING

W ithin days, Tom was on a flight to Bermuda along with a team of agents who he'd briefed on the case. Getting the FBI's approval to move forward was easier than he'd expected, especially given the fact that he was a cousin of one of the victims. Getting the Bermudan authorities onboard with the rescue plan proved more challenging.

Local law enforcement on the island were hesitant to let an American team armed with guns anywhere near their citizens—until they found out that the owner of the mansion in question wasn't a citizen—he was an American himself. A doctor, in fact, who had lost his license to practice in the United States for over-prescribing narcotic pain medications. Upon learning this background, the Bermudans were much more accommodating.

As the plane circled the airport and prepared to land, Tom felt a familiar twang in his gut. He wiped his clammy hands against his trousers, hoping nobody around him noticed. He wasn't a nervous flier, but he was always nervous about going into situations blindly. In about an hour, he could break open an international trafficking ring that nobody in the world knew existed. He could save his cousin and her friend, as well as countless others who might have been kidnapped and victimized over the years.

Or, he could be walking straight into his own execution. His odds in either case were about the same.

"All good, sir?" asked the man next to him, watching him rub his sweaty palms against his legs.

"All good," he replied with a tight smile.

On the ground, they were met by an envoy of Bermudan police who escorted them to the mansion in a very conspicuous line of military vehicles. They had no idea what to expect once they reached the property, and were prepared for anything. Or, so they thought.

As they drove up the side of a hill along a secluded road, an acrid smell lingered in the air.

As they parked their vehicles and approached the property in question, they saw the source of the smell; half of the mansion was a blackened ruin. Smoke seeped from the broken windows. Whatever had happened here, appeared to have happened somewhat recently.

Tom removed his gun from its holster and held it out in front of him. As he stepped through the gate, which had been left wide open, a quick movement to his side had him aiming the gun at a man running toward him.

"Freeze!" Tom barked.

CHAPTER 47
WHAT NOW?

ndrew had a disappointing day at the market. He'd been looking forward to a beef stew for dinner, but the usual butcher was out for the day. He approached other stands and shops but couldn't find a decent cut of meat at any of them. He begrudgingly settled on a vegetarian dinner.

He browsed the many vegetable carts and again found himself uninspired by what he saw. Misshapen carrots, turnips, and some wilted herbs rounded out his purchases for the day. He didn't have a clue what that night's dinner would amount to, but Clarissa always had a way of pulling together something from nothing. He considered stopping by the local bookseller's shop, but was already running late from having to search so long for decent ingredients. Instead he slung his bag over his shoulder and began his bike ride home.

The way to the mansion was long and winding. The house sat on a steep, rocky hill that overlooked the nearest town, which was just over four miles down, by the shoreline. Once Andrew left the cobblestone streets of the town's market, it was mostly dirt roads and boulders all the way back. Though he was grateful to have the bicycle, it didn't make the uphill journey much easier.

As he rounded the bend that led him to the high brick wall surrounding the property, Andrew sensed that something wasn't right. The air was too still. A shrill shriek shattered the stillness and without thought, Andrew leapt from the bike and ran toward the gated entrance. Just as his hand reached the lock, a loud bang from inside the house froze him in place. Another bang a moment later jolted him back to reality. He didn't know what to do. Through the wrought iron bars of the gate, he saw movement in the garden. People. Men.

Instinctively he ran backward and hid low behind some bushes at the base of a large tree. He wondered if anyone would see the bike and come looking for him. It was off to the side, against the wall—visible only if you were walking along that way. He didn't have time to risk finding a better hiding place for it.

He heard more movement, then glass shattering and haughty laughter. Not long after, his nostrils filled with the smell of smoke. Eventually, he heard brusque voices and what sounded like a small explosion as the gate's lock was blown apart by a close-range rifle shot. The gate was kicked open with a clash and a group soon emerged. Huddled in the middle of a circle of well-armed figures were three familiar faces. *At least they made it out*, he thought. Remembering the two gunshots from moments before, he didn't have to wonder about the others.

They headed in a different direction than the one Andrew had just returned from, avoiding the crowds of the town. Fortunately, that also meant they avoided stumbling upon his bike and the bag of groceries he'd dropped alongside it. He followed them at a distance, careful not to get too close and risk being seen or heard. He found an outcrop of stone and watched as they continued downhill. There was no well-worn path where they were going, just steep craggy rock and small bursts of vegetation. It was a more direct, albeit more dangerous, descent than the one he often took. Down at the shore, a solitary speedboat waited in the shallow water, away from the regular fishing vessels closer to town. Whoever these people were, it was unlikely they'd been seen by anyone but him.

He watched them board the boat from his vantage point. As the boat reversed and sped away, Andrew contemplated his next move. There would be little left for him at the mansion, but where else was there to go?

He could barely feel his tired legs as they carried him back to the gate. He looked up and saw the heavy smoke plume up through the roof and windows. Without much thought, he went to the garden and turned on the spigot, aiming the hose up as far as the stream of water could go. He didn't know if it was worth the effort, but what else was there to do?

He carried the hose along the back of the house and continued his efforts. Briefly, he considered going inside to see if Clarissa or the Master were still alive, but the sounds he'd heard earlier stuck in his mind. Even if they were still breathing, he wasn't sure he could handle the sight of them. His imagination conjured up images of blown out skulls and mutilated faces covered in blood. It wasn't how he wanted to remember them, but somehow, he knew that his memories would be forever stained by the events of the day.

Andrew wasn't sure how much time had passed, but the feel of soggy shoes brought him out of his reverie. He looked down to find that he'd been holding the hose limply over his feet, which were now soaked in a muddy patch of lawn. He dropped the hose to turn off the spigot. As he walked, he heard voices again, and the sound of the gate slowly creaking open.

He crouched down behind a rosebush, unaware of the thorns scratching at his bare arms. He watched as local police flanked by other military-looking officers entered the garden. A wave of relief surged through him as he rushed toward his saviours. A well-aimed firearm stopped him short.

"Don't shoot!" he cried.

"Who are you? What's happened here?" Tom barked, his gun pointed stiffly at Andrew.

"I-I-I live here," he said. "I was out at the market and when I got back, there were people all over. Th-th-they killed people, I think," he choked, barely able to breathe. "They shot them, and they burned the place down."

"How many people were shot?" Tom snarled. "What were their names?"

"Two people, I think. The Master and Clarissa. They're the only ones who didn't leave."

Tom let out a slow breath. "Was there anyone else at the house before? Two other women?"

"There were three other women," Andrew told him, his voice breaking and tears rolling down his face. "They took them to a boat down by the docks," he said, gesturing toward the rocky hill and away from the house. "I watched them leave. I tried to put out the fire with the garden hose," he said, looking in the direction of the soggy patch of lawn.

"What were the other women's names?" Tom asked.
"Tabitha, Lisa, and Geri."

Tom led his team through the house after the local fire department was called to assess the safety of the situation. Inside, they were taken aback by the opulence of the place, even underneath layers of ash and debris.

Upstairs, they found two charred bodies. Despite the burns, each had obviously been shot at close range through the head. The team took pictures and collected evidence before moving on to the other rooms. In the basement, they found what appeared to be a fully-stocked pharmacy—or, a formerly fully-stocked pharmacy. The shelves had been ransacked, leaving rows of antibiotics and allergy medicines. On an average day, this find would have been a welcome surprise for any investigator. Today, it just added another complication to an already head-spinning case.

Back outside, Andrew told Tom everything he knew, which wasn't much. He confirmed that the Master had purchased everyone at auction, and that they had all been taken from various cruise ships over the years. While they all understood that they'd been victims of trafficking, Andrew conceded that their lives here in Bermuda left little to be desired. He'd come from an abusive household and had been kicked out by his parents at the age of 16. He went from being homeless on the streets of New York City, to washing dishes in the back of a restaurant for cash, to waiting tables, and eventually winning a free cruise in a bar lottery.

Andrew told Tom that the cruise was the best thing that ever happened to him. Even when he was starving on the island, and near death on the boat taking him here, it was still better than the life he'd had back home. The Master had brought him to paradise. Where would he go now?

That was a question Tom couldn't answer. He had too many questions of his own that were more pressing; mainly, where were Lisa and Geri now? Were they still alive?

Andrew described the boat, a small speedboat with a distinctive red symbol that resembled an eye. Immediately, Tom knew which group had been there, and who had taken the women. It was a well-known drug cartel that mostly kept to themselves in Latin America. What would draw them all the way to Bermuda? And why would they take Lisa and Geri with them instead of killing them on the spot?

CHAPTER 48
AN HOUR EARLIER

As Geri banged on the door and screamed for help, Lisa didn't know what to do but watch. Geri stopped after a few seconds, and was surprised to hear… nothing.

Down the hall, the intruders looked at each other through face-masks that obscured everything but their eyes. It was hard to gauge one another's expressions, but one of them slowly walked toward the source of the sound. The floor creaked beneath his combat boots.

Geri inhaled sharply upon hearing the footsteps.

"Hello? Are you there? Can you help us?" Geri begged through the door. She was never much of an actress—she couldn't even lie to her parents without smiling in nervous guilt—but her life depended on this performance and she knew it. She needed them to be the heroes in this scenario. Maybe then, they wouldn't kill her.

Her pulse throbbed in her neck as the footsteps got closer to the door. Her whole body felt hot and she thought she'd faint on the spot as she saw the doorknob turning.

The door opened slowly, pushing aside the debris they'd piled up in front of it only minutes before. On the other side stood a tall man in combat gear with a large rifle ready to fire. Instinctively, Geri lifted both hands in surrender and looked to Lisa to do the same.

"Are you here to rescue us?" Geri asked shakily.

"Where's Ximena?" he demanded.

"She's on the island," Geri quickly responded. "Not here, the one we came from."

"What island? Which one?"

"I don't know the name of it…" she answered truthfully.

"They didn't tell us much on the cruise, but I don't think the places they took us would be frequented by many people," Lisa chimed in.

"So how does that help me?" the man asked roughly. More men joined him to see what was going on.

"There's another woman here who might be able to help," Lisa suggested. "She's been here longer and might know where the Master keeps his records."

The man stepped into the room, grabbed Lisa by the arm, and threw her out into the hallway. He then did the same with Geri.

"Take us to her," he said, pushing each forward with the barrel of his gun poking their backs.

Together, they led the men through the house to Tabitha's chambers. The walk felt longer than usual. As they passed through her sitting room, Geri saw one cat hiding under a chair. They opened the door to her bedroom, and found Tabitha calmly stroking another obviously terrified cat, its eyes wide and fur standing up.

She'd heard the horror upstairs, but realized the futility in making a fuss in her room that locked only from the outside. She was trapped. And even if she could have broken her window, she saw the men outside and thought better than to struggle.

Tabitha looked up at the group without a hint of fear or emotion.

"Hello," was all she said.

"Tabitha, do you know where the Master keeps his records? And where the island was where we were all sold?" Lisa asked.

"Of course," she answered. "I can show you where he keeps the drugs too."

Without another word, Tabitha rose gracefully from her chair, placing the cat that had been on her lap delicately on the ground. It ran under the bed as soon as its feet touched the carpet.

To see Tabitha in her large flowing gown was to see what life might have been like hundreds of years ago. Geri silently wondered what the men thought as they watched her glide from the room in her hoop skirt and old-fashioned coif.

"What kind of place is this?" one of the men asked.

"You know, I still haven't quite figured it out myself," Tabitha answered, leading them out of the room.

She led them back upstairs toward the Master's study, finding his and Clarissa's bodies still leaking blood and brain matter into the carpet. She paused at the sight, taking a moment to catch her breath. She attempted to step into the room, then stepped back.

"The maps and paperwork are all in the second drawer on the right side of the desk," she told them with a faltering voice.

"Afraid of a little blood?" one of the men asked snidely as he pushed past her.

"I'm not afraid of anything except God," she answered, turning around to wait back in the hall as two men stepped over the bodies to search through the desk. They came back out a moment later with an armful of papers.

"Alright, now where are the drugs?" the lead man asked.

"In the cellar," she replied, leading them back downstairs and down another set of stairs that neither Geri nor Lisa had ever used before. They descended the creaky wooden steps and entered a cool, dark, dungeon-like place. It had a low ceiling but was expansive in every other way, like a claustrophobic cave. Along every wall were shelves filled with bottles.

"Opiates are on that wall," Tabitha directed. "Mood stabilizers are there," she motioned, "and the good stuff is there," indicating the natural remedies the Master had secretly been growing, hallucinogenic mushrooms among them. "Take what you want, and if you have any health problems, take what you need for that too."

The men began filling the oversized cargo pockets on their pants.

"By all means, take a bag," Tabitha offered, walking to a small counter and reaching below to produce a handful of tote bags. At least two guns were drawn on her as she reached down. "He used to charge extra for these," she said, handing them out calmly as the guns were lowered. "Might as well get your money's worth." She smirked.

While the majority of the men were ransacking the place, the leader stood under a dim light, trying to make out what was on the maps.

"It doesn't make sense, this island doesn't exist," he said through his teeth, using the map feature on his cellphone to try to locate the scrap of land in the sea.

"Oh, it exists," Tabitha assured him. "It's privately owned and only recently acquired, but it does exist. Take us with you and we'll show you where to find it."

"We can also show you where on the island they're keeping Ximena," Geri piped in, feeling her face flush under the attention. She thought she saw the corner of Tabitha's mouth briefly rise in an almost-smile.

"And more drugs," added Tabitha.

The man squinted his eyes at her. "Why do you want to go back to the island?" he asked.

"Honestly, I don't," she answered, and it was the truth. She assumed Geri and Lisa had a good reason for suggesting it, so she was simply following their lead. "But, I do want to live, and as long as I'm useful, that's a step in the right direction."

At this the man chuckled, rubbing his hand over his masked jawline. "If this is a trap, I'll kill you all," he said, then paused. "But, if you do lead me to Ximena and whatever else is there, I'll let you go on the island."

"Fair enough," she answered.

The other men had made quick work of emptying the shelves of all that was valuable. Once they were satisfied with their haul, they made their way back upstairs and through the main floor. As they walked out the front door, a few of them hung back inside, while a handful of others ran along the sides of the house. Once the main group, with the women in the middle, had reached the gate, the lead man turned around and let out a long, loud whistle. A moment later, explosions shook the ground as men ran from the house, hooting and laughing ahead of the smoke and debris.

Geri, Lisa, and Tabitha all ducked and instinctively covered their heads as the first explosion rocked the earth beneath them. Geri turned back and saw flames bursting through upstairs windows.

"The rabbits!" she screamed, lunging herself toward the wreckage. Lisa extended her arm and grabbed her ankle, sending Geri crashing to the gravel driveway. She clawed against the ground but Lisa held her firmly as Tabitha got up and stepped in front of her, crouching down. Geri was in hysterics, tears streaming down her cheeks and crying out without any awareness of anyone else around her.

Tabitha gently lifted Geri's chin to face her, revealing her own eyes filled with tears. She smiled painfully down at Geri, then took her arms and lifted them around her in a warm embrace. Lisa let go of Geri's ankle, seeing that she was now secured by the other woman's loving gesture.

"My cats are all in there too," Tabitha said softly. "Hopefully they'll find their way out. I'm sorry for all that you've lost today."

"I'm sorry," Geri choked, still sobbing uncontrollably.

"It's okay, we'll figure this out. Everything will be okay." Tabitha rose, guiding Geri with her. They looked up at the house, holding each other's hands, before being shoved away down the driveway. Lisa put her hand on Geri's back, tears forming in her eyes now too.

Silently, they walked with the rest of the group out the gate. Though none of the women had ever seen the land around them, having been unconscious when they were each brought here, they were blind to it now. Each looked alternately down at the ground or straight ahead at the men in front of them. If anyone had asked which direction they'd come from, they wouldn't be able to answer. Eventually, they somehow ended up on a small beach in front of a speedboat.

Without any thought or emotion, they boarded.

CHAPTER 49
LUCK

*T*om didn't have a boat, nor did he have the means to procure one from the local authorities, who seemed relieved to find that the disgraced American doctor was no longer their concern.

Every second that passed meant Lisa and Geri were getting further away, if they were still on the boat at all. In the open water, it'd be easy to dump a body and wash away any evidence that a person was there to begin with. Tom kept picturing weighted bundles being dumped into the ocean.

All his life, Tom followed the rules. Now, he was getting increasingly frustrated by rules that had him standing around doing nothing. The local police didn't seem to care that a human trafficking scheme had brought people to Bermuda. Nor did they seem to care much about who'd killed the man who purchased them.

Back in the U.S., Tom's superiors seemed slightly more interested in the case, but didn't have the same sense of urgency about it that he did. They wanted to review all of the evidence before they sent him anywhere else. He understood the need for diligence, but time was of the essence, and people's lives were at stake.

With time slipping away, he was running out of options. He pulled his team together for a quick huddle.

"Look, we don't know where they went, or exactly when, but we know they left by boat not too long ago. We'll get a boat, and we'll track them down," he said, neglecting to mention his lack of transportation, as well as orders from the FBI to do so. "McGuinness, you brought a pocket drone, right?" he asked.

"Yes, sir!" a skinny young agent answered.

"Alright, once we're on the water, let's see if we can get that thing in the air and find these bastards."

Tom smiled confidently and told the team to gather their supplies. While they were busy, he found Andrew and asked him to lead him to the local fishermen. He had some money on him, and he hoped it was enough to charter a ride. When Andrew understood his plan, a mischievous grin brightened his face, before being replaced by a wide-eyed realization.

"What is it?" Tom asked, suddenly on alert.

"The boat!" Andrew yelled, running toward the attached garage.

"Wait! Don't go in there!" Tom shouted after him, before following him to the massive garage door.

"I don't think they touched the garage, it might be okay," Andrew quickly said, failing to explain his train of thought. He patted his pockets, then looked up at Tom. "I don't have the key. There's a boat inside, behind the cars."

Now Tom understood. He looked around them briefly

and pulled out his handgun, causing Andrew to gasp and recoil in fear. Tom fired a round and destroyed the lock. Andrew took a moment to catch his breath before rejoining Tom at the door, then slowly, the two of them lifted it with some effort.

Immediately, Tom was struck by the smell of polish and leather. It was the scent of luxury, still strong despite all the smoke hanging on the air around them. Hundreds of thousands of dollars' worth of cars were neatly arranged in front of them. As Andrew had hoped, none of them appeared to have sustained any damage in the enclosed space.

"I don't suppose he kept the keys around here?" Tom asked hopefully.

Andrew again smiled. "On that wall," he pointed with his thumb. Indeed, a row of keys hung along a row of hooks, all thoughtfully labeled. Awestruck, Tom walked through the cavernous garage alongside Andrew until they were face to face with a speedboat named Ariana Grace. Tom walked slowly all around the vessel, trailing his hand against her smooth hull.

"Who's Ariana Grace?" he asked quietly.

"They were the Master's daughters," Andrew answered softly. "Ariana and Grace. They were kidnapped and murdered about 30 years ago... It's why he brought all of us here, to save us from the others," he paused. "That's why he did it," he looked down at the grey floor as he spoke.

"Why didn't he just report the whole thing? Take it down?" Tom asked.

"I think he wanted to build a new family from it," Andrew answered honestly. "It's kind of what he ended up doing. We became like his kids," he said thoughtfully.

"It wasn't like we were victims here, not at the house. This was the best life I ever had."

To this, Tom had no response. He kept his hand on the boat a moment longer, then turned to get the keys from the wall. He also got the keys to a large, silver pick-up truck that he doubted had seen much use in its pristine condition. Today, it had a job to do.

As his team gathered their equipment and readied themselves for the next stage of their mission, Tom drove up towing their mode of transport behind him. He was greeted with hollers of ascent as they all admired the streamlined vessel. If it had ever been taken out onto the water, it certainly didn't show. Andrew confessed that he'd never even seen it outside; it had been sitting in the garage for as long as he'd been at the house. Still, he'd been dutifully polishing it once a week and performing regular maintenance and inspections along with all of the other vehicles that otherwise sat in disuse.

The group followed the trail down the hill behind Tom as he drove carefully down the steep and winding road. He filled the boat's gas tank down at the shore, and launched into the water just as the sun was setting on the horizon.

Andrew waved goodbye and wished them luck. He knew it was risky to leave so late in the afternoon, but he wanted his people found safely. Any further delay could put them in more danger—and surely Tom knew the risks of being on the water at night. He just hoped that the search would have a good outcome, and that everything would work out well for everyone involved. He wondered if he'd see any of them ever again.

CHAPTER 50
ISLAND BOUND

*G*eri, Lisa, and Tabitha all had their hands bound with duct tape behind their backs. They were led below deck, where they then had their ankles bound for good measure.

"If you make too much noise, I'll tape your mouths shut too," said a gruff man before he turned to leave, heavily stomping up the steps. All of the men still had their face masks on in the women's presence. Tabitha took that as a positive sign.

"You know," she whispered once they were alone, "if they were planning on killing us, they wouldn't care if we'd seen their faces."

"Do you think they'll just leave us on the island?" Lisa asked quietly.

"I don't know, but I think there's a chance, at least," Tabitha answered.

"But what then?" Geri asked. "Even if they let us stay on the island, how long until the next group finds us there?"

Tabitha paused. "How long were you at the house with us? About a month?" she asked. "So, either the next group will find us very soon once we get there, or we'll have about two more weeks to figure out our next move," she calculated.

Geri huffed in response. "How are you so calm about everything?" she asked impatiently.

Tabitha sighed. "Because I learned a long time ago that there's no point in being anything but calm. It doesn't do anyone any good to worry about what might or might not happen."

As the boat began moving, Geri focused on keeping her breaths long and steady. They knew it was a long journey back to the island—none of them had been conscious enough to know exactly how long it had taken to get them from the island to Bermuda. They all sat quietly with their backs against the wall of the boat, rocking to and fro and bouncing on top of the choppy water beneath them.

Though she tried to push the image from her mind, Geri kept imagining Clarissa laying on the ground with a gaping wound spilling blood all over the carpet. She knew that the mind often made things seem more grotesque than they actually were, but in the end, Clarissa was dead because a bullet burst through her skull. Even if her mind did dramatize the sight, the actual event was no less horrifying.

She sat, remembering when she first met Clarissa and how kind she was throughout their stay. She wasn't as close with her as she was with Lisa, but she considered her a friend nonetheless. Clarissa was a good person. She was young. And now she was dead.

Geri's eyes burned. She held them tightly shut as if to

stop the tears that were already gathering. She sniffed, and again tried to focus on her breathing, which was getting deeper and louder despite her best efforts. It didn't help that the up-and-down motion of the boat made it evermore difficult to control each breath. Lisa sighed. Tabitha pretended not to notice. There was no comfort to be had or given here. If their hands were free, Lisa would have at least reached out to offer some support. Instead, she simply leaned her head back and pretended to sleep, her head continuously banging against the rocking stern.

Up on deck, the men finally peeled off their masks under the setting sun, their faces pasty with sweat. They each had a turn looking at the odd maps and fought over the best course to the island.

"How do we know this isn't a trap?" asked a wiry man.

"If it's a trap, we kill them," said the leader, a barrel-chested man.

"Why don't we just kill them now? We know where we're going?" said another.

"Because the island is a big place, and we don't know where to go when we get there," the leader said through clenched teeth. He left the group to move alongside the man steering the boat.

"You know where we're headed?" he asked roughly. The man at the helm simply nodded.

"Good. At least someone does."

Though they were on a relatively large speedboat, it continued to bob in the choppy water. The ride to Bermuda had been considerably smoother; the weather seemed to be shifting now. Looking up, the captain saw the clouds rolling in thin long strips—not a good sign.

The darkening sky meant that a storm was likely coming, in addition to nightfall.

The helmsman appeared to realize the same.

"Sir, maybe we should turn around?" he suggested cautiously.

"We're not going back," the captain said sharply. "Police will be looking for us and probably already have the other islands on alert. We're not stopping until we get to the island on the map."

"Yes, sir."

The captain didn't bother turning toward the other men, but could hear the nervousness in their voices, as well. This would be a rough night, but there was nowhere to go but forward.

The wind continued picking up as the first tiny drops of water began spraying from above. Just as most of the men on deck began heading down the narrow stairs with the maps in hand, one of them looked up for a moment, toward where they'd come from. He squinted against the fine mist and held a hand over his brow.

"Captain, I think we're being followed!"

CHAPTER 51
OLD FRIENDS

*M*ary had been lounging at home, spooning ice cream straight out of the container and into her mouth while watching a nature documentary on TV. She hadn't bothered getting dressed in days; it wasn't like anyone was going to see her now anyway. She did, however, take to wearing sneakers throughout the day—though she didn't plan on venturing out any time soon, one could never be too prepared in case of emergency. She'd learned that well enough after her last little adventure.

Tom texted her updates when he could, but they were rare and sparse. She knew he was heading to Bermuda, but didn't know exactly when. She had a sense that he'd left already and hadn't seen or heard him in the halls for about two days. She still didn't have her laptop, but Tom did provide her with a cheap little tablet computer that was marginally more comfortable to use than the clunky phone he'd given her. She'd been absentmindedly scrolling through Facebook (actively *not* posting updates) between spoonfuls of ice cream when a knock rapped at her door.

She froze, spoon still in her mouth. She listened, then heard the knock again. She swallowed the cold mouthful and returned the spoon to the container. She placed the container down on the couch and loosely put on the lid before rising from her seat.

Another knock sounded at the door, louder this time, followed by an oddly familiar voice.

"Mary, are you there?"

Mary crossed the room quickly and peered through the peephole in the door. Without another thought she unbolted each of the locks and swung open the door.

"Trish!" she exclaimed, gathering Lisa's friend in a tight embrace before recoiling in pain from her burned arms.

"Hello, Mary," the woman said formally, caught off guard by the sudden rush of affection. "I'm here about Lisa," she said, before noticing Mary's bandaged arms and hand. "Are you okay? What happened?"

Mary paused, unsure of how much she should tell. She invited Trish in and hastily put the ice cream container back in the freezer. Trish sat uncomfortably on the couch, as if she didn't intend on staying long to catch up. Mary sat at the other end of the couch, at first not meeting Trish's eyes.

"Where is Lisa?" Trish asked softly, trying to be patient with her friend's younger sister.

"I don't know." Mary decided that she'd be truthful, without giving away too much. She wished Tom were here to take control of the conversation or offer her some advice on what to say.

"When was the last time you saw her?" Trish asked.

"Before she left for the cruise. I saw her the day before," Mary answered, glancing up at the woman and then looking away again.

Trish exhaled from her nose. "And what happened to you?" she asked, looking at her arms again. "What happened to your apartment?"

Mary explained that there'd been a fire, and she got burned while escaping. She didn't mention her kidnapping or that anyone had intentionally set the fire. Suddenly, she looked up at Trish suspiciously.

"How did you know where to find me?" Mary asked pointedly.

"I was keeping an eye on Lisa's apartment, and when I didn't see any sign that she'd been there for a while, I went to yours," she explained. "I saw the place burnt to a crisp. I didn't know what happened to either of you..." she trailed off. "Let's just say, I have friends in high places. I had them look into footage from the town's street cameras and when they found your face, they followed it back here. I've known you were here for about a week, I just wasn't sure if I should barge in or not. I'm worried about Lisa, so I didn't want to wait anymore. That's why I'm here."

Mary didn't know what to say. She wondered who these friends were who had access to public cameras and facial recognition technology. She wondered what else they had access to.

"Your friends," she began. "Do you think they could help us find Lisa?"

"If they know where to look," Trish said with a nod.

CHAPTER 52
NO TURNING BACK

*T*om was never good at reading the weather, but even *he* knew that a storm was coming. A big one. The wind continued to pick up and frigid droplets pricked at his skin like a thousand tiny needles. He squinted through the sharp, fine mist of rain and could see the clouds rolling ominously above.

"Sir, do you think we should turn back?" one of the men asked, looking at the darkening sky.

"Not yet," Tom said. "We've gotta be close. If we turn around now, we'll never find them."

"Yes, sir," the man said, turning around and shaking his head at the men behind them.

They continued on through the chopping water, wondering if the luxury boat they were in was even tested for these kinds of conditions.

"McGuinness! You got that drone?" Tom asked without looking back at his miserable crew.

"Yes, sir! But I don't know how well it'll work in these conditions," the young man answered.

"Well, there's only one way to find out," Tom replied.

The team created a makeshift tent using their jackets to keep the tablet receiving the video feed dry from the rain. The drone itself was meant to be weatherproof, but nobody knew how accurate the claim was, or what type of weather was implied.

Once they had everything set, McGuinness pulled out the controller and got under the jacket-tent with the tablet to guide the drone. Tom watched intently as he pushed some buttons and the small device buzzed to life, lifting off the bounding deck and hovering in the air. It was guided higher and higher and then forward as fast and far as it would go. Everyone was concerned that it would be thrown into the waves within minutes, so they wanted to get as much visibility as they could before then.

At first, the landscape was all varying shades of blue and grey. Nobody could tell if they were looking up at the sky, or ahead through fog, or below at the water. McGuinness continued guiding the craft where he thought forward would be, and was silently praying that they'd see something soon that could point them in the right direction. In a few more minutes, his prayers were answered.

"There!" he exclaimed, pointing to the screen. "There's something there, in the water!"

Tom peered under the low tent and looked at the screen. In the water, somewhere in the distance, a boat bobbed in the rough sea. He looked up to make sure the drone wasn't lost and looking at their own boat.

"That's it, sir, that's the boat we're following," McGuinness said, still pointing at the screen.

Tom ordered the group to continue on their path, and told the wiry McGuinness to recall the drone to prevent it getting lost or giving away their position. The rain began to fall heavier now, and the wind whipped hard enough to throw the men and the boat off balance. Not a minute later, and the drone was declared lost to the water beneath them, tossed effortlessly like a leaf in the breeze. Tom was sorry to have lost the equipment, but was glad that it had done its job.

The men crouched low in the boat to keep from being knocked over the sides. The helmsman put all of his effort into keeping the wheel straight against the pounding waves, the muscles in his arms bulging against the strain.

Tom stayed close as a show of solidarity, he knew that nobody wanted to be here, that nobody thought it was a good idea to continue. He himself felt that way. But they'd come too far to turn back—and even if they turned back now, they'd still be stuck in the same storm. It was too late to do anything but stay afloat.

After what felt like hours of being pummelled by waves, the rain finally lessened and the wind slowed down. The waters were far from calm, but didn't seem nearly as deadly as they had moments ago. The helmsman squinted at the expanse in front of them and called out.

"Something ahead!"

Tom scrambled up next to him and pulled a small pair of binoculars from his jacket, holding them to his eyes.

"There it is!" he pointed with his free hand before patting the helmsman hard on the back.

"You did it. Keep on them at a distance for now. Once the weather clears we'll worry about getting closer. Good job, man," Tom said, patting him again.

Eventually the rain turned to a fine mist and Tom

directed the helmsman to continue forward at a brisker pace, taking advantage of the fair conditions. Though the sky continued to darken as night fell, it was clear enough to see a reasonable distance ahead. They were in the middle of nowhere and they'd likely been spotted already anyway. Might as well prepare to engage.

The boat advanced. Surprisingly, the boat ahead of them didn't seem to take any notice. It continued at the same pace, allowing Tom's team to quickly meet them in the sea.

"Hello!" Tom shouted as they got too close to ignore, unsure of what else to say. He hadn't planned this part of the mission—the mission that had never been ordered.

Nobody on the other boat answered. As they drew closer, Tom saw that they were all pulling on face masks. *Not good,* he thought to himself.

CHAPTER 53
VISITORS

*O*n the belly of the boat, it was difficult to know how much time had passed. They'd been tossed by the sea for what felt like hours, and were so jarred from the constant thrashing that neither Geri, Lisa, nor Tabitha had the ability to feel or fear anything but water crashing down over them.

At times, it felt like they were about to capsize. Again, Geri was reminded of the fact that she couldn't swim. She quickly scanned the room for life preservers, and was unsurprised not to find any. This was how she'd die; trapped on a boat with a bunch of armed drug traffickers, yet still managing to get killed by Mother Nature.

After being hurled from one side of the boat to the other every few seconds and bruising just about every inch of their bodies in the process, things finally started to calm down outside. They were sticky with dirt and seawater, and every part of them ached and stung. Their arms and legs were still duct taped, meaning they'd had no way to catch themselves as the boat swayed. Geri took in a deep, painful breath.

"Do you think we're almost there?" she asked, almost choking on the words.

Lisa scoffed, then winced. "No, not even close."

"You'd think somebody would've checked a weather report before starting a long trip like this," Tabitha mused. "I mean, just because *we've* been cut off from the outside world, that doesn't mean *they* couldn't check the damn weather before we left."

"Ain't that the truth," Lisa concurred.

The boat rocked more gently now, almost enough to lull them to sleep. And then the yelling started.

"Anybody speak Spanish?" Tabitha asked the others, unable to understand what was being said above them.

"A little," Geri answered. After listening a moment, she could make out a few words and sentences. "There are people," she translated. "Another boat."

"Interesting," Tabitha said.

There was more yelling, then the engines cut off. Now there was silence.

"I don't think this is good," said Lisa in a whisper.

"Me neither," said Tabitha. "Let's all try to get ourselves back to the corner over there," she said, gesturing with her head.

They all wriggled back to where they'd initially sat when they were led down into the boat. The effort left them heaving and breathless and wincing in pain.

Things were mostly quiet again, with just the sound of shuffling feet and some hushed voices up on deck. Then, a clear voice cut through the muffled sounds with a simple "Hello." There was no response.

The voice spoke again, hesitating now. "We're

looking for people. We're wondering if you might have seen them."

Geri and Lisa's eyes got wide as they found each other. "Tom?" they both asked in tandem.

"It sounded just like him."

"How could he find us here?"

"It can't be him."

"What does he do again? Isn't he a cop?" Geri asked.

"I don't know exactly what he does, just that he works for the government," Lisa said quickly. "It's been a family joke for years," she said, unable to catch her breath.

"Shhh!" Tabitha piped in. They were quiet, listening. Nobody was saying anything now. Then, suddenly there were screams and loud pops and more screams.

"Oh God," Tabitha said.

Lisa closed her eyes tightly and held her breath. Geri did the same, and crumpled into Lisa's shoulder.

"Oh God," Tabitha said again, gasping for air. "Oh God."

There was running and grunting and crashing and pops and bangs and screams and splashes. The boat tipped and jerked under the activity, and collided with the other boat more than once. After a few minutes, things were relatively quiet again, and there were footsteps clumsily clunking down the stairs.

Geri opened her eyes now and saw the feet coming down the steps. One step, then another, then another. And there was Tom, being led toward them, his head hung low and his jaw tense. She looked at him, then looked away. She looked at Lisa, who still had her eyes closed, and nudged her with an elbow. She then turned to Tabitha, who's eyes were open but focused on nothing at all ahead of her. Then Geri saw the blood.

"Tom!" Lisa shouted in disbelief.

"Lisa, you *are* here!" he answered just as incredulously.

"Tabitha," Geri said urgently. "Tabitha!" she yelled, turning to Lisa.

Lisa turned to look, her face quickly darkening as she took in the scene. Tabitha had been shot. A bullet had pierced the bow and worked its way through the boat's body and her own, tearing through metal and flesh indiscriminately. A small puddle of red-tinged seawater was slowly spreading beneath her body.

The man leading Tom followed the women's gaze and muttered under his breath. He hastily taped Tom's hands, legs, and mouth and shoved him to the wall across from the other captives. He then roughly dragged Tabitha, still warm despite the chill in the air, and still breathing, if only barely. Geri cried as she watched her friend pulled up each step without any thought or care. A moment later, a heavy splash was the only closure they'd get.

More men were led down and similarly taped and gagged. The small hole that Tabitha's fatal bullet had emerged from was lazily duct taped over too. Lisa and Geri kept their mouths closed as much as they could given the circumstances, though a stray gasp or sob occasionally broke from Geri's throat—they were hoping to at least avoid the same treatment that the men were getting. Fortunately, they were paid no more mind. Four ragged-looking men now sat across from them, all splattered with blood. Whatever rescue mission this was meant to be had obviously failed.

CHAPTER 54
EXPEDITION

*T*wo days later, the energy on the boat seemed to change. While all of the captives were increasingly lethargic due to limited food and water, the crew suddenly appeared in high spirits.

The male captives still had their mouths taped shut most of the time, but were given some reprieve to allow them to eat and drink sparingly, once a day. Geri wondered why they were being kept alive at all—she'd seen and heard their captors kill others, so why not these men too? Once feeding time was over and the traffickers returned up to the deck, she quietly asked Lisa what she thought of the situation.

"I think," Lisa began, meeting Tom's eyes for confirmation of what she was about to say, "that they're hoping to ransom the men." Tom nodded curtly. "I can't think of any other reason they'd keep them here... unless they wanted to auction them on the island, but I doubt they're dumb enough to risk getting involved in that mess," she added with an eye roll.

Soon, there were excited shouts above and a flurry of activity.

"I think they found the island," Geri said, trying to make out what was being said.

Within an hour, they lurched to the side as the boat's bottom hit a sandbar.

"We're ba-ack," Lisa sang softly with a wry laugh. Here they were, back on the island that nearly killed them once before. *Funny how life comes full circle sometimes,* Geri thought numbly.

They sat in silence for some time while footsteps ran in all directions above them. Eventually, the masked man who usually brought them their rations of food and water came down the steps with a roll of bungee cord. He deftly cut the tape that had been keeping their ankles painfully joined together for the past two days, and paired off the captives, starting with Geri and Tom. Geri's cheeks flushed ember and she thought she'd faint from the sudden heat flooding through her. It was the first time they'd been that close since their failed date so long ago. The one that wasn't really a failure when she thought about it—just another nice date that she ran away from before it had the chance to become anything more.

Throughout the boat ride, Geri had actively avoided looking at Tom directly. She felt guilt every time she saw his dirty face, and the line of duct tape across his mouth didn't help. Here he was, risking his life to save her and Lisa, and she hadn't even given him a chance those months ago.

There was also another feeling tempering her guilt, but she couldn't tell if it was attraction, admiration, or humiliation. It was probably a mix of all three. As they were pushed up the stairs, Geri was aware of each time their hands and arms and hips brushed up against each other, which was frequent given the tight nature of their current bondage.

Once the pairs were all up on deck, they were given a makeshift leash to be held by one of their captors. It wasn't the first time she'd been leashed, but she hoped it would be the last.

Geri noted that each of the largest men was paired with a woman, while the two smaller men were paired together. She doubted it was accidental. The traffickers wanted to make sure that the strongest men would be weighed down by the supposedly less capable women if they tried to run. Unfortunately, in her own case, it was true. But clearly they didn't realize that Lisa could out-run any of them, even if she'd had sandbags tied to her ankles. She wondered if they'd have a chance to witness the folly of their assumptions first-hand.

The pairs were awkwardly loaded onto an inflatable raft, their hands still tied behind them, and were lowered into the shallow water. One man behind them paddled, while another man in front stared back at them through his mask, cradling his black machine gun.

While she was sure it was loaded and ready to kill at any moment, Geri focused less on the gun than the water beneath them. She really should have learned to swim, she chided herself. The water probably wasn't more than five or six feet deep, yet still, that's what terrified her more than anything in that moment.

Fortunately, the raft found the island's sand quickly, and they were clumsily led ashore on legs that hadn't held any weight for days. She briefly wondered if it'd be easier to walk on the sand if she shrugged off her shoes, but then remembered the walk through the forest they'd soon be taking, over knotty roots and craggily stones. Better keep them on and have sandy shoes than none at all, she reasoned.

They were shoved along toward the tree line and told to lead the men to Ximena. Geri and Lisa didn't bother looking at each other, they simply followed the way as best as they could remember back to the volcano. They had no idea what would happen once they got there—either it would be empty, or full of more captives and different captors with guns. Neither knew which would be worse to stumble into. At least there was no sign of other boats anywhere around. Less chance of a gun-fight to be caught between that way.

"Freeze!" came a sudden voice from the trees, followed by the sounds of guns being cocked.

Geri didn't know whether to laugh or cry. She did both.

CHAPTER 55
RUN

*I*n her fit of hysterics, Geri didn't notice the first elbow prod at her arm. Or the second. Finally, a sharp elbow found her ribs, and she looked up to see Tom looking down at her, eyes burning with intensity. She almost melted on the spot before she realized he was trying to say something beneath the duct tape.

"Mphh"

She continued staring.

"Mrphnn"

Still, no idea what was happening.

"Uhh, tphuh…" She saw that he was lowering his body, his legs slowly moving into a sprint position until he got to "thrph!" at which point Lisa, who had been following along a few feet away, yelled "Run!" and they bolted. Geri wasn't ready for the sudden jolt, and was dragged helplessly for a few seconds before she was able to get her feet under her and haphazardly follow Tom's lead. Whoever had been holding their leashes had been distracted enough not to follow. Gunshots sounded but Geri was too focused on her feet to pay them any mind

They headed clumsily into the trees and didn't stop until they were hidden in dense brush. Geri bumped into Tom's sweaty back as he stopped abruptly to listen. In the distance, they could hear shouts and shots being fired. They didn't seem to get any closer, so Tom crouched down where he was. Geri followed his lead. He nudged her with an elbow.

"Umphh."

Once again, she was at a loss.

He jerked his head around toward her back, looking at her hands as dramatically as he could, then pushing out his chin.

My hands, his chin, she thought. "The tape? My hands to take off the tape?" she asked, feeling stupid as she fumbled the words. He nodded emphatically. *Okay, at least she got something right,* she thought to herself.

She stood, her hands still taped together behind her. Self-consciously, she backed herself up until her hands felt his nose, then worked their way down to his covered mouth. As she had been on auction day, Geri was very much aware of the fact that it had been days since she'd showered. She was sure Tom had the same awareness now. She traced the tape across his cheek with her fingertips until she felt a corner of it. Slowly, she gripped the corner and pulled.

If she could have ripped it off in one quick motion, she would have, but her own limited range left her pulling off the tape about as fast as if she were pulling a wad of gum from her hair. In fact, she could practically feel every follicle of Tom's stubble being plucked from his face. To his credit, not a whimper escaped his raw lips. She left the rest of the tape hanging from his other cheek once his mouth was free, not wanting to drag out the process any more than necessary.

"Thanks," he said hoarsely, rubbing his free cheek against his shoulder.

"You're welcome," she answered quietly.

"I have a knife hidden in my vest, but I can't reach it," he said. "If you reach in, we can get our hands free and separate ourselves."

Tom guided Geri to the hidden pocket inside his vest. Her hands brushed past his collarbone and then his chest hair until she felt the bulge of metal. Her fingers worked their way into the pocket and pulled out the folded utility knife.

"Cut through yours first, and then you can do mine," he instructed.

Though it was difficult to maneuver the knife blindly behind her, Geri was able to spring it open and eventually use it as a saw to break through the tape at her wrists. It took longer than she'd hoped, and she was sure Tom was judging her ineptitude despite his silence. Once her hands were free, she stifled her proud smile and worked on his. The task became much easier now that she could see what she was doing. A moment later, they were both free.

"What do you think happened back there?" Geri asked, pointing her head back toward the direction they'd come from.

"I don't know," Tom replied, stretching his arms out on either side before pulling what was left of the tape off of his cheek with a grimace.

"Should we go back?" she asked.

Tom thought for a second, his mouth pinched to the side. "Well, I don't hear any more shots, so whatever it was sounds like it's over. We can go back, slowly and quietly and see what there is to see."

As he suggested, they walked back, with Tom leading the way. Within minutes, a rustling sound to their right had them freeze in place, Tom's knife held out in front of him.

"Hey! It's me!" Lisa whispered, happy to again see her cousin and friend. She was still tied up with the man she'd been paired with earlier. "Can you help us out?" she asked, turning around to gesture toward her wrists.

"Yeah, I got ya," Tom said, getting to work on her taped hands. "What happened to you?" he asked, now noticing her dirty bandages.

"Long story, not important now," she said curtly as Tom freed her hands. He moved on to her partner, who Tom introduced as Bolton before ripping the tape from the man's mouth. They all went through their introductions before continuing on to where they'd come from as a group.

It didn't seem like they'd gone too far while they were running, but now, it felt like they could be miles away from shore. Geri tried to recognize anything from her surroundings. She looked down at gnarled roots and palm fronds, and then spotted something that stopped her in an instant. She gasped.

"What is it?" Tom asked, before following her line of sight.

"Oh," he said, taking in the butchered remains of what was once a body. All that remained were the hands, feet, head, and skin. Everything else appeared to have been removed, leaving a deflated version of the person that once was.

"That's Brett," Geri said, her voice shaking. She

continued looking, unable to pull herself from the grotesque sight. Finally Lisa nudged her forward, and the group solemnly continued on their journey.

Minutes later they approached the clearing, and everyone tensed. It was too quiet.

With some hesitation, they came upon the scene. Scattered bodies were visible on the ground, the sand below them stained scarlet.

"Welcome back, Tom. And good to see you too, Lisa," a commanding voice called out.

CHAPTER 56
FRIENDS IN HIGH PLACES

Once again, Geri was on a boat. If she ever got home, Geri never wanted to see another boat again—although by this point, she was pretty sure she'd found her sea legs.

At least now, she was free to walk around the deck if she so chose to. She could also eat and use the bathroom whenever she needed to, in private, by herself. On this boat, she was a passenger, not a prisoner.

She and Lisa continued to share a bunk, just like back at the mansion; it had been so long since either of them had a moment apart, that they weren't sure how they'd cope once they got back to their individual residences in Boston.

Trish, whom Lisa had long-considered one of her best friends, had personally briefed them on where they were heading now—another small island with a private airport —and what to expect along the way. To Lisa's amazement, the friend she thought she'd known so well had been a high-ranking leader in the CIA for years. She'd suspected something along those lines from her cousin, Tom, but not her friend. How could she have missed that?

"Ladies, let's talk," Trish said, suddenly appearing at their doorway. She pulled out the chair from a small desk that remained as yet unused in their cramped quarters, and closed the door behind her.

"I'm sure you have a lot of questions," she said, looking pointedly at Lisa. "I can't answer all of them, but I can tell you some things that I'm aware of," she said seriously. "Lisa, first of all I want you to know that while I am so happy that you're okay, I wasn't supposed to be here. You're not supposed to know about my job, neither of you," she looked between Lisa and Geri. They both nodded without a word.

"But, being that I am here, as a friend, I'll fill in a few gaps for you both. Lisa, Mary is okay, but she's been through a lot since you've been gone. Tom's been taking care of her and set her up in a new apartment. You should thank her when you get home, she helped me track down your cousin to find you." She smiled genuinely. Then, her face darkened as she turned to face Geri directly, who was sitting on the adjacent bed to Lisa's left.

"Geri, the news isn't as good for you, and I'm so sorry to have to tell you," she began, then hesitated. Geri stared unblinking, her face expressionless.

"Your parents knew something wasn't right, and they did what any good parent would do, they asked questions. Unfortunately, those questions made them... vulnerable. I'm so sorry, but your parents were both killed."

Though Geri already knew what Trish was about to say, hearing the word "killed" caused her to gasp, her hand involuntarily touching her mouth. She tried to hold back her tears until she could be alone later, but felt her lower lip quivering and her face contorting as the sobs caught in her throat.

"It was fast," Trish continued. "I know they couldn't have felt pain, and they died together, in their home." She paused, giving Geri time to process everything. "We have good news too, but I wanted you to know what to expect back home. We'll have plenty of time to talk later, but I am here if you need anything. *Anything* at all, tell me and I'll do what I can," she said as she rose from her chair. Without another word, she opened the door, walked through, and closed it again behind her, leaving the two women alone.

Geri cried openly now. Lisa crossed the room to her bed and sat next to her, pulling her into a hug. No words were said between them. There was nothing left to say.

CHAPTER 57
HOMECOMING

*M*ary sat on a bench, waiting alone at the train station. She'd brought a book to read, but couldn't focus on the words in front of her. A week ago, she'd learned that her sister and cousin were found and safe. She didn't know what had happened between then and now, only that there was some kind of administrative work to be done before they could all come home.

The train was due at the station at 1:47 p.m., and Mary checked her phone every few minutes as the time drew closer. As 1:47 came and passed, she bit her fingernails and reassured herself that they were probably gathering their bags and making their way across the platform. At 1:50 p.m., she looked up and met Lisa's gaze. It took her a moment to realize that it really was her sister approaching—in just under two months, Lisa's skin had gone from bronze and freckled to ghostly white. Her blonde hair now had grey roots growing in. Geri had a similarly haggard appearance, but the two of them together, along with Tom, allowed Mary to recognize them in the crowd.

She ran to them and was immediately embraced by the sister she'd been working so hard to find. They held each other tightly, neither realizing just how much she missed the other until that moment. As they parted, they each looked each other up and down.

Lisa's arms, legs, and neck were mottled with old insect bites and scars. Her hand was freshly bandaged.

"What happened to your hand?" Mary asked, holding Lisa's arm to inspect it.

"Long story," Lisa brushed it off. "I'll tell you later. What happened to you?" she asked, now noticing her sister's own bandages.

"Long story," Mary scoffed. "Come on, are you hungry? We can talk while we eat."

The four of them found a quiet café near the train station. The lunch crowd had mostly departed, giving them much of the place to themselves. Lisa and Mary scooted into a booth next to each other, leaving Tom and Geri to do the same. They smiled awkwardly at one another before Geri quickly dove into the menu in front of her.

"So, where were you this week?" Mary asked. "I know they said you were 'back,' but wouldn't tell me where. Trish said it was just standard practice but wouldn't tell me anything."

Lisa laughed. "Yeah, talking to Trish used to be a lot easier, huh?" she sighed. "I don't even know how to describe the place. It was like a hospital, but not. They took a bunch of samples, fixed up my hand," she said as she held it up for inspection. "I was shot, straight through."

"Oh my god," Mary breathed. "What happened? What happened to all of you? Nobody would tell me anything."

A waitress came to the table with four glasses of water and a notepad to take their orders. Geri was the only one who'd been looking at the menu since they'd sat down.

"Could we have a few more minutes? Thanks," Lisa dismissed the woman. They were all silent until she returned to the counter.

"Alright let's just figure out our orders and then we can get into everything," she said. They all quietly poured over the standard café options. Lisa and Mary each ordered turkey club sandwiches with extra bacon, while Tom ordered an egg white omelet stuffed with every vegetable on the menu. Geri ordered a grilled cheese sandwich.

"Wait!" Lisa called out as the waitress began to walk away. "Can I also get a Diet Coke? It's been so long since I've had a Diet Coke."

"Oh, and an iced tea for me!" Geri added. She'd forgotten how much she'd missed the simple pleasure of fountain soft drinks.

After the beverages arrived at the table, Lisa leaned forward to continue explaining what had happened, only stopping to sip her cola.

"God, that's strong!" she said, her face puckering from the sweet fizz. "Anyway, the cruise was a front. They took people who either had no family, or didn't speak to people much," she said, briefly looking at Geri, who looked down and stirred her drink with her straw.

"They have an island where they bring people to sell. Geri and I were separated, I still don't know why—"

"Oh, we figured that out, actually," Tom chimed in. "They knew you're an athlete. They separated the strongest people and drugged them to make them easier to move."

Everyone looked at Tom as though they'd forgotten he was there until that moment. "Sorry," he said.

"Well, that explains things…" Lisa said with an eye roll. "So I was with all the doped up people, and they were leading us off the ship. I didn't even know that Geri was gone at that point, but I knew that whatever was happening wasn't good. I jumped into the water, and they shot me."

"God," Mary said quietly. "And you were still able to swim after that?"

"I didn't even know what happened, between the adrenaline and the drugs, all I knew was I had to get away and hide, so that's what I did. Eventually I did get to the island without being seen, but a *dog* found me and led them to me. Then Geri and I saw each other, and she said that I was with her, and thank God the Master went along with it. I think they would have killed me for good measure if that hadn't happened that way."

"The Master?" Mary asked, perplexed.

The waitress returned with their meals, and the table went silent again until she walked away.

Lisa hesitated, trying to find the right way to describe it.

"He's the one who bought them on the island," Tom answered.

"Well, bought Geri," Lisa replied. "I was more of a two-for-one special," she snorted.

"None of you knew his name, did you?" Tom asked.

"I don't know, I don't think so," Lisa replied. Geri

also shook her head. Now that she was back in a group setting, her old quiet habits returned.

"He was a doctor, you know," Tom continued. "American. Dr. Albert Desola."

"Albert," Lisa repeated softly. "He looked like an Albert." At this, Geri laughed. She had to agree, he did look like an Albert.

"He wasn't a bad guy," Lisa said. "He took care of us. It wasn't a bad place, where we ended up."

"It was a beautiful place," Geri finally said. "There was a garden, and flowers, and animals. It was like a fairytale." She blushed as she wondered what they all thought of her, saying that her time in captivity was like a fairytale.

"I'm starving," Mary said, breaking the silence. They all began to dig into their meals, and didn't raise their heads to talk again until every plate was clean. They'd been so invested in the conversation that none of them even realized how hungry they were until they began eating.

Once they were finished, Lisa signalled the waitress to request the check. Once it was set down on the table, her hand instinctively went to her back pocket.

"Shit," she hissed. Lisa and Geri's possessions had been left on the cruise, and nobody had any luck tracking them down. Now that they were home, they had a long task list ahead of them that involved requesting new credit cards, checking on all of their bank accounts, and seeing what state their lives were in now.

"I got it," Tom said, pulling out his wallet.

"Let me handle this one, you guys have been through enough," Mary said, putting her new credit card on the table.

Lisa looked at it, furrowing her brows. "Alice? Who's Alice?"

Mary laughed in sudden recognition, realizing she'd forgotten to mention her new identity. "Yet another long story!" she said. "I'll tell you when we get back to my place."

CHAPTER 58
NEW BEGINNINGS

*T*he group shared a cab ride back to Mary's new apartment. As they got out and walked toward the unit, Mary explained that there wasn't much in the way of seating, but they could all squeeze on the sofa or spread out on the bed.

"Ah don't worry about it," Tom said. "I'll be heading home myself, plenty of room for you on the sofa without me."

"Absolutely not," Lisa said commandingly. "We've all been through something together, and we'll all fill in the gaps for each other together. You played a big role in this, Tom, you can't just leave now."

"Okay," he chuckled. "I'll stay for a bit."

"I have wine!" Mary added cheerfully.

In truth, Geri wasn't sure where she wanted to be. She hadn't been home in months now, nor had she had a moment to herself. Part of her wanted to hide under the covers of her own bed and bask in its solitary comfort. But a larger part of her was afraid to be alone now. Did she really want to go home, by herself, to an empty house?

As the others discussed all that had happened since Lisa and Geri went missing, Geri largely tuned out the conversation. She got bits and pieces, and the realization that Billy had played her struck through her like a dagger. When she'd heard that he targeted Mary next, and almost killed her, all she felt was white hot rage.

"Where is he now?" Geri asked sharply, speaking for the first time since they left the café.

"In custody," Tom responded. "Don't worry, he's headed to prison. In the meantime, he's helping us track down other people involved."

"You mean, he's helping Trish track down other people involved," Lisa corrected him.

The muscles in Tom's jawline tightened. "Yup. That's what I meant."

Mary's face twisted in confusion. "What do you mean? You're not on the case anymore?" she asked Tom.

He sighed. "Nope. Not anymore," he said, first looking up at the ceiling, then down at the floor, then downing the glass of wine in front of him.

"Tom went rogue," Lisa said with a devious grin. "He came to save us before getting any orders."

"Wow," Mary said, taking it all in. "And Trish is on the case now? She's FBI?"

"CIA! Crap!" Lisa exclaimed. "No. You never heard any of this. None of us know anything and this conversation never happened."

They all laughed and continued filling each other in on all that happened. As the sky outside darkened, and more lights were turned on throughout the small apartment, the topic of leaving kept coming up without much resolution.

"You know what, can we sleep over here tonight?" Lisa eventually asked.

"I don't have a spare bed or anything for you..." Mary said, not wanting to kick them out but not wanting to seem a bad host.

"We've slept on more bare floors than I care to remember," Lisa said, answering for herself and Geri. "As long as you have a blanket or two, we'll be fine."

Geri was silently thankful for Lisa suggesting it, she didn't want to admit that she was now afraid to go outside in the dark. By sunrise, she was sure she'd feel more comfortable about returning home.

"I have an air mattress at my place," Tom added. "And a futon cushion we can bring over here for you."

"Great!" Lisa beamed. "You can take the futon cushion and Geri and I'll get the air mattress!"

Geri and Tom both looked at Lisa with eyes bulging.

"Uh, I have my own bed to sleep in just across the hall..." he said.

"Oh, but why spoil the fun now? Let's have a slumber party while we're all here! We're all alive, and we're all here," Lisa said, still smiling and looking among the bewildered faces.

"Alright," Tom conceded. "Just for the night."

Together, Mary and Lisa retrieved the large cushion and dragged it through the hall, laughing all the way at their pathetically bandaged hands that made it difficult to grip anything. Tom followed with the rolled up air mattress and a pump to inflate it. Once it was all done, the entire living room floor was turned into one large haphazard bed. Mary decided to join everyone by sleeping on the couch. Lisa insisted on taking the side of the air mattress closest to the couch, leaving Geri on the side closest to Tom's cushion. Geri knew it was intentional, but she didn't mind.

For the first time in weeks, Geri slept soundly. And from the sound of things by the time she woke up, everyone else was sleeping comfortably too, despite the lack of actual beds or pillows. As she opened her eyes, she saw Tom's face startlingly close to hers. She also realized that their hands had been gently touching as they slept. She slowly pulled back her hand now, careful not to wake him, while taking in the utterly peaceful expression on his sleeping face. He looked younger, almost boyish. She couldn't help staring.

As light trickled in through the window, the others began to stir. Mary took a sofa pillow from under her head and put it over her face as she rolled over, blocking the light so she could steal a few more moments of sleep. Lisa opened her eyes next, and slightly nodded her head at Geri as a way of greeting. She then pulled herself up and walked across the apartment into the bathroom to take a shower. At the sound of water, Tom opened his eyes. Geri was sitting up with her knees to her chest. She'd been watching him, and quickly turned away once he woke up, sure that he'd caught her looking.

Mary was still asleep—or pretending to be—and just the two of them were now alert in the room. Tom lay still for a moment, looking up at nothing, before getting up from the cushion and leaving the apartment.

"Hmmph," Geri said aloud, offended that he hadn't even acknowledged her presence before he left. She continued sitting where she was. She didn't feel comfortable walking around someone else's home, even if that someone was only two feet away on the couch. So she sat, and she thought. Back in quarantine, Trish had mentioned that Geri's parents had listed her as a beneficiary for their investments, bank accounts, and life insurance policies. She didn't have an exact number, but she knew it was a lot. Her father had alluded to it before, letting her know that she'd always be taken care of, no matter what. They'd also left her with their mountain-side house in Virginia. And then there was her own house to consider. Suddenly, she went from having nothing in the world, to having more than she knew what to do with.

Just as her heart began racing with dread and possibility, the front door opened and Tom returned with a large bag full of fresh bagels and a box of hot coffee. Lisa emerged from the bathroom wrapped in a towel just as he set the breakfast on the table.

"Mmm, that smells good!" Lisa said, immediately heading to the cabinets to find plates and mugs.

"Eurgh," Mary moaned from beneath her pillow. "Mugs and dishes are on the top shelf," she said sleepily, reluctantly removing the pillow from her face and propping herself up on one arm.

Geri took the opportunity to speed into the bathroom and wash her face. She wished she'd had a toothbrush. Instead, she squeezed some toothpaste on her finger and rubbed it across her teeth before slurping up some water for a quick rinse. She searched for actual mouthwash but didn't see any. It would have to do. She checked herself in the mirror to make sure there wasn't any toothpaste left on her face, then returned to the main apartment, where everyone was now smearing bagels with cream cheese or butter and sipping fresh coffee.

"Good call with the bagels," said Lisa through a full mouth.

"Yeah, sorry I don't have much in the way of food here," said Mary sheepishly.

"It's no trouble," said Tom. "I was thinking we should all talk anyway, about what we're all going to do from here. Mary, I don't think you'll have too much trouble getting back to work once you're healed, but Lisa and Geri, you both might have some issues."

"I'd been thinking about that, too," Lisa confessed. "Apparently we 'resigned,' and it would be hard to take that back with the whole situation being hush-hush."

"Why is it hush-hush?" Mary asked, holding the warm coffee cup in both hands.

"Oh!" Lisa looked startled. "Can we…?" she asked Tom.

Tom bobbed his head side to side, weighing the options. "Okay, but you can't tell anyone. Anyone…" he said seriously to Mary, who nodded in reply. "We can't let anyone know what's happened, because the case is still open, and it's bigger than anyone realized. There are foreign dignitaries involved, and we need more evidence before we can do much. A lot more evidence," he said with a deep sigh.

"Wow," was all Mary could say.

"Yeah," Lisa agreed. "So anyway, it's complicated. I don't have a job, and frankly I don't know how I'm going to catch up on rent at this point."

"You can stay with me," Geri said suddenly, surprising even herself. "Um, I mean, I have my house, and my parents left me everything. I have more than enough room, and my mortgage will basically be paid."

Everyone stared at her unblinking. She looked down at her untouched bagel and took a quick sip of coffee.

"That would be amazing," Lisa smiled, putting her

hand over Geri's. "Seriously, thank you."

"So, what do you think you'll do now?" Tom asked Geri.

"I don't know," she said, her face burning from all the attention. "I can do whatever I want, I guess."

"You can write a book," he suggested with a chuckle.

"Yeah, actually, I can."

EPILOGUE

With Geri's sudden windfall, she paid off her mortgage and finally gave her home the renovation it needed. The floors no longer creaked, the walls no longer peeled, and every room had its own unique theme and palette of colour to suit her tastes. Though she could now afford a landscaper, she continued to tend to her garden herself, enjoying the fruits of her own efforts.

During the home renovations, Geri and Lisa stayed with Mary. Occasionally, Geri stayed with Tom.

Initially, Geri planned to sell her parents' home, afraid to even step inside for months. Once she did work up the courage to return, she found herself unable to part with the secluded mountain retreat. Instead, she kept it as they'd kept it, and returned regularly to work on her Great American Novel in uninterrupted silence, surrounded by nature.

Three years later, *The Harvest Cruise* hit store shelves, just as the international human trafficking ring of the same name was finally exposed to the world and brought to justice. Within weeks, the book was a bestseller.

Lisa continued to live with Geri even after entering a new field as a trauma counsellor and motivational speaker. Together and separately, they'd attended therapy sessions to overcome the sudden panic they'd feel during everyday activities, and Lisa decided that she wanted to help others in similar positions.

Mary eventually got back to work and built her career as an investigative reporter with the *Boston Globe*. She re-claimed her birth name and became a well-respected journalist, travelling the world to root out corruption and tell the stories that others brushed off with indifference.

Tom continued working for the FBI, with the understanding that he wouldn't lead any more international missions. He happily accepted those terms.

ACKNOWLEDGEMENTS

First, I would like to thank you, the reader. Thank you for trusting me to deliver an escape (teehee) from daily doldrums.

Next, I would like to thank my dedicated publisher, Alanna Rusnak, without whom this book would not be in your hands right now. Thank you, Alanna, for believing in this story and bringing it to life. I am truly grateful.

Thank you Chris, my devoted husband and biggest cheerleader. There have been so many times and in so many ways that I've felt like a failure, and you've always managed to pull me from that spiral. You've supported my ambitions while encouraging me to reach higher, and you've been my beacon through every storm. Thank you for filling my world with light.

Thank you to my parents for the immense support you've provided throughout my life. I've accomplished every goal thanks to your generosity, dedication, and unwavering help. Thank you for always giving me a place to come home to.

Thank you to my sisters and my in-laws for giving me inspiration, laughter, and joy.

Thank you to the Benisons, Hoffmanns, Hellmans, Hersches, Vizelters, Scibellis, Plotnicks, and everyone in between. Over the years you've all contributed so much to my growth and well-being. Whenever Chris and I have needed help, a hand was raised before we could even reach out. Thank you all for showing us, and especially me, that we have so many people in our corner. It's so appreciated.

And lastly, thank you to my daughter. You are my greatest pride.

Rebecca Benison is a New York-based writer. A professional storyteller, her weekdays are spent connecting with audiences on behalf of brands, while her nights and weekends are devoted to fiction. Her work has been published in the *Workers Write!* literary journal, *Empyrean Literary Magazine*, *Newsday*, the *Long Island Herald*, and a host of other publications. *Harvest Cruise* is her debut novel.

When she's not at her desk, Rebecca can often be found in her garden.